Dra

The Lake

The Chronicles of Brawrloxoss

Book 9

By

J. R. Knoll

Artwork by

Sandi Johnson

Edited by

Kim Stewart

Dragon of the Lake is a work of fiction and all of the characters, places and events come from the really messed up mind and imagination of the author. Any resemblance to any persons, living or dead, is purely coincidental. The places are all made up as well, so don't go looking for them. They are only in your imagination and mine, just like everything else here.

For my Mom
Joyce Lee Knoll
30 January 1940 -9 March 2021

Hers was an amazing story of strength and perseverance, of adapting to changing times, driving the best in her children to encourage us to see our better selves. She faced life at the side of my Dad, Clifton Knoll and together they paved the way through adventures that most will never know. Even through the lean times, we never went wanting and never knew the struggles she endured to keep us happy and healthy.

May your spirit join the greatest of our ancestors, and may you continue to fill all our hearts with strength, love, and joy.

CHAPTER 1

It's long been told that dragons will wisp away with human maidens and hold them as part of their hoard, use them as leverage against a human kingdom from which they want gold or favors, or even to keep them in their lairs where the maidens will sing to them. I know of no such dragons in my experience who do this, and yet the stories persist. I don't know if this has ever been seen or experienced by any living humans, but still the stories are told, many claiming to be of long ago and involve dragons who were slain by some brave knight or warrior looking to make a name for himself. I find the idea that any human, no matter how mighty or brave, can defeat a dragon of my species in single combat to be ludicrous, but humans will tell their stories.

In any event, there is one instance of which I am familiar, one that I know to be true, a story that tells of a dragon who would sweep a human girl away from her people and into a long journey that neither could have ever foreseen, and two simple lives would be forever changed by unforeseen circumstances beyond their control.

Across the Abtont Forest, through the desert and sweeping across the Territhan range to the sea, Autumn would come to announce the inevitable arrival of Winter. Winds blew from the north and brought with them a chill in the otherwise hot or warm air.

A certain borderland, one made of mountains on the west side of the Hard Lands, had once shared a vast lake that was dotted by islands that had once been mountain peaks. This lake, on the southern tip of the Hard Lands, was usually a tranquil place, and would prove to be disputed territory between two powerful dragons, one from the west that was known as Terrwrathgrawr the Terrible, and on the east by the one creature in the world he feared: Agarxus the Tyrant, likely the largest and most powerful dragon in the world.

This dispute would be settled after a deep crossing into the realm of Agarxus by Terrwrathgrawr, who it seemed was pursuing a fleeing dragoness of his. The battle that led to this would push the recognized border thirty leagues to the west to the very mountains that begin the Territhan Range.

But that is a story for another time.

A large island in this lake, one connected to the nearby western shore by boats that ferried goods and people many times a day and a long, rickety bridge of timber and planks, was home to a population of humans and a few gnomes, the latter living inside caves and tunnels carved into the stone of the island. These humans lived mostly on fish and whatever vegetables and herbs they grew in their gardens, and the occasional crocodile, and these crocodiles were much a part of their daily problems as the food they provided, especially the largest of them that were too big to be taken by creatures as frail as humans.

This is where our story has its origins, an island settlement of humans and gnomes.

Far away from here, far to the northeast and into the tallest peaks of the mountains that ran like a spine down the middle of the desert, a dragon swept against the northern winds, stroking his wings for height before he would angle down and ride the air currents. His dark blue eyes swept the mountainsides and the ground, black scales reflecting deep red and maroon back as the sun hit them just right. His dorsal scales, running from between his horns all the way to the end of his long tail, were suddenly scarlet, as were the tips of his horns and his long claws. This dragon was not fully an adult, not close to as large as he would grow and, at only thirty seasons old, was still very much an adolescent. Still, he was very big for his age, well-muscled but lean for our kind. This was a healthy dragon, a formidable drake for those his own age, but one that had only recently learned to avoid larger dragons.

Clutched in his red claws and held close to his chest was a human girl, one who also watched the terrain below them. She wore a long, heavy green cloak that flapped in the passing air. One arm was pinned to her by the dragon's grip while the other clung to one of his powerful fingers. Her legs were held together tightly by his other hand. Her black hair was long and unruly in the rapidly passing air and her eyes were squinted against it. Cocooned in the cloak and in the dragon's grip, she did not fidget or struggle, but instead seemed to have accepted her fate, that she was a captive in his talons until he decided otherwise, that and if she managed to struggle free, the ground was very far below them.

The dragon's right wing angled upward and he banked and turned toward what appeared to be the tallest mountain in eyeshot, and he angled himself toward a flat outcropping that was more than large enough to allow a dragon of his twenty-pace wingspan to land. Lowering his feet, he swept his wings forward in many air-grabbing strokes, slowing his descent and expertly settling his clawed feet onto the gray stone below him. Once his weight was on his feet and off of his wings, he folded his wings tightly to his back and sides and lurched over, gently lowering the maiden he carried to the ground.

Laid to her side, she rolled away from the dragon, facing him as her wide eyes were locked on him, and he backed away a step and turned away from her, grasping the cliffside that led to the mountain's peak as his flanks heaved for breath. The shoes she wore were not well suited for any time in the wilderness, but she pulled her feet to her, hugging the cloak to her as well as she sat up and stared at the mighty beast that had taken her high into the mountains. She was a pretty girl for her kind, seventeen seasons old and marrying age, and as she reached from within the cloak to comb her hair out of her face, she revealed a lean build that was considered desirable to her kind, a well-muscled and healthy body that came from a good diet of fish and vegetables and a life of work. Fingernails were short, worn down by her labors and slowly combed easily through her hair as she stared up at the dragon. Slowly, she leaned forward and stood, full attention never leaving the dragon before her. As she stood fully, the cloak blew open to reveal a torn white shirt, one without any sleeves that dropped nearly to her knees, and a leather jerkin died green in some effort to match her cloak. Her legs were largely bare, her thighs only half concealed by her long shirt. Dark blue eyes studied the dragon and for a long moment she could not speak.

The dragon, still leaning against the cliffside, closed his eyes and drew in deeper breaths to catch his wind, and the last few growled out of him as his other hand slid across his belly to grasp his side, that side closest to the cliff on which he leaned.

Her voice betrayed lingering youth as she observed, "You don't look so good."

Annoyance found his eyes as he opened them and looked down at her from nearly four heights, and he growled back in a deep voice that also betrayed youth, "I'm fine. Just let it go."

She raised her brow and folded her arms.

He pushed off of the cliff and took three long strides to the edge of the outcropping, squinting slightly as he scanned the distant land beyond, a green land past the desert.

"You need to eat something," she insisted.

"I could eat you," he suggested.

"I'm serious!" she barked. "When was the last time you ate?"

"We can go for long periods without food," he informed. "You know that." Looking down at her, he observed, "You haven't eaten for a while, either, and you should eat two or three times a day."

She stared back at him for long seconds, then demanded, "What are we doing?"

He looked east again, scanning the land beyond as he replied, "We are surviving."

"Barely," she snarled back.

He growled again. "You'll forgive me if I never took instruction in how to care for a human girl." He looked back at her, looking her up and down. "We'll need to find you some new clothes. You'll never survive winter in those."

"I'm sure we'll have to trade money for clothes," she said frankly, "and I think you're the one dragon in the world without a hoard."

He raised a scaly eyebrow, then looked east again. "There's a lake in the distance. I'm sure we can find food there."

"And crocodiles," she added grimly.

"Like I said," he went on, "food."

"You know I don't like crocodile meat."

He nodded. "Starving, and still a picky eater."

She heaved a heavy breath and reached from within the cloak to pull it closer to her. "I don't want to argue."

He looked back to her and this time raised both eyebrows.

Looking up at him, she barked, "It isn't my fault we're out here!"

"No," he corrected, "it's your fault that *you're* out here."

She looked away again.

He turned his attention east again. "All you had to do was not talk. That's all you had to do. But as always, you just couldn't help yourself."

"It wasn't right of them to banish you!" she cried. "It wasn't right."

"It was my problem," he snarled. "You should have just stayed out of it."

Her eyes strayed to him again and she asked, "And if they wished to banish me, what would you do?" When he did not answer, she prodded, "Well? What would the mighty Farrigrall do?"

The dragon heaved a hard breath and still did not answer.

She finally approached and gently reached up to place a hand on the side of his leg. His knee was as high as her shoulder. He was a huge, formidable beast with the longest of his sharp teeth as long as her forearm. Still, she had no fear of him and insisted, "I'm with you until the end. I've never known a time without you and I hope I never will."

He lowered his eyes.

She turned her attention from his face to the wound on his side that was stubbornly slow to heal, and her lips tightened to a thin slit. "It wasn't your fault," she assured.

He heaved another hard breath.

"Once you heal up," she continued, "we'll go back and you'll—"

"We aren't going back," he growled. "It's over. We'll start over out here somewhere."

She nodded. "Okay. We start over out here." Looking beyond them, toward greener and more fertile lands, she insisted, "I'll bet all kinds of adventure awaits us out there."

"And all kinds of dangers you'll walk right into," he grumbled. Reaching to her, he gently picked her up and held her to him as he had before, opened his wings, and leapt from the outcropping.

"It won't matter," she assured. "I'll be right at your side."

He just growled in response.

"You know," she began slowly, "there are stories where people ride dragons into great ad—"

"No," he interrupted.

"But I'm sure we could find someone who could make a saddle that—"

"No."

"Oh, come on! If I were riding on your back you—"

"No."

"You wouldn't have to carry me all the time!"

"No."

**

Within an hour they landed in a field of beige and light green grass on one end of the vast lake he had seen. A river that fed into the lake was very wide here and ran slowly and the surface of the water was calm and tranquil. Surrounded by hills and trees, it was a beautiful place, and as he set her into the knee-deep grass, she looked around her with wondrous eyes and wore a big smile as she insisted, "This has got to be the most beautiful place in the world!"

He just looked down at her, then he sat catlike and scanned the area around them, alert for any danger that might approach.

"I'm parched," she informed as she waded through the grass toward the water.

Farrigrall just watched her as she approached the water's edge, wearing no readable expression. As she was nearly there, his brow shot up and he raised his head, then he sprang up and shouted, "Josslee!" as he ran toward her with long steps.

The girl was just about to crouch down by the water's edge when she heard her name and half turned to see him charging forward, and a splash from the lake alerted her to something deadly and horrible and she stumbled away, screaming as her eyes were filled with the vision of white teeth inside the gaping jaws of a huge crocodile! It lunged toward her and she stumbled and fell to her back. Just the crocodile's jaws were as long as she was tall and it would swallow her with one gulp, but it turned to the right and backed away, its jaws still open as it retreated.

Roaring like something from a nightmare, Farrigrall stomped toward it with his own jaws gaping, scaly lips drawn away from his own long, menacing teeth. The crocodile was huge, but was clearly not up to dealing with a dragon today and whipped around to splash back into the deep of the lake.

The dragon stood fully, his complete attention locked on the retreating crocodile that nearly matched his own length, then he grasped his side as he turned very annoyed eyes down to the girl.

She stared back up at him, managed a strained smile and offered, "Thank you?"

He growled, then turned and strode into the water until it lapped just above his knees. "Get your drink if you have to."

Josslee stood and brushed herself off, then set her hands on her hips and complained, "Of course, now that you've made the water all muddy."

His jaws clenched together and he grumbled, "I should have just let the crocodile eat you."

She strode a few paces away from where he had waded in and knelt down beside the water's edge, finding clean water in which to dip her hands. "Then you'd have to answer to Mama."

In a low voice, he mocked, "Then you'd have to answer to Mama." Looking up, he observed, "Nearly high sun. I'm going to fly over the lake and see if there are any fish out there to catch." He turned toward her, pointing to the tree line. "Go over there, stay over there, stay out of trouble, and don't move until I get back."

She slurped a handful of water into her mouth, then another, then she looked that way, back up at him and insisted, "I'm going to stay in the sun where's it's warm."

Growling again, he turned fully, strode to the girl and plucked her from the water with one hand around her chest and midriff, walked her about ten steps from the water's edge, and dropped her where she crumpled into the tall grass there.

She got back to her feet, combed a hand through her hair and glared up at him.

He poked the tip of one of his claws into her chest just hard enough to make her lurch backward and ordered, "Stay!"

"Fine!" she barked back.

With yet another growl, he turned and strode away from her, his tail sweeping just over her head and close enough to make her duck.

"Hey!" she shouted.

Farrigrall opened his wings and took flight, soaring over the lake and flying only about three or four heights from the surface.

Josslee watched him and huffed a hard breath, then sat down and crossed her legs. She was fairly well concealed in the tall grass and knew that he was only trying to protect her. Still, about a quarter hour later, she found herself pinching seeds from the stalk of one of the tall grasses that grew around her, still a little frustrated with him and, worse, feeling horribly bored.

At this low level, the wind was but a breeze coming off of the lake and only the distant sounds of the air in the trees and the singing and chirping of birds reached her. None of this was of interest. She was hungry, still not quite warm, and still bored. Another quarter hour later, she found herself missing her family, missing her home, and suddenly feeling alone and a little vulnerable. She would not allow fear to overtake her, but stories of giant forest cats in these parts, tree leapers, and flesh rending Dreads could not be pushed completely from her mind.

Another quarter hour of nothing to do but pick seeds and try to rid her mind of terrifying thoughts and she finally heard that familiar whoosh of wings through air and she turned her eyes toward the lake, raising her chin slightly as she realized this comforting sound was coming from behind her. Turning at the waist, she looked over her shoulder, her eyes widening as they were filled by an approaching dragon, but not the one she was expecting.

Scarlet scales glistened in the sunlight and the ocher breast and belly of this dragon were like fire against the blue of the sky and the few clouds that floated by. Somewhat smaller than Farrigrall, this dragon had a different shape to its body, leaner limbs and a slenderer head, neck, and tail.

Josslee's spine went rigid as she saw the dragon soaring right toward her. The dragon's feet lowered to land, and the dragon's attention was focused ahead of her. Frozen where she was, the girl watched as the dragon glided over her almost close enough to touch, and she turned as she watched the great beast settle to the ground halfway between her and the water's edge and fold its wings to its back and sides. That crawl in her stomach became even worse as it turned toward her, sweeping its tail just over the tops of the grasses as it looked her way—and up!

Turning, Josslee drew a gasp as she saw a second dragon, a burgundy beast with black claws and horns, approaching and lowering its feet to land, and sweeping its wings forward almost frantically as it tried to slow itself, and she turned with the dragon as it passed about ten paces on her right, hit the ground hard with its feet and stumbled forward.

This landing did not go well and this smaller dragon could not keep its balance, tried to run into its momentum and finally crashed head-first into the shallow water near the lakeshore with a huge splash.

The scarlet dragon had also watched this and was shaking its head as Josslee looked back to it, and a growl rolled from its throat.

The other dragon was slow to push itself up, shaking its head as it also growled its annoyance. Struggling back to its feet, the burgundy dragon's brow was low over its eyes as it looked to the scarlet.

"Really?" the scarlet barked in a feminine voice. "You were able to do this yesterday!"

Shaking more mud and water from it, the burgundy dragon turned and folded its wings to itself, stomping toward the scarlet as it snapped back in a younger feminine voice, "You said it would take time!"

"You've had a month," the scarlet snapped back. "I swear, hatchling, an ogre learns faster than you!"

Through clenched teeth, the burgundy pointed out, "It is not as easy as it looks."

"Even wyverns can do it," the scarlet pointed out.

"They do it by instinct," the burgundy dragoness spat.

The scarlet raised her brow and folded her arms.

The two stared at each other for long seconds.

Lowering her eyes, the burgundy dragoness admitted in a low voice, "I'll keep trying."

"Just don't kill yourself," the scarlet snarled as she turned—right toward Josslee!

Scarlet dragon and girl locked eyes.

The burgundy dragon looked to the scarlet, then to the girl who held her attention.

Silence thickened the air all around for long seconds.

The dragons looked to each other, then back to the girl.

Josslee forced a little smile and waggled her fingers to them in a nervous greeting.

Drawing her head back slightly, the scarlet dragon observed, "I've never seen humans in this part of the land before. It is far too thick with predators that eat them."

The burgundy dragon lowered her head and started to step toward the girl, but something jerked her backward and she stumbled toward the lake with wide eyes. Swinging around, she roared as she saw the large crocodile that had her tail in its jaws and was dragging her into the water.

The scarlet dragon looked that way as her smaller companion was pulled into deeper water, then she looked to the girl and asked, "What are you doing in this part of the forest?"

Wide eyed, the girl raised her brow and looked to the splashing battle that raged in the lake.

Glancing that way, the scarlet dismissively assured, "Oh, she's fine. How did you get here on your own like this?"

"I'm not alone," Josslee assured. The fighting crocodile and dragon drew her attention back to the lake as the two rolled in the water, each looking to get in a good bite, and finally they were in deep enough water to submerge, though they still violently disturbed the surface at times. "Are you sure she is all right?"

"She does this all the time," the scarlet dragon informed. "We both wrestle crocodiles from time to time. It's actually quite a sporting time. Now back to you."

The burgundy dragoness surfaced and roared again, then plunged back into the water with gaping jaws.

Josslee finally stood, her attention on the battle that raged in the lake. "Um..." Looking back up at the scarlet dragon who drew closer to her with hesitant steps, she asked, "Uh, you aren't one of those dragons who eats people, are you? That would not end well for either of us."

The scarlet seemed to smile and assured, "I have no appetite for humans, no. In fact, I have friends who are humans."

A little smile curled the girl's mouth and she admitted, "That's a relief. I was afraid—"

A deep roar shook the land around and the scarlet wheeled to the left, her dorsal scales standing erect as she half spread her wings and held her claws ready for battle. She stepped back and roared a response as Farrigrall swept in and slammed onto the ground only ten paces away. The scarlet retreated a few steps as she realized this intruder was larger than she was and she roared again, then she looked to the lake and a roar escaped her as she called, "Revillee!"

The burgundy dragoness' head surfaced long enough for her to shout back, "Busy!" before disappearing below the surface again.

The scarlet snarled, "And useless." She looked back to the drake before her and roared again, trying to make herself look as big as possible, but she retreated a few more steps as he advanced.

Farrigrall angled himself between Josslee and the scarlet dragon and bared his teeth, holding his ground there as he faced her down with a deep growl.

The girl stepped to his side and looked up at him, calling, "Farrigrall, wait. She is—"

"I can handle this!" he snapped, his full attention still on the scarlet dragoness. "Just stay behind me."

"You never listen!" the girl shouted. "She is friendly and she doesn't eat people!"

The black drake glanced down at the girl, then his focus returned to the scarlet dragoness, his brow low over his eyes as he assured, "She is definitely not eating one today."

Her own eyes narrowing, the dragoness demanded, "What are you doing here?"

"This human is mine," he insisted.

"I am not interested in your pet human," the dragoness insisted.

Josslee stepped forward and raised her hand before her, correcting, "I'm not his pet. I'm his sister."

The scarlet's eyes found the girl and she informed, "That raises more questions than it answers."

A growl rolled from Farrigrall and he took another long step toward the dragoness. "I am not here to answer your questions. It is time for you to depart."

The sound of rushing water drew his attention and that of the other dragon and they both looked that way to see the burgundy wading ashore, water cascading from her as her chest heaved in an effort to catch her breath.

Stopping about twenty paces away, the burgundy sat catlike in the tall grass and complained, "My tail is going to be sore forever." She looked the black dragon up and down, raising her brow as she declared, "Wow! You are a handsome dragon!"

The scarlet growled and ordered, "Focus, Revillee." Studying the black dragon before her, she half turned her head and asked, "Have we met before? There is something familiar about you."

"I've never seen you before," Farrigrall assured.

Revillee seemed to smile and said, "That's a pity." She looked to Josslee and raised her brow. "Is that your pet girl?"

"I'm not his pet," Josslee cried, "I'm his sister!"

Looking to the scarlet, the burgundy dragoness mumbled, "That doesn't make any sense."

The scarlet's brow arched and she mumbled, "Coming from you?"

Laying to the ground to bring her head closer to the girl's eye level, the burgundy dragon gave the girl her full attention and introduced, "Hi. My name's Revillee. This is Falloah. What is your name?"

"Josslee," the girl answered. "This is Farrigrall."

Drawing her head back, the scarlet dragoness demanded, "Where do you come from? Where?"

"What does it matter?" Farrigrall snapped. "Look, we just stopped to find something to eat and—"

"Where?" Falloah demanded again.

Black dragon and girl exchanged glances, and Josslee answered, "Peak Island village, south of the desert."

Falloah's eyes found the black dragon again, her jaws hanging open as she stared in apparent disbelief.

Another roar sounded from above and behind the scarlet dragon, a much deeper roar from a more powerful dragon. All looked that way and Revillee stood, mumbling, "Uh, oh."

Descending sharply, another dragon swept his wings forward and slammed onto the ground hard in a clear challenge, his dorsal scales erect as he gaped his jaws and roared through bared teeth. Dark green scales darkened to black on his back and belly. Horns that swept back from behind his eyes had black tips and faded to that dark green as they approached his head. Dark green eyes found the intruder quickly and he bared his teeth, holding his nose downward slightly as he stomped toward the black dragon with heavy steps. He was larger than Falloah, thicker built, larger than Farrigrall, and with his claws curled and his back arched, he was spoiling for a fight. This was a young drake with much to prove to his superiors, especially the landmaster who had allowed him hunting range in this territory, and he would make certain all knew of his strength.

Farrigrall had no intention of fighting this other dragon, but stood his ground as the larger dragon approached.

Josslee backed away, horror in her eyes as if she were reliving something terrible.

It was Falloah, the scarlet dragoness, who stepped in front of the approaching drake, blocking his path, and when he went to roar at his foe again, she clamped a clawed hand over his nose and mouth and ordered, "That is enough. There will be no combat today."

The drake pulled his nose free of her grip and growled, "It is my duty to the Landmaster—"

Falloah roared, "I have said no! Back away."

His brow lowered over his eyes and he looked down at the scarlet dragoness as patience drained away.

Revillee approached him next, cooing at him, and informed, "They are friends, not invaders."

"They?" the green dragon demanded.

"Josslee and Farrigrall," she replied. "Josslee is his human."

The green dragon's eyes finally found the girl, then turned back to the black dragon with a blink. "It makes no difference if he has a human pet or not. My orders from the Landmaster are clear."

"And I have said no!" Falloah hissed.

"You have no authority here," the green drake growled. "Stand aside, or I will move you."

The scarlet's eyes narrowed. "I am certain that my own drake would not look favorably on that. Perhaps I can summon him and you can try to move *him*."

He spat back, "Always hiding behind Ralligor's wings, aren't you?"

Revillee informed, "A crocodile bit my tail."

"The quicker you learn your place," Falloah informed, "the quicker you will know who you should and should not challenge."

"It really hurt," the burgundy dragoness added.

A deep growl rolled from the green dragon's throat as he stared down the scarlet, and finally he tore his eyes away from her to look to the young burgundy dragoness.

Revillee glanced at Falloah, then her attention found the drake and she went on, "I fought it off as usual. I guess it's fine."

He drew a deep breath and forced it out through his nose with a snort. His eyes found the black dragon again and he demanded, "What is this dragon to you, anyway? Why would you protect him?"

"That is none of your concern," Falloah snarled. "The unicorns will be here soon and you will not want to be here when they arrive."

The green drake's eyes narrowed again, then found the black drake once more. "The unicorns do not concern me. If Ralligor wishes to keep pets then that is his problem."

"Then you can tell him when he arrives," Falloah added.

Revillee approached another step, close enough to grasp his arm, and she suggested, "Lornoxez, perhaps we can spend some time together. I hardly get to see you anymore."

"You can see me anytime you wish," he growled. He huffed another breath, then turned and bade, "Come along, Revillee."

She happily followed, looking over her shoulder, and she waggled her fingers at the young black drake as she said, "Bye, Farrigrall. Bye Josslee. See you later."

The three who remained watched the two dragons take flight and soar toward the east, and silence gripped the grassy floodplain.

Falloah turned and gave the black dragon a long, awkward stare, then she strode past him, toward the lake, and laid to her belly near the water, staring out over the lake with her arms crossed before her.

Farrigrall and Josslee watched her for a long moment, and the girl asked, "What do you suppose is wrong with her? Should we go talk to her?"

The dragon grasped his side as he stared at the scarlet, and slowly shook his head. "Give her time to think. Whatever is on her mind will come out in time if she is willing."

CHAPTER 2

An hour or so ago Farrigrall had laid down to sleep as he often did following a long flight. How he could sleep after what had just transpired was a mystery. He faced the lake, laying on his belly with his arms drawn to him, his legs straight out on each side of his tail, and from time to time, he would snore and shift ever so slightly.

Josslee sat beside him, leaning against his neck near his head as she stared at the scarlet dragoness over fifty paces away, a dragoness who stared across the lake and did not seem to move otherwise. Farrigrall had said she would speak of it if and when she so desired, but the girl was not all that patient.

Pushing off of the dragon's neck, she stood and approached the dragoness with slow, hesitant steps, her eyes never leaving the great predator. No longer fearing the crocodiles that inhabited this lake, not with dragons about, she found her steps rhythmic and almost automatic, as she neared, and could almost hear her own heart beating.

Nearly there, she froze as the dragoness half turned her head toward her, her eyes widening as the dragoness' jaws parted.

"What happened?" Falloah asked.

"What do you mean?" the girl countered.

"You are too young to leave home and live alone. Something happened to drive you and him away. What was it?"

Josslee glanced back at the black dragon, who continued to slumber away, then she looked to the scarlet dragoness and tried to answer, but was unable to.

"Start from the beginning," Falloah ordered. "How did you come to call a dragon your brother?"

Drawing a deep breath, the girl looked to the ground before her, then sat cross legged in the tall grass and plucked at a few of the stalks before she finally answered. "My mother found him near the lake when she was just a little girl. He was still in his egg and she snuck him into her house and kept him hidden in the corner of her bed until he hatched." She raised her brow. "She's told me the story of that many times, how my grandfather was afraid and upset, but he did not have the heart to tell her to cast him out. He was raised around the house in secret for many seasons and grew very fast, and turned out to be much smarter than anyone expected he would be. By four seasons old he was as tall as any man, talking and actually helping with the chores around the house, but they had to keep him hidden."

Falloah turned her head fully to look down at the girl.

Josslee went on, "When the rest of the village found out about him, he was able to hold conversations and quickly won the hearts of most of them, and in time was too big to sleep in the house, so he slept by the docks. Still, there were those who did not like the idea of a dragon living in the village and were afraid he would turn on them and eat some of them. That, and food was a problem." She raised her brow. "He eats a lot. The people of the village mostly live on fish and whatever small crocodiles they could harvest, and little gardens for vegetables and herbs, but you can guess that the big crocodiles would sometimes come in very close and eat some of the villagers. Several of these bigger ones were a real problem, and one summer my grandfather was taken by one. I never got to meet him." She drew a deep breath. "Two other people were taken that day, but Farg was very close to my grandfather by this time six seasons later, and he was already eight paces long himself. Mamma said he mourned for many days and people could hear him crooning into the night." She finally looked up at the dragoness. "Eight days later the big crocodile returned, and Farg was waiting for him."

The dragoness just stared down at her with no readable expression.

"As the whole village watched," Josslee went on, "there was a great battle, dragon versus crocodile, and Farg drove the big crocodile away. He tried to kill him, but he was not quite strong enough.

"Over the seasons, as he grew larger and stronger, he killed many crocodiles, big snakes, any threat to the village. The houses and shops along the shoreline on the west side of the lake were once troubled by Dreads and barbarians, but he drove them away, too."

"And now?" Falloah pressed.

Josslee turned her eyes down again. "About ten days ago, a bigger dragon appeared. Farg tried to fight him off, but the other dragon was too big and too powerful. Part of the village was burned, people died, and the other dragon ate half of the stores of fish and other food, and made it clear that he would be back for more." She huffed a hard breath. "He also made it clear that if Farg remained, he would kill him and burn most of the village down, so the village elders banished him. I spoke out against this, but I'm just a silly girl."

"They banished you as well?" Falloah questioned.

"I argued too much," the girl replied. "They said if I was not happy with their decision then I could just go with him, so I did."

Falloah smiled. "A little too head strong for your own good. I know other humans like you."

Also smiling, Josslee looked up to the dragoness.

"So, what now?" the dragoness asked.

With a shrug, Josslee replied, "I don't know. We're just trying to live day by day."

"When did you eat last?" the dragoness asked.

With a shrug, Josslee looked down and confessed, "A couple of days, I think. I am most worried over Farg. He was injured in his fight and it seems slow to heal."

Falloah turned her attention to the black dragon who lay slumbering fifty paces away. "Has he eaten of late?"

"I think he got a fish today," the girl replied.

The dragoness nodded in slight motions, her eyes fixed on the slumbering black dragon. Something caught her eyes and she looked a few paces beyond the girl, to the big bay unicorn with the black mane, tail and beard who stared at the girl with a blank expression.

"Good to see you," Falloah greeted.

The unicorn just turned his eyes up to her and did not respond.

"This is not what it looks like," the dragoness defended.

Josslee turned at the waist, her eyes widening as they filled with the magnificent unicorn behind her, and she drew a loud and deep gasp.

Looking back to the girl, the unicorn mumbled, "No, it never is." He turned and whinnied toward the forest, and paced that way, looking over his shoulder as he informed, "You know the rest of the herd will not emerge as long as there is a strange dragon about."

"Except Shahly," the dragoness added.

The unicorn paced on. "Except Shahly." He stopped and looked back at her again. "What about crocodiles?"

"Revillee tangled with one earlier," Falloah reported, "and I haven't seen any others since I got here. We can make certain so that your herd can drink safely."

The unicorn nodded to her and offered, "Appreciated as always, Falloah." He paced two more steps, then stopped again and looked to Farrigrall, then to Falloah.

"I'll take care of it," she assured, "and explain everything to you."

He nodded again, then turned to pace on.

Josslee watched as the unicorn walked toward the trees, and slowly she shook her head and breathed, "A unicorn."

"You'll have your chance to marvel over them," Falloah assured. She pushed herself up standing with her back and tail nearly parallel to the ground and her arms held to her, then she turned to the black dragon and strode toward him with long steps. "Come along, human pet."

Josslee also stood and followed the dragoness, correcting, "I'm not a pet, I'm his sister."

"Whatever," Falloah grumbled.

They reached the slumbering black dragon and Falloah nudged him until he stirred, then she sat catlike and stared down at him.

A low growl rolled from him and he opened his eyes, then turned them up to the dragoness with a raised brow.

"You need to go," Falloah informed.

Farrigrall pushed himself up and nodded.

"We will talk more," she added, "but you need to hurry and get somewhere else. Not south and not west, just—" She was cut off by a sharp whinny, and tightly closed her eyes, grumbling, "It's too late."

"What do you mean?" the young drake questioned.

Galloping hoof beats drew their attention to the little white unicorn who raced toward them, the gold ribbons in her horn glistening in the sunlight as she ran. Around her neck was a gold chain suspending golden talons that gripped an emerald orb about the size of a bird's egg, and as she reached the dragons, her attention went to the black drake, then to Falloah, then to Farrigrall, and back.

"Who is your new friend?" the little unicorn asked, youth still in her voice despite the added girth around her middle that hinted of pregnancy.

Falloah heaved a heavy breath and looked down to the little unicorn, and she replied, "This is Farrigrall. Farrigrall, Shahly."

"Nice to meet you," the little unicorn offered. Turning abruptly, she whinnied to the forest, "It is all right! He is a friend to Falloah!"

Farrigrall watched the little white unicorn gallop to the tree line and kept his eyes on her as she disappeared into the shadows of the forest, then he looked to the scarlet dragoness and asked, "You are friends with unicorns? A whole herd of them?"

Her eyes slid to him.

"I had always heard our kind and theirs were, well, not on the best of terms."

She just stared at him, and finally ordered, "Fly along the shoreline and a quarter league out into the lake and see to it there are no threats to the unicorns. They wish to play in the water once more before winter comes."

He seemed perplexed, but finally glanced down at Josslee, shrugged and turned to take flight.

The girl watched him go, then she turned her attention up to the dragoness and asked, almost begged, "May I stay?"

Falloah looked down to her, her brow tensing as she demanded, "Why aren't you afraid of me?"

Josslee shrugged. "I grew up with Farrigrall."

**

A couple of hours later found a herd of about two dozen unicorns frolicking in the water, on the shoreline, or grazing in the deep grasses of the field, many of them nibbling on the seeds that were temptingly at the tops of some of the taller stalks.

From time to time, Farrigrall would soar overhead, his attention on the water as he maintained his vigil for crocodiles or any other threat to the herd of which Falloah was so protective. While he did not understand all of the fuss over a bunch of unicorns, he could see that Josslee enjoyed their company, and that was good enough for him.

The scarlet dragoness had, once again, strayed from everyone else and lay on her belly as she stared out over the lake. One could assume that she was also keeping watch for crocodiles, but she seemed more lost in thought. The girl glanced at her often, and though consumed with the company of the magical unicorns who wanted to play with her, many of the younger ones mobbing her for attention from time to time, she found herself more and more distracted by the dragoness.

Only two unicorns played out in the water and most were grazed peacefully in the field, and with all of them distracted with eating or those few still playing in the water, Josslee looked to the scarlet dragoness again, and this time approached her with more confidence than she had before.

As she reached the great, scarlet predator, she stopped at her side, well out of eyeshot, and just stared out at the lake as well, unaware that the dragoness had felt her approach until her head swung around and she looked down at the girl.

Raising her brow, Josslee offered, "I don't mean to disturb you."

"You aren't," the dragoness confirmed as she looked back to the lake. "That dragon that attacked your village. You didn't catch his name, did you?"

"He announced his name," Josslee replied. "Something the Terrible, I think."

Falloah raised her head, her eyes widening slightly as she guessed, "Terrwrathgrawr?"

"Yes!" the girl confirmed. "Do you know him? Can you talk to him?"

"I know him," the dragoness confirmed, "but I will not be talking to him." She stood and looked around her, to the unicorns, out into the field, then back to the lake. Raising her nose, she opened her jaws and sent forth a high-pitched call, not a roar, almost a trumpet, and clearly not as loudly as she was able. She turned abruptly, careful not to step on the girl, and she strode to the unicorns, her eyes quickly finding the big bay, and she called, "Vinton!"

The bay raised his head and looked that way, then he turned and trotted to meet her.

They stopped only about ten paces apart, Falloah lowering her head to come almost eye level with the big unicorn.

"Something troubled you in a hurry," the unicorn observed.

"I need to go somewhere," she informed with a certain franticness to her voice.

He nodded. "This has something to do with your visiting dragon, doesn't it?"

"It does," she confirmed.

A little out of breath, Josslee finally caught up and bent over to grasp her knees as she caught her wind.

"Will you be leaving the other dragon?" the unicorn asked.

"I need him along," Falloah replied, then she motioned to the girl and added, "And her. Something is happening to the west that I should investigate."

The unicorn's eyes narrowed. "Shouldn't Ralligor be the one to—"

"No!" the dragoness barked, raising her head. "I must do this myself. He does not need to know, not yet."

"Not like you to keep things from him," Vinton observed.

Falloah looked away from him. "I just need to find out for myself. That's all."

"It's about another dragon," Josslee volunteered.

Her brow low over her eyes, Falloah swung her head around and growled at the girl with her nose within arm's reach, and the girl cringed under the dragoness' anger.

With a slow nod, Vinton observed, "Another dragon that you don't want Ralligor to know about."

Falloah looked back to him and defended, "It is not like that at all! This other dragon has crossed the border and—"

"Is Ralligor's responsibility," the bay unicorn finished for her.

The two stared at each other for a long, tense moment.

Farrigrall swept in behind the dragoness and swept his wings forward in air grabbing strokes, touching his feet gently to the ground about fifty paces away, then he looked to the scarlet and asked, "You called?"

Falloah stared back at Vinton a few seconds longer, then she swung around and stood fully, announcing, "I need to go. Come along, Farrigrall, and bring your pet human with you."

Josslee barked back as she followed the dragoness, "I'm his sister!"

"Whatever!" Falloah shouted back to her. Stopping suddenly, she half turned and ordered, "And Ralligor is not to know about this. Any of this!"

Vinton's eyes narrowed.

"Promise me!" the dragoness insisted.

"I don't like this, Falloah," the big unicorn informed.

"Just promise you will not tell him," the scarlet said again, her voice laced with desperation.

Vinton heaved a hard breath, looked out toward the lake as two more dragons soared into view who he knew to be Revillee and Lornoxez, then he turned his eyes back to Falloah, assuring, "I won't tell him. I promise."

The unicorn watched with tense eyes as the scarlet dragoness turned and strode to the waiting black dragon, who had scooped up the girl and held her in his hands and arms, and he watched longer as the two dragons took flight and flew directly away from him, toward the west and south, and his eyes narrowed slightly.

An old gray unicorn with a white horn and a long white beard, mane and tail paced up from behind Vinton and took his side. This unicorn was not quite as large as the bay, but his eyes betrayed many more seasons, much more experience, and he asked in a low voice, "Troubles among your dragon friends?"

Vinton heaved another hard breath and confirmed, "I'm not sure, but something is definitely amiss."

CHAPTER 3

The mountains were ten days travel by foot, but only a few hours on the wing. Falloah flew off of Farrigrall's wingtip and as they flew southeast, she glanced frequently to the right, to the desert beyond as if she were expecting something from that way, and hoping never to see it. The young drake, holding his human tightly to him as he always did, was quiet for most of the journey, his eyes finding the dragoness seemingly every few moments as they flew. Josslee was also silent, watching the coming horizon for the most part, but her eyes would slide to the dragoness from time to time, and anxiety welled up within her with each league behind them.

Finally, Farrigrall spoke up. "This is not a good idea."

"Just take us there," Falloah growled back, her attention ahead of them.

"We were banished," he reminded. "We can't just return there and expect a warm welcome."

"Your human needs to eat," the dragoness informed. "If they draw offense by your return then they can speak to me about it. I wish to see this village." She squinted slightly. "That is the lake ahead. Your village is on one of the larger islands south of here?"

"Yes," the young drake confirmed. "You've been here before?"

"A long time ago," she replied, "before you hatched."

He glanced at her. "Do you think the village will remember you?"

She glanced back at him and did not respond.

Ahead of them was the lake they sought, a vast lake surrounded by the green of grasses and patches of forest. Islands that had been mountain peaks long ago, long before even any living dragon, seemed to be in a line near the center of the lake, mountains that had once been a divide between river valleys but were now mosty under water. Some of these islands were very small, only peaks of plant covered rock and soil that were white and gray near the water and perhaps only a hundred paces across. Others were much larger, some a league across, some this size flatter and covered with forest and no doubt many animals. The largest, off in the distance, was the only one settled by humans and their kin, an island about a league and a half wide at its widest point and about four times that long. There were still many trees and plants, but also many houses and stone buildings, including what appeared to be a castle near the center where the island was tallest.

These islands were not evenly spaced at all, and this largest of them, about twenty leagues from the southern shore, was only a league and a half from the western shore and connected to a village there by a long bridge that was built of stone and wood. Half a league north of it was a much smaller island peak, mostly stone but with a good amount of forest and growth on the southern side. The peak itself was some kind of granite, and a flat area, one that looked as if it may have been quarried for stone once, faced the approaching dragons, and Falloah descended toward it, approaching low and keeping this smaller island between her and the island she sought. Farrigrall followed, eying the dragoness almost suspiciously as they approached the mostly bare rock of the smaller island, an inviting place to land that was about fifty paces wide and thirty deep to the peak of the stone hill in the island center.

Setting down gracefully and making very little sound when she did, Falloah's attention was on the ground below her as her feet settled, and she quickly folded her wings and strode to the cut stone of the cliffside before her. Farrigrall landed behind her, also folding his wings right away as he followed.

The cliff was about ten paces tall, too high for the dragoness to see over, but she dug claws into cracks and crevices and easily climbed toward the top with expert form. Farrigrall set the girl gently to the ground and also climbed, stopping beside the dragoness as she peered over the top.

He glanced at her, then to the village in which he had grown, and he grumbled, "Now you are afraid to be seen?"

"Quiet," she hissed.

He whispered back, "This is not a good idea."

"A worse idea is for you to keep talking," she whispered back, her attention on the activity in the village, and the smoke that rose from the west side. Her eyes squinted as she drew far away vision close to her.

Farrigrall did the same, and he raised his head as he saw the big form moving about on the far side of the village, near where the smoke was rising.

Falloah watched the big, dark copper colored form stomp among the modest wooden and stone structures of the village, then she slowly lowered herself back down to the ledge where the girl waited, turned and leaned her back against the cliff side, her wide eyes staring blankly forward into nothing.

Still hanging from the top, Farrigrall looked down to the dragoness, then he also clamored down and stood there staring at her.

Slow to approach, Josslee wrung her hands together as she stared up at the dragoness, and she asked, "He's there, isn't he? That other dragon."

Staring blankly ahead, Falloah just nodded.

Farrigrall growled and insisted, "We can take him together."

The dragoness turned her eyes down and corrected, "No, we can't, not that dragon." She drew a breath, and snorted as she released it. "I need to think." Her eyes found the girl and she added, "And you need to eat something. Will your people at least let you have a meal?"

"I doubt it," Josslee answered grimly. "My family might, but the others, especially the village elders... " She shook her head and turned her eyes down. "I made my feelings clear when they banished Farg. I don't even want to go back."

Falloah drew another deep breath and released it in a growl, looking up as if to see the village over the cliff. "We need to get out of here before he smells us." She stepped away from the cliff and opened her wings. "Come along, Farrigrall. Collect your human and follow me."

**

They flew northeast this time, very low and changed direction often. The scarlet dragoness seemed to be trying to avoid something, perhaps being seen by a larger dragon. In any case, they flew for a long while, past the lake, and eventually veered due north.

Josslee held her cloak close to her as they flew, trying to keep warm against the chilly air they passed through, and eventually she spotted a mountainous castle of white and gray stone ahead of them. She had heard of castles and had read stories about the great kingdoms of the lands, the sieges and great battles fought around them, and the nobles and royals who called them home. What she knew of them were in these romanticized stories and her heart fluttered within her as she wondered how true the stories were, if the royals who lived there really threw extravagant banquets and balls and if knights and ladies were really quite as numerous within as the stories told.

Farrigrall had different feelings about such things and stroked his wings to take the dragoness' side as she descended over the turning trees of red and orange and brown and tan, over fields and creeks and a river, and he said, "We're not really going to that castle, are we?"

"We are," the dragoness confirmed. She glanced at him and ordered, "Just relax. I know these humans and the one who leads them."

"I've only ever heard of dragons attacking castles," Farrigrall grumbled.

"I'm sure," Falloah mumbled back. "Land gently on the wall with me and make sure you don't land on one of them."

As they approached the four height tall stone perimeter wall that surrounded the huge palace, Farrigrall grew more uneasy and held the girl tighter to him. As guards on the wall fled their path and they lowered their feet to land, the young drake growled, "I'm not liking this."

They landed gently atop the perimeter wall and watched as humans in the courtyard below cleared the center, but lingered along the edges to watch the dragons. When there was a large, clear place to land, Falloah leapt from the wall and stroked her wings forward, settling gently on the ground below, and as she closed her wings, Farrigrall followed, setting down behind her only to stumble forward and right into the scarlet's back.

Falloah turned and growled at him and he backed away a step, raising his brow as he retreated from her. Though larger than she was, he still felt a little intimidated by her for reasons he could not know. He had never interacted with other dragons socially before, only the one battle with the large dragon that had driven him from his home, and he found himself learning quickly that there was a specific pecking order, and he still did not know where he stood in that order.

Most of the humans did not approach and were content to admire the dragons from a safe distance. One, however, who had been standing near the huge timber gates that led into the palace itself, strode toward the dragons seemingly without fear, her eyes locked on the scarlet as she strode toward her. This was a tall woman, a little taller than an average human man, and her long red hair was worn in a single braid that hung nearly to her lower back. She was dressed in a brown fur mantle that seemed to have come off of a bear and wore tall boots nearly to her knees that had metal armor covering the fronts of them. Similar armor was around her forearms and covered her chest, form fitting to her chest and bosom. Her trousers were black and baggy around her upper legs, held in place by a thick belt that suspended a long broadsword on the left, dagger and sword breaker on the right, and an assortment of pouches and a drinking horn that hung just behind her sword.

Dark eyes were fixed on the dragoness as she rested her hand on her sword and smiled ever so slightly, greeting, "I was hoping you would return here on my watch. I have never seen a dragon closely before. You are as magnificent as I had imagined."

"You honor me," Falloah said with a nod. "I need to see Princess Faelon."

"Already on her way," the tall, muscular woman informed. "I am Mir'Karra, Guard Captain from Zondae."

"I am called Falloah. With me is Farrigrall and his pet human Josslee."

"Sister," the girl snarled.

The warrior nodded and said, "I know who you are, Falloah the Scarlet. Many kingdoms do. Welcome to Caipiervell."

Falloah nodded again, then her eyes shifted to the palace doors and she raised her head slightly as she saw a girl about Josslee's age with long black hair and wearing a bright yellow dress emerge and run toward her. Her guards, dressed in polished armor and tunics bearing the castle's crest, trotted behind to try and keep up, but seemed apprehensive about approaching a couple of dragons in their courtyard. The girl was just below average height for her age and gender but built as a girl of sixteen seasons would be. Her movements were as well and she swung her forearms back and forth as she ran, a big smile on her lips which seemed to accentuate her already pretty face.

Out of breath, the girl reached the dragons, stopping about thirty paces away, and her eyes darted from Falloah to Farrigrall and back before she greeted, "Welcome back, Falloah! It has been so long since I saw you last!"

Falloah drew her head back and countered, "Faelon, it's only been a few weeks."

The girl set her hands on her hips and raised her brow. "That is a long time to miss someone. Do you bring word of the unicorns? Are they returning today?"

"Probably tomorrow," the dragoness informed. "They were still playing in the lake when I left. I need to ask a favor of you, if I may."

"Of course!" the girl exclaimed. "Anything!"

Looking to the black dragon at her side, then to the girl he still held, Falloah explained, "Farrigrall has a human in his company that needs to be fed and needs to spend some time in the company of her own kind." She looked to the Princess. "And she needs to tell you her story. May I leave her here with you for a day or two?"

Princess Faelon answered, "I would be honored to host her for as long as you need me to." She looked to the girl and waved to her, loudly greeting, "Hello!"

Josslee hesitantly waved back, still gripping the dragon's thumb with her other hand. Loudly clearing her throat, she looked to Farrigrall and raised her brow when she had his attention.

A little growl rolled from him and he bent over to gently set her onto the ground, and when she was standing on her own, he nudged her forward with the backs of his fingers.

She shot him an irritated look over her shoulder, then strode toward the waiting princess with hesitant steps.

Faelon met her halfway with outstretched hands and Josslee reached from within her cloak to take the other girl's hands in hers. She was taller than the princess by half a head height and was not sure what to do, so, remembering what she had read in storybooks about greeting royalty, she bowed her head and greeted, "Your Magesty."

"None of that," Faelon scolded. "You are a friend to magnificent dragons and I'll not have you bowing to me." She looked to Falloah and smiled again. "Not to worry, Falloah. I shall see to it she is well cared for." She looked the girl up and down. "And maybe dressed appropriately."

Josslee admitted, "I did not have time to change before..." She looked over her shoulder to the black dragon, her brow high over her eyes and arched in concern.

"Be at ease," the scarlet dragoness advised. "You will be well cared for here." Her eyes flitted to the Princess.

"Of course," Princess Faelon assured. "You will be my guest here for as long as you like." She also looked to the black dragon, and nodded to him.

"She has not eaten for a while," Farrigrall informed. "Perhaps you will attend to that first."

"We shall," the Princess assured. Tugging on the girl's hands, she urged, "Come along. Our midday meal will be served soon." She looked to the dragons again and nodded to them. "She shall be well cared for until you return."

Falloah informed, "We should return in a day or two."

"Hopefully," Faelon added, "you will be able to stay longer."

"Perhaps," the dragoness said as she turned to the castle wall. "Come along, Farrigrall."

The black dragon gave Josslee a long look again, then he nodded to her and turned to follow the scarlet dragoness.

The Princess tugged on Josslee's hands again and urged, "Come on. I want to hear all about your adventures!"

**

Falloah led the way back south, but not to the lake where she had found the black dragon. She also did not speak as they flew. Her eyes were hard and directed forward. Farrigrall flew just off of her wingtip and a bit behind her, taking advantage of the air that spiraled from her wingtip in his flight, but also not wanting to provoke her anger. He could not help but feel that she was not usually so quick to temper or so impatient, but that was all he had seen of her, so he wisely remained silent for most of their journey.

Almost an hour later, the silence got the best of him and he finally said, "This is beautiful country."

She only glanced at him and did not reply.

"You've lived here your whole life?" he asked.

"You are very large for your age," she finally observed.

"Good diet," he informed. "I eat a lot of fish and crocodiles. Most of the fish I eat are the giant carp that feed on the lake grasses and come near the surface in the morning. The villagers don't like to eat them, something about their flavor and they are way too bony." He glanced at Falloah again. She did not respond or even look at him. "I also eat crocodiles that are foolish enough to approach the village, and sometimes I will catch a whisker fish. They can get as big as horses. No scales so they go down easily."

Still, Falloah did not respond.

"You never answered my question," he prodded.

She glanced at him again, and finally replied, "I hatched on the Territhan Range on the other side of the desert and came here when I was, well, I suppose about your age."

"I've heard of Territha," he said. "There's supposed to be good hunting there. Not sure why you would leave."

Falloah banked slightly and began to descend to a clearing in the forest where the grasses had gone brown and tan. At the edge of it was a cliff and a creek below it, then more trees and bushes and a trampled down field of stone and gravel just outside of what looked like a cave. Farrigrall followed and landed on the grassy field just behind her, folding his wings to his back and sides as he trotted off the last of his speed and stopped beside her.

He looked to the cave and nodded. "The secret lair of the fierce Falloah the Scarlet, just as I thought it would appear." He finally turned his eyes to her.

She looked back at him, and appeared annoyed.

"Is that how you are known?" he questioned. "Falloah the Scarlet? It suits you. Do all dragons have such titles?"

She growled and strode to the edge of the field, opened her wings and jumped down, gliding to the mouth of the cave below.

Farrigrall followed, again landing behind her, and this time patience was leaving his voice as he demanded, "Have I offended you?"

Not looking back at him, she lowered her nose, folding her wings as she heaved a heavy breath.

Stomping toward her, he veered around her right and stopped in front of her, now displaying his superior size as he continued, "You see to it my human sister is cared for, you stop another dragon from attacking me, you show interest in where I am from, and yet you seem to regard me as an enemy, and I want to know why!"

She turned her eyes away from him, turning her head ever so slightly.

"And now you bring me to your lair," he growled. "You've already said you have a drake of your own so I'm certain you don't see me that way."

She heaved another breath and shook her head. "I don't, Farrigrall, not that way."

"Then why are you so hostile?" he barked loudly.

"Lower your voice," she hissed back.

"Why?" he roared.

She reached to him and tightly closed her hand around his nose, and finally turned her eyes to him. "Because the Landmaster is only about ten leagues away from here, and if he hears you then you will receive a very unwelcome visit from him and you'll not live to see morning."

He pulled his snout from her grip and demanded, "Who? Landmaster? Is this your drake?"

"No," she replied. Heaving another heavy breath, she shook her head and looked into the darkness of her cave. "You've not spent enough time among your own kind to know of our ways. I'll teach you what I can, then you... "

He leaned his head. "Then I what?"

She just stared into the cave, and admitted in a low voice, "I don't know. I just don't know. I have to keep you hidden for a while, just until I figure something out."

"From this landmaster and your drake?" Farrigrall questioned.

"Yes," was the dragoness' reply, just over a whisper.

"Is your drake as big as that Lornoxez from this morning?" he asked.

"Much bigger," she replied, "much stronger."

A little crawl began in Farrigrall's belly, a rare pang of fear, but still he said, "I am not used to hiding from anything."

"I know," she confessed. "You are much like... " She lowered her nose again and closed her eyes.

"Like... " he pressed.

Another dragon called from south and overhead, and Farrigrall could make out the name, "Falloah," in the loud trumpet. This was a female dragon, a very young one, not the burgundy dragoness before, but another one, and he looked up to see.

Soaring low overhead was another small dragoness, about the size of Revillee, but with a light blue belly, and as she banked to turn and land on the grassy field on top of the cliff, she betrayed darker blue, a royal blue over her back and down her tail. She turned hard, lowered her feet and landed in the middle of the field, trotting off her speed all the way to the edge of the cliff, then she hopped down and landed just on the other side of the creek before folding her wings. Her light blue eyes caught the scarlet dragoness quickly, then darted to the black drake in her company, and she froze where she was. Looking the drake up and down, she slowly folded her wings to her and drew her head back, her jaws slightly ajar as she studied the black dragon carefully.

Falloah snorted, then growled, and finally called, "Kyshira!"

The small female tore her eyes from the drake and looked to Falloah, then back to the drake.

"Kyshira," the scarlet repeated. "Why are you looking for me?"

"Um... " the blue stammered in a young voice.

Farrigrall stared back at the blue with a little curiosity in his eyes, and he also looked her up and down with great interest.

With another growl, Falloah strode to the blue dragoness, took a horn tightly in her hand and forcibly turned the younger dragon's face toward her own. "Kyshira! Why do you need me?"

The blue shook her head and drew away, and when the scarlet released her, she reported, "The Landmaster sends word that another dragon has been seen to the west." She looked to Farrigrall again. "This one, I suppose. He wishes to know if it is an invading drake or a wandering dragoness. I suppose I should tell him—"

"You will tell him nothing," Falloah interrupted. When the younger dragoness turned bewildered eyes to her, she raised her head and repeated, "You will tell him nothing. Does he expect you back this evening?"

"He did not say to return right away," the blue reported, "but I can assume he wants me to tell him what you said. He also said to tell Ralligor and Lornoxez to patrol the western border and to remind them not to cross it, and if the other Landmaster comes across he is to be told and no other dragons are to challenge him."

A deep grunt escaped the scarlet and she shook her head. "Tell Ralligor not to challenge Terwrathrawr. I may as well tell the wind not to blow."

"He was very specific about that," Kyshira added.

"You haven't had time to get to know Ralligor," Falloah grumbled. She heaved a heavy breath and looked fully to the young blue. "Lornoxez and Revillee have flown north. Go that way and try to find them, then go back to your lair. I will report to Agarxus myself."

Farrigrall raised his head and asked, "Should I go with Kyshira?"

"No!" Falloah suddenly, loudly barked. "No. Just stay here for now."

"I could use the company," the blue informed, her eyes on the Farrigrall. "It could be a long flight alone."

"I said no!" the scarlet insisted, anger in her voice now. "Go north and find Lornoxez." Her eyes found the black dragon, her brow low over them. "And you stay here."

He growled, then finally complied with a nod.

Kyshira opened her wings and swept them as she jumped up on the cliff, then looked over her shoulder at the black dragon, wearing a little smile as she informed, "I'll be back as soon as I can."

Farrigrall smiled back and watched her take flight, and stared that direction even after she had disappeared.

"Just stay here," Falloah ordered. "I'll be back later."

The black dragon growled and shook his head as he watched her take flight, then he raised his brow and sat catlike as he stared at the sky and began his long, patient wait for the little blue dragoness.

CHAPTER 4

Josslee was soon to realize that Princess Faelon was not the typical royalty that she had always heard of. Taken into the deep of the castle and up two flights of stairs, she found herself trying on many different dresses, and this princess seemed to have an endless supply. Still, those that fit her best were dresses that belonged to a tall, rather thin servant girl of the castle, one who was present with the princess during these fittings, one about her height, and one who seemed to be almost on equal terms with her castle's ruler.

At long last, and with the consensus of the tall girl and another of the castle servants along with the Princess herself, a yellow dress was decided upon that accentuated Josslee's womanly curves and had a low neckline that was trimmed in white lace, as were the short sleeves and the four bells of the skirt. Often, Josslee would fuss over this low neckline, tugging it upward almost absently as she was led from the little fitting room and into the corridors of the palace. She had never worn such a dress before and this one displayed much more of her bosom than she was comfortable showing. Still, she would not complain. The castle was warm for the most part, the dress was fairly comfortable and she was being taken to where she would have her first meal in a couple of days, and this is what she looked forward to the most.

Expecting to sit in the cavernous dining hall of the castle, she was instead led through it, through the kitchen area and into a back room that seemed to be a small storage area for dishes and baskets of roots. This room had a single window, a door leading outside, was about four by five paces in size and had a little wooden table right in the middle. Bowls and eating ware were already in their places at the four chairs that surrounded the table and a pot of some kind of stew was in the center, as was a plate of cut bread with a knife waiting by the half that was not cut.

Each took their seats, the servant girls on each side, the Princess at one corner and before she sat, she extended a hand to the seat right across from hers.

The tall girl looked at the table and declared, "I thought we were going to have wine!"

Princess Faelon turned her eyes to the tall girl with a blink and said, "Darree, who is supposed to bring wine down here?"

The tall girl huffed a hard breath, pushed away from the table and stood, and as she turned and walked toward the door, she grumbled, "I have to do everything around here."

"Do your crying in private!" Faelon called after her as she left the room.

With wide eyes, Josslee asked, "You get to have wine with your meals?"

"Of course!" the Princess confirmed almost dismissively. "I'm the ruler of the kingdom. I can have wine when I want to."

The other servant girl added, "Who is she going to answer to?"

Raising her brow, Josslee looked down at her empty bowl and said, "My parents have always said I am too young for wine."

"You're not here at Caipiervell," Faelon informed with a smile.

Darree returned with a carafe that she set onto the middle of the table near the pot, then she turned to the shelves behind the Princess and began plucking glass goblets from it, setting them on the table one by one.

Looking to her guest, Princess Faelon observed, "You must be starving. Let us not tarry with useless etiquette. Please, enjoy our hospitality."

"Thank you," the girl offered shyly.

They dished out the stew and bread, wine was poured and the girls engaged in conversation fitting their age, laughing and enjoying one another's company, and finally the Princess rested her elbow on the table, her cheek in her palm, and gave her guest a hard stare as she asked, "Okay, so we are all wondering if you have a special boy in your life."

The other girls giggled and also looked to Josslee.

A little flattered and a little embarrassed, Josslee did not know she was blushing as she stared down at her bowl and picked at the scant contents that remained. She shrugged ever so slightly as she replied, "I seem to have the attention of a couple of the boys at the village, but they don't dare come too close to me."

Drawing her head back, Darree barked, "Why not? You aren't diseased, are you?"

Faelon and the other servant giggled and Josslee smiled broader and shook her head. "No, not diseased, it's just that Farg tends to be a little, um, protective of me."

"Farg?" the shorter servant girl asked.

The Princess answered, "Her older brother. He's a dragon." Also looking to her bowl, she raised her brow and continued, "I cannot say I blame the boys of their village for keeping their distance, not with a dragon guarding you all the time."

"Um," the black-haired servant girl stammered, "how did that happen?"

Josslee glanced about at them and drew a deep breath before she answered. "My mother found him as an egg when she was just a little girl and took him back to the village. She managed to keep him hidden and safe until he hatched, and kept him a secret for many days even after that. My grandfather was not happy having a baby dragon in the house, but he did not have the heart to order my mother to cast him out, so in the house he stayed."

"So," Darree began hesitantly, "he was like a house pet."

Shaking her head, Josslee corrected, "No, more a member of the family. He learned to talk and even helped out with chores around the house."

Faelon asked, "And when your village found out?"

With a little shrug, Josslee stared into her bowl and replied, "Of course many were frightened at first, but as he grew and they got to know him, he was accepted as just one of the villagers. Eventually he was too big to sleep in the house and spent his evenings sleeping on the docks. Fishermen would give him the parts of their catch that people don't eat and he would gratefully gobble them down." She raised her brow. "He eats a lot. He was also able to help out with things around the village.

"By the time I was born he was helping to protect the village. Then one day a really big crocodile took my grandfather. He and Farg had become very close, and Farg did not take it well. He just laid on the docks for days and people could here him crooning in the night."

The other girls exchanged pitiable glances.

"One day," Josslee went on, "the crocodile returned to find another easy meal." Her eyes narrowed. "And Farg was waiting for him. The two fought in a spectacular battle and when it was over the crocodile swam away as fast as he could. Farg roared loudly as if to tell other crocodiles that he would do the same to them."

Faelon clapped and declared, "Yay!"

Josslee looked to the Princess and smiled. "By the time I was born he had quite a reputation as a crocodile killer. He also drove away barbarians who would raid the village, snakes, anything that was a threat to the village. A wyvern even attacked us once and he met it in flight and killed it over the lake, and he shared his kill with the village like he always did." She loosed a hard breath through her nose. "And then, about ten days ago, another dragon, a bigger dragon attacked our village. Farg tried to fight him off, but he was too big, too powerful, and... " She just shook her head.

Faelon reached across the table and took the girl's hand. "This other dragon will be attended to."

Nodding, Josslee informed, "Falloah said the same, but she seems to be afraid of this invader. She did say that her landmaster, whoever that is, would fly in and take care of it and another dragon's name was mentioned a few times. I don't know. I want to go home." She looked to the Princess and smiled. "But now I am getting to meet nice new people, like you."

Faelon smiled back and squeezed her hand.

Darree took a sip of her wine and declared, "I'll bet the Desert Lord will dispatch this other dragon. He is powerful and mighty and he even saved this kingdom, and I've never seen a bigger dragon than him."

Josslee turned her eyes to Darree and raised her brow. "Desert Lord?"

The Princess answered for her, "That is his title. His name is Ralligor."

Raising her brow, Josslee informed, "That is the name of the other dragon that was mentioned. I think he is Falloah's husband."

The black-haired girl took a drink of her wine and confirmed, "He is. He even rescued her from a dragon slayer this spring."

"That is its own story," Princess Faelon declared, "and we have all evening to tell you." She pushed away from the table and looked to the empty carafe. "Right now, I think we need more wine."

**

The sun was just touching the treetops to the west and long shadows crept ever so slowly across the ground below the castle wall. Horses grazed in the turning grass beyond and darkness filled the surrounding forest to create deep voids of blackness beneath the trees. Even in this late season with the air growing colder, crickets and other insects could be heard singing and chirping beyond. Even as the light retreated, it was a beautiful sight.

Still, Josslee missed home, and without Farrigrall about for company, she missed it even more. She missed her family. She missed her old life, though she was becoming accustomed to the absence of the smell of fish all of the time.

Staring out over the darkening forest from atop the castle's perimeter wall, she drew a deep breath and was slow to release it, hoping that it would somehow lift her heavy heart. The dress she had been given was now covered with a shawl made of wool that would keep the cold air at bay and she held this close to her as her mind drifted from thought to thought, memory to memory.

The unmistakable sound of boots on stone sounded from behind her and she looked over her shoulder to see the Zondaen captain striding toward her at a casual pace.

Mir'Karra stood beside the girl and folded her arms as she looked out over the darkening forest, and she nodded in slight motions. "You seem lost in thought up here."

Looking back to the forest, Josslee confirmed, "Just thinking."

"About your dragon friend?"

"And home," the girl confessed.

"Some special boy waiting for you there?" the Zondaen captain asked with a little smile.

Josslee's mouth also curled into a little smile and she replied, "No. Farg scares them all away."

"You should speak to him about that."

The girl glanced at her Zondaen companion. "I have. Ever tried talking sense to a four height tall dragon?"

Mir'Karra smiled a little broader. "I see. Well, since he's not about tonight, this would be the ideal time to find a boy that appeals to you. Plenty around here."

Josslee turned her eyes down and shrugged.

The Zondaen's eyes swept the darkening forest again. "Princess Faelon was wondering what had happened to you. She is determined to keep you safe and well cared for until your dragon brother comes to fetch you." She looked to the girl. "Assuming that is the plan."

Josslee raised her eyes, her mouth falling open as this thought hit her like a landslide.

Mir'Karra finally looked to the girl, her brow high over her eyes.

Shaking her head in quick motions, Josslee insisted, "No. He wouldn't do that. He'll be back for me in the next couple of days, you'll see."

"Unless," the Zondaen captain added, "he brought you here to ensure you would be cared for. I cannot see you faring well among dragons, and I'll wager he is looking to protect you more than anything."

Josslee turned her eyes down. "No. He'll come back for me."

With a shrug, Mir'Karra looked back to the forest. "You know him better than I do."

The girl nodded, then looked to the forest beyond, barely aware that soldiers marched by behind them carrying torches, and some of these torches were placed in iron holders in the wall behind.

Mir'Karra glanced at her again. "You're tall enough to be Zondaen. You come from a place called Peak Lake?"

Josslee nodded and confirmed, "Yes. I've lived there my entire life."

"Any warrior training?" the Zondaen asked.

The girl considered, then, "A couple of old warriors who settled in the village showed some of us how to fight with a staff and I can shoot a bow. I'm better at the bow than the staff."

"How good?"

"I can shoot fish at more than thirty paces, even smaller ones."

An owl spoke in its characteristic question of "Who."

Mir'Karra glanced around them, then she took the girl's arm and turned her, leading her toward the steps that led into the courtyard. "Come along, little girl. Let's get you to cover before something swoops down and eats you."

"What would do that?" Josslee asked, a little disbelief and a little fear in her voice.

"Oh," the Zondaen sighed, "perhaps some wyvern that did not migrate, or a giant predatory bird. Something like that. No telling what's out there at night."

"Farg killed a wyvern once," Josslee informed. "It tried to attack the village and he met it in the air and fought it until he killed it."

Mir'Karra turned and folded her arms, her brow high over her eyes as she asked, "Is Farg here?"

The girl just stared up at the Zondaen, then she glanced about before hurrying around her to the step that led down into the courtyard.

Following, Mir'Karra smiled slightly and shook her head. "You like that dress?"

"Yes," the girl replied. "It's very pretty and really comfortable."

"You don't seem the kind of girl to indulge in such girly things as our princess and her attendants do."

"I suppose I never had the opportunity," Josslee said as she started down the stone steps. "My life was mostly about helping my family gather food and... Well, there were a lot of chores to do and little time to be prim and proper."

"I understand," Mir'Karra assured.

They reached the bottom and the Zondaen took the girl's arm and pulled her a different direction, urging, "This way. I want to show you something."

**

"How is that?" Mir'Karra asked as she set her hands on her hips.

Somewhere deep in the castle near one of the armories was a large room that was well lit with oil lamps about every two paces high on the walls and eight more oil lamps hanging from the arched ceiling. All around the walls were racks of weapons and armor, shelves of folded clothing, leather belts and even some black and brown leather boots. The place seemed to be a depository for the army, but the center of the room, which was twelve by twelve paces, was empty of all but a single stone column right in the center of the room, a column that also had oil lamps hanging from it on four sides only an arm length from the ceiling, which seemed to be the inside of a dome and was over two men's heights tall at the center where it met the column.

Josslee stood near this column, now sporting Zondaen clothing and dark brown boots that reached nearly to her knees. The trousers were dark green and fit tightly around her upper legs, hips and buttocks. The shirt she now wore was the same dark green and seemed rather form fitting, dropping only to about the middle of her hips. The sleeves were a little baggy around her arms, but from her wrists to her forearms were black, heavy leather bracers that were laced tightly in place, and formed to her arms. A black leather belt was tightly around her waist, accentuating her shape and the shirt itself, with grommets for laces, hung open halfway down her chest, revealing much of her bosom for likely the first time in her life.

The girl looked down at herself, her eyes sweeping around her legs and the new boots she wore, the trousers that were not modest at all, and how her new clothing showed off her shape, and she looked to the Zondaen captain with mixed emotions.

Mir'Karra smiled and nodded in slight motions. "Now you are going to *need* a dragon to keep the boys away." She glanced about, finally seeing what she sought, and turned toward one of the of the racks and strode that way. "You said you had some training with a staff?"

"I'm better at the bow," the girl admitted.

"I remember you telling me that," the Zondaen recalled as she took two long, wooden staffs that were leaning against the stone wall and turned back toward the girl. She hurled one toward the girl as she strode back toward her, then she reached up and unfastened the fur mantle she still wore, shrugged out of it and pulled it from her shoulders. This she tossed behind her toward the wall as she watched the girl catch the staff smartly with one hand. "You'll find those clothes allow you to move very freely." She stopped a pace away and held her own staff ready with both hands, raising her chin as Josslee did the same, and a little smile curled her mouth. "Let's see what you know. Defend."

Josslee drew a shrieking breath and stepped away as the Zondaen swung right at her head, and instinctively she raised her weapon and met the Captain's staff at arm's length. Mir'Karra brought the other end of the staff up swiftly and Josslee, who seemed to anticipate this, brought her own staff down to meet it.

This sparring continued for several moments and it was soon clear to the girl that this warrior she faced could strike her much harder and much faster, and she was secretly glad she did not.

Finally, Mir'Karra backed away and held the staff level before her with both hands to show the girl that this bout was over, and Josslee did the same. Both lowered one end of their weapons to the ground, staring at one another intently, and the Zondaen smiled slightly and nodded.

"Well done," Mir'Karra commended. "You seem to be very well trained.

"Thank you," the girl offered, raising her chin with just a bit of confidence in her eyes now.

A large man who had entered unnoticed scoffed, "It was not a terrible display." The two women turned to see him, and an uneasy crawl began in Josslee's belly.

He was a very tall man, very broad shouldered, and he wore a thick beard on his heavy jaws. His hair was black and long and streaked with silver, as was his beard, and he had a very rough appearance about him. He wore dark gray trousers, black boots and a fur jerkin that left his extremely thick and muscular arms bare. Around his waist was a broad belt from which hung a few pouches, a dagger on his left and a battle axe suspended from an iron ring on his right. His dark eyes were on the Zondaen as he added, "A good bit of sparring with a stick, vixen. How do you handle a real weapon?"

Mir'Karra smiled and raised her chin, replying, "Oh, I think you know." She gestured to the wall with her chin.

He looked that way, then raised his brow and looked back to the Zondaen, a little smirk on his mouth as he strode to the weapon rack and took a wooden broadsword, clearly a training weapon, and turned fully on the big woman.

Josslee retreated from them and found her back pressed against the stone column.

The big man, a head height taller than the woman, took the axe from his belt and tossed it down at the base of the shelves where it made a loud ring on the stone floor, and he smiled as he stalked toward the Zondaen, his weapon ready. With a mighty yell, he swung it hard at her head.

Mir'Karra easily knocked it away, and with speed she had not demonstrated before, she swung the end of the staff toward his gut. He easily warded it off and struck back.

Josslee watched in amazement as the two sparred in what appeared to be a deadly game, but she noticed that each of them wore expressions of almost joy. This was a game between them, one that they clearly played often, and she grasped her staff with both hands as she now leaned on it, giving the combatants her full attention.

Several moments later, he blocked with his sword, and when she swung the other end at his head, he caught the staff in his big hand and stopped it cold. They both paused and just stared at each other for long seconds.

He observed, "Supposed to get cold tonight."

She raised an eyebrow. "I'll keep you warm as always."

They both smiled.

Josslee slapped a hand over her eyes and grumbled, "Oh, for God's sake."

They looked to her, and the Zondaen introduced, "Josslee, this is Rokar of Enulam, our former enemy. He is among those of us charged with Princess Faelon's safety and the continued training and rebuilding of her army."

The big Enulam soldier turned fully to the girl and nodded to her. "You are another Zondaen?"

Josslee shook her head. "No, I am from Peak Lake Village many leagues from here."

He nodded. "The girl who came with the dragon. I heard of you, and this dragon you call your brother." He glanced at Mir'Karra. "I see you are getting some training in. That's good. Got to be ready to defend yourself when your dragon brother is not nearby." He huffed a laugh. "Especially with all these young men about."

She smiled shyly and nodded.

"There you are!" Faelon announced as she strode into the room. "I've been looking everywhere for you!" She paused and looked the girl up and down, then she turned fully to the Zondaen captain and barked, "You are trying to make her a warrior?"

Mir'Karra smiled. "A warrior she already is." She looked to the girl and added, "Just needs to have her training finished."

"Well," the Princess announced as she set her hands on her hips, "it is time for dinner and we are eating in the dining room tonight. You two are, of course, welcome to join us, since you are both emissaries of your kingdoms."

The two warriors looked to each other and Rokar shrugged and said, "I can eat."

"You can always eat," Mir'Karra grumbled as she rolled her eyes.

Faelon strode to the girl and took the staff from her, leaning it against the column before she took her hands and pulled her along. "Come along, sister of a dragon. Let us go to the dining hall and have a grand meal!" She looked to Rokar, to Mir'Karra. "And I want to hear more of your adventures."

The Zondaen took the practice sword from the Enulam warrior and turned to return them to their places on the weapons rack, and she mumbled, "Careful what you wish for, Princess."

CHAPTER 5

A dragon sleeping sprawled in the open on a grassy field was not so unusual a sight in this part of the land, not for those who knew where to find dragons. Farrigrall was not a dragon to sleep curled in a semicircle as many imagine we sleep. His arms were splayed out, his legs parallel behind him flanking his tail and his neck was curled slightly as he slumbered with his head rocked over, stopped by one of his horns which had dug into the soft, grassy ground he lay on. He also snored in deep rumbles with each breath. This was ultimately to the ire of the scarlet dragoness, but she did not disturb him as she returned to her lair to sleep just inside of the cave and facing out, her eyes growing heavier and heavier as she watched the top of the bluff where the black dragon slept until they finally closed and her mind was pulled into a misty place of the dreams of a dragon.

The coming of the sun did not wake either of them, nor did the black dragon stir in his sleep. The only movement from him was the rhythmic rising and falling of his back as he took slow breaths. His presence did not go unnoticed and, as the sun rose to reflect dark reds and blues from the dragon's scales, they also reflected the many blues of another dragon who lay near his head and silently watched him sleep.

Eventually, warmed by the sun more than an hour after it rose over the treetops, Farrigrall's eyes slowly opened and he blinked the sleep from them, then they slid to the blue form that watched him.

Kyshira just stared back, smiled slightly, and offered, "Good morning, strange dragon."

Without really raising his head, he grumbled back, "Good morning. How long have you been here?"

She shrugged. "I don't know. I awoke before the sun and flew this way when it was still just a glow to the east and found you still here, so I waited for you to wake."

The youth in her voice was not lost on the young drake. What was lost on him was the interest in her eyes and how she stared at him.

The young dragoness glanced over the bluff and into the cave where the scarlet dragoness still slept, then she looked to the black drake and asked, "What do you want to do today? We could hunt, or maybe catch a fish by the lake. Revillee and I will go to catch fish sometimes in the mornings when the big grass eaters come to the surface. They're bony but they taste really good."

"I had one yesterday," he informed dryly.

"You aren't hungry again?" she asked. "I like to eat every day when I can catch something." She glanced away. "Revillee really does not have to hunt much with Lornoxez about. He hunts for them both a lot." She looked to the cave across the creek again. "I'm a good hunter. I've always had to be. I like fish, but I could often go for a good Grawrdox or something like that from time to time. I like them better." She looked back to the drake and laid her head down, her big yellow eyes fixed on him. "You look like a good hunter. Do you ever hunt Grawrdox?"

"I've never had one," he replied, staring back at her.

She turned her eyes away from him again. "Oh. I thought for sure you would take them regularly since you're so big. Lornoxez boasts all the time that he could take any game he wants and would even eat a Drakenein. I've never eaten one of those before. I'm afraid of them."

"What about crocodiles?" he asked.

Her eyes shifted back to him and she blinked. "Falloah and Revillee will wrestle with them sometimes, but the really big ones frighten me. I'm afraid a really big one could surface and eat me. Same with wyverns. Big wyverns eat little dragons like me."

Farrigrall raised his head and closed his eyes as he stretched his neck, then he shook his head and blinked a few times to awaken fully. With a big yawn, he admitted, "I've only had a couple of run-ins with wyverns. They were not such the threat to me that they wanted to be and both paid with their lives when they attacked my village."

The young dragoness raised her head and seemed to smile, her eyes wide as she observed, "You have the look of a mighty wyvern slayer."

His eyes found her again and he boasted, "I've killed many threats to my village, including wyverns and big crocodiles. The smart ones keep their distance when I'm about."

Her brow tensed and she raised her head slightly. "Your village?"

"The village I protect," he explained. "I was raised there from the time I hatched about thirty seasons ago."

She leaned her head. "You protect humans? Why would you do that?"

Realizing that she, as a dragon, was having difficulty understanding why he would protect a village of humans, he raised his nose and used a harshness in his words as he explained, "They took me in and fed and protected me from the time I was an egg. It is a debt I shall repay by protecting them for as long as I can."

"You aren't there protecting them now," she pointed out.

He growled and looked away from her, his brow low over his eyes.

Her eyes widened slightly and she drew her head back, then she looked down and offered, "I'm sorry. I did not mean to offend you." With a glance at him, she offered, "Should I go?"

Farrigrall drew a long breath and released it in another growl, looking to the tree line on the other side of the field, then he shook his head and grumbled, "No, you don't have to go. Just forget it."

Her voice was slight as she asked, "What happened?"

The young drake snarled back, "Another dragon, one larger and stronger than me." He forced a hard breath through his nose and turned his eyes down. "I was driven away by a stronger dragon and now I have to find a way to defeat him."

Falloah slammed onto the ground on his other side and roared, "You will do no such thing!"

He swung his head around and looked up at her, then growled and turned away again. "You don't understand. I have to—"

"It is the dragon way!" Falloah cried. "Farrigrall, you fought a landmaster, one who crossed the border into this territory. You will let our Landmaster attend to him!"

He pushed himself up and turned fully on the scarlet, his head almost a full man's height over her. "That is my village to protect, Falloah! And since when do you care about them, anyway? How do I know your Landmaster won't do the same thing this other one has done?"

She glared up at him, baring her teeth at him as she growled back, "You are not to return there and you are to remain as hidden as possible while you are here. Do you understand?"

He also bared his teeth. "And now you think you are in a position to order me about. You aren't, dragoness, and you'd better realize that! I will do as I will!"

"You'll do as I say!" Falloah cried. "Don't you understand that I am doing this to protect you?"

He stomped toward her, one step. "I don't need your protection." With that, he turned, opened his wings and swept into the air, climbing away from the sun and in the direction of the lake.

Falloah watched him go with a low brow and grumbled, "As stubborn as..." Looking to Kyshira, she ordered, "He seems to like your company. Keep an eye on him and see if you can keep him out of trouble. I have something to do."

The little blue watched Falloah take to the sky and turn north, then northwest, then she looked to the black drake who grew more distant, opened her wings, and swept herself into the sky to follow.

**

Farrigrall returned to the lake and landed about a hundred paces from the shore, stumbling slightly as he tightly closing his eyes and grasped his side. The pain was still there and grew worse when he flew fast. He growled deeply and fell to his knees, catching himself on his palm as he fell forward. A deep growl rolled from him as he struggled to catch his breath against the pain from his ribs, and finally he was aware of the approach of another wing born creature and pushed himself back up, turning as he looked skyward to see the little blue dragoness sweeping in low and lowering her feet to land.

Kyshira swept her wings and set down gently and gracefully, her eyes on the black drake as she folded her wings to her back and sides. Hesitantly, she approached him cautiously, holding her body low as she did.

Farrigrall motioned behind her and grumbled, "Is she always so bossy?"

The dragoness shrugged and admitted, "I do not know her that well."

He growled and turned toward the lake, folding his arms.

She took his side and also looked out toward the lake, and there was silence between them for long moments. Finally glancing at him, she observed, "You seem hurt."

He growled back, "It's fine."

With a nod, she looked back to the lake. She drew a deep breath as she stared out over the water, then said, "There is a lake like this where I come from. Lots of fish in it as well. The water is not as warm and there are not so many crocodiles and they are not as big—"

"You sure do talk a lot," he suddenly observed.

They looked to each other.

He raised his brow slightly. "I never knew dragons could be so chatty."

She lowered her head slightly, her brow arching between her eyes. "I'm sorry."

"No," he assured. "It's not a bother at all." Looking back over the water, he raised his brow and said, "You remind me of someone else, just much less annoying."

"Is that good?" she asked.

He nodded and confirmed, "I suppose so."

"Another dragoness?" she questioned almost shyly.

He shook his head. "No."

A little smile curled her mouth and she sidestepped slightly toward him. "You've chosen no dragoness."

"The three of you are the first I've ever seen," he informed.

"That sounds almost sad," she said with a sympathetic tone, sliding one foot a little closer to him. "I can imagine that you have missed a lot, not being close to your own kind your entire life."

He shrugged, staring out over the lake. "I had my humans to take care of, crocodiles to deal with. My time was well spent. Other than the big drake that attacked my village, Falloah and Revillee were the first other dragons I had ever seen, and the first who did not try to kill me."

"I wouldn't try to kill you," she assured.

He looked down to her, realizing he was a height and a half taller. "I'm much larger than you, so even trying that would not be a wise thing to do."

"And you are much stronger," she observed, not looking at him. "Only really strong dragons can deal with large crocodiles."

"Revillee fought one yesterday," he informed.

"It was not that big," she scoffed.

"You were not even here!" he barked. "How would you know how big it was?"

She heaved a heavy breath and looked up at him, a strange look somewhere between confusion and disbelief, and almost a little disappointment. Finally, she said, "Dragonesses talk, Farrigrall."

He looked back to the lake and just shrugged.

Even as silence surrounded them again, she slid just a little closer to him, and ultimately growled a low growl before she spoke again. "I've never eaten a crocodile."

Hesitantly, he turned his eyes to her.

She looked up at him and asked, "What do they taste like?"

He glanced about, then replied, "Like crocodiles, I suppose."

She gave him that hard stare again, then raised her brow. "So, you really have a pet human. Did you ever eat a human?"

"Never ate a human," he replied dryly.

"I've always been told the flavor is very foul," she rambled on, "so I never ate one. My old landmaster and a couple of his drakes used to eat them from time to time, but I never did. I would have a difficult time eating anything that can talk to me."

Farrigrall nodded.

Kyshira lowered her head, looking sheepishly up at him as she mumbled, "I'm talking too much again."

"No," he assured in a low voice. "I don't eat creatures that can talk to me, either, like the humans of my village."

"They think of you as their guardian," she observed.

"They did," he growled, his brow lowering over his eyes. "I could not best that other dragon, and I need to find a way to."

"Agarxus will attend to him," she assured. "If he crosses the border again then the Landmaster will sweep in and teach him a harsh lesson, maybe even kill him."

"This other dragon is awfully big," he snarled.

She smiled slightly. "You've never seen the Landmaster, have you?"

"No," he replied in a sigh, "I haven't. I also get the impression that he may not welcome me here, nor will this Ralligor or any of the other dragons who call this place home."

"I welcome you," Kyshira assured.

He glanced at her again, and a little smile curled his scaly lips.

They both stared out at the lake again as the morning sun slowly rose over it, and the little dragoness' eyes darted about, eventually landing on some strange ripples on the water's surface. Slowly, she stood, her dorsal scales growing erect as she growled and took a step back.

Farrigrall looked down at her, then to the ripples in the water that held her attention, and his eyes narrowed.

There, slowly cruising toward the shore, was yet another large crocodile. Just his eyes and nostrils and the tips of the scales of his back and tail broke the surface as he moved slowly toward the dragons. Judging his size with most of him submerged was difficult, but the young drake could tell from experience that it was a sizeable beast, likely as large or larger than the dragoness at his side, but was much smaller than the drake.

With a growl, Farrigrall lowered his body and stomped toward the shore to meet this old adversary, and the crocodile paused in the water. The dragon did not break stride, his feet hitting the water with heavy steps and as the crocodile opened its jaws and rose from the water, Farrigrall lifted a foot and stomped down hard on the big crocodile's head. Though powerful in its own right, the crocodile thrashed and tried to roll away from the dragon's foot that held it in the mud and rocks of the half height deep water, and it finally managed to roll its bulk fully and release its head from the dragon's foot.

With mighty splashes, the crocodile turned as fast as its bulk would allow and swam fast back into open water.

Farrigrall watched its retreat, then he turned back to the dragoness and raised his head, sporting a victorious and rather cocky expression.

A little dreamy eyed, the little dragoness stared back at him, and for a moment she basked in the attention of this mighty young drake, a dragon close to her own age and another newcomer to this territory.

The black drake strode from the water and right up to the little dragoness, the morning sun reflecting brightly from the red dorsal scales that ran down his back and glistening from the water that continued to drip from him. About four paces away, they stopped and sat catlike before her. His eyes narrowed slightly as he sternly informed, "I regularly fight much bigger crocodiles than that." Now he was just boasting, and he poked his chest out slightly more as he continued. "After so many seasons of driving them away from the village, only the biggest of them will challenge me these days, and even they learn I am not to be trifled with."

The little dragoness simply nodded, and smiled ever so slightly. As if she heard something, she looked over her shoulder, raising her head as her eyes widened slightly. Her eyes turned downward, then she drew a breath and looked back up to the drake at her side. "Um," she stammered, "I, um... I need to go do something."

He glanced down at her and shrugged. "It doesn't look like I'm going anywhere."

"Maybe we can catch fish together," she suggested.

He nodded and looked back over the lake. "Sure. Sounds fun."

He was clearly distracted by his own thoughts and she backed away, then turned and opened her wings, taking to the air in rapid strokes, and flew toward the north.

CHAPTER 6

Kyshira's flight was not a long one, not even half a league, and she lowered her feet and descended toward a clearing in the forest, one where trees had been knocked over many seasons ago and the land had been taken over by grasses and clumps of bushes. Settling gently where there were no fallen logs in her path, she folded her wings and looked around her, her eyes fixing on something dark and shadowy hiding in the trees. A nervous crawl began in her belly as she turned that way and strode with slow, hesitant steps toward the tree line, holding her body low, her wings clamped tightly to her back and sides, and anxiety in her eyes that few dragons would ever know.

Nearing that place, she watched as smoke drifted from the shadows between the trees and settled toward the ground, disappearing there as if the earth was sucking it below ground.

A deep and raspy voice, one that sounded as if it was made of evil and fearful things, reached from the shadows and greeted, "Kyshira. You seem to have made a new friend."

She settled to her belly on the ground, her attention fixed on the glowing yellow eyes that peered back from the shadows.

"You were given a task," the voice reminded from the shadows.

Kyshira nodded and turned her eyes down. "I know. I am trying."

"Yet you have time to court a new drake," the voice observed.

The little dragoness growled. "If he wants me to do this then he has to know—"

The voice interrupted in a horrible, shrieking hiss, "He wants progress, not your endless excuses!"

Cringing, Kyshira looked aside and complained, "What he demands is not fair."

It drew closer, and more smoke rolled from the shadows to descend to the ground and be swallowed into the grass and earth. A clawed wing emerged, dark gray and black and slate blue, and two clawed fingers dug into the ground near her head. "You were allowed to live, dragoness, but Mettegrawr's generosity has its limits."

She closed her eyes, tensing up more.

"What news do you bring?" it demanded. "What can I take back to him to convince him to spare your life a few days longer?"

Kyshira opened her eyes, still looking away from the smoky, shadowy form as she replied, "I have nothing for him today. These things take time, and he has to understand that."

"You'll have to do better than that," it informed coldly.

Her brow lowered over her eyes and she snapped back, "It is all I have. Just tell him I am working on finding out what he wants."

"Not good enough," it snarled. "Your life is about to grow very short. You should be grateful he has not killed you already."

"He has not killed me," she snapped back, "because he fears what would happen to him if he crosses into this territory again."

It hissed loudly, and a growl rolled forth as it scrambled quickly from the shadows. This was a wyvern that seemed to drip smoke and black mist, one twice her size and much heavier built, more heavily armored. It's thick, serpent like head directed yellow serpent's eyes down on the dragoness as it clamored out on the claws of its wings and slammed the talons of its feet hard onto the ground. A lean, scaly body had three rows of bronze spines from between the blunt horns behind its eyes all the way to the end of its long tail which matched the length of its body, making it more than eleven paces long from nose to the end of its tail.

One of those clawed wings slammed down onto the dragoness' back, crushing her to the ground as its neck snaked around to bring its nose less than a pace from hers. A long, forked tongue jetted forth to taste her, then it leaned its head and observed, "You are becoming too spirited. Perhaps it is time to just end you and tell him you were killed because you failed!"

She crooned submissively, her chin pressed against the grass she lay on, and she assured, "I am trying! I really am! I have to get close to them to do what he wants!"

Another deep hiss escaped the big wyvern and it moved its head along her neck, tasting her with its tongue all the way to the shoulder of her wing, then it drew back and opened its jaws, striking down to clamp its horrible, dagger like teeth shut around the middle of her neck.

Kyshira shrieked, her hands making tight fists and scooping earth and grass into her palms. Smoke descended all around her, settling around her body and her head, and when she opened her eyes, it was all she could see.

After long, horrifying seconds, it withdrew its teeth and hissed loudly right beside her head, into her ear. "One bite," it reminded. "Just one bite and you will be paralyzed and you will endure the pain of my venom, and I will swallow you alive and leave you to smother in my belly as I digest you."

A whimpering croon escaped her, and a tear slipped from her eye.

He bit her neck again, right behind her horns, then withdrew his teeth and whispered to her, "You have been promised to me, and I will feast on you if you get too spirited again." Long, clawed fingers wrapped around her neck and throat and it hoisted her from the ground and threw her hard to the center of the clearing where she landed on her back and rolled away from it. It watched as she drew her hands and feet under her and stood, and it hissed, "I will be watching and I will return soon, and if you have nothing for me to tell him, I will hunt you down and eat you alive."

Looking to the ground with wide, defeated eyes, she could only nod. When she finally mustered the courage to look that way, all that remained of the horrible wyvern was settling smoke. Her eyes darted about and she raised a hand to her neck where it had bitten her, relieved to feel no blood and no wounds. With another fearful croon, she opened her wings and swept herself into the sky.

CHAPTER 7

Kyshira returned to the lake to find the black drake still sitting at the shore, staring out over the water as if he were daring any crocodile to come close enough to challenge him. From over a hundred human men's heights high, she could easily see into the clear water of the lake, and did not see anything even close to the shore where the dragon sat.

She circled behind him once, quickly descending toward the ground, and she landed very softly about fifty paces behind the drake, stepping down as quietly as she could. He appeared to be lost in thought, and she found herself distracted by her own.

Farrigrall was, indeed, lost in thought, but he was not distracted by his longing for his home nor the welfare of the human he called his sister. She was in good hands, it seemed, and it also seemed that bigger dragons would be on their way to his village to dispatch this intruder. Now, his thoughts bounded about a little blue dragoness who reminded him of a puppy eager for his attention. As dragons go, she was extremely easy on the eyes, her coloring, her shape, her face and her cute little snout... Feelings stirred within him for the first time.

Hearing footfalls behind him, he recognized them as a small dragon, of the very dragon he was thinking about, and without looking back at her, he asked, "Is this important task complete?"

She stopped right behind him, looking up at him with confusion in her big eyes as she countered, "Huh?"

Farrigrall finally looked back at her. "Whatever important task you flew off to take care of."

"Oh!" she declared, then she strode the rest of the way to him, took his side, and sat down beside him, wrapping her tail around her on the ground as she confirmed, "Yes, it has been attended." She finished in a mumble as she looked away from him, "For now."

He nodded and looked back out over the lake.

She swallowed hard and looked that way herself, glancing behind them once as she could almost feel eyes on her. Farrigrall was far bigger than the smoke wyvern, clearly more powerful, and new thoughts invaded her mind.

For a time, they quietly sat on the shore and watched the ripples on the lake, each distracted by their own thoughts, and it was the drake who finally looked to the little dragoness and observed, "You're suddenly very quiet."

Her eyes darted to his, and as they met, she could not look away, and a quick excuse burst from her. "I thought I might be talking too much and..." She tore her gaze from his and looked back to the lake. "I don't want to irritate you with my constant babbling. Some dragons say I talk too much and I can be a bother and I..." She looked down. "I want you to like me."

Humans were never so abruptly honest. They tended to avoid such honesty whether they feared him or wanted his attention. Such honesty from this little dragoness was both unexpected and refreshing, and he could not stop a little smile that curled his mouth as he looked back to the lake. "Oh, chatter away, little blue bird. I don't mind."

She hesitantly looked up at him.

His eyes slid to her. "Do you want to do something other than just sit here?"

A little smile curled her mouth.

Falloah landed in the field behind them and appeared to be a little out of breath. The two younger dragons turned toward her as she strode to them, folding her wings, and she walked around the young dragoness and right up to the water, fell to all fours, and began to drink with loud splashes, raising her head and snout over and over as she gulped down large amounts of water.

Farrigrall and Kyshira glanced at each other.

Her thirst finally quenched, Falloah stood and turned to the young dragons, looking to the drake as she informed, "I have a few more things to attend to. I just wanted to see to it that you are staying out of mischief."

Still sitting catlike beside the little blue, he shrugged and informed, "All is quiet. What are you doing that is so important and exhausting?"

"None of your concern," she snarled back. "Just stay out of sight until I get back." Without waiting for a response, she opened her wings and strode past them again, easily sweeping herself into the air and flying toward the north.

The two younger dragons watched her fly away, then looked to each other.

Kyshira observed, "Something is definitely on her mind."

The drake nodded and looked toward the departing dragoness. "Regardless, I need to fly to that castle and see that Josslee is okay and staying out of trouble."

"Your human sister?" the young dragoness guessed.

He nodded. "Falloah assured me that she is in good hands and I do trust her, but I still feel I should check in on her."

"Can I come?" Kyshira asked eagerly.

Farrigrall sighed, "I suppose so. The company would be welcome."

Both turned and opened their wings, sweeping themselves skyward with air grabbing strokes of their wings, and she remained beside him and just a little behind his wing as they began this first little adventure together.

CHAPTER 8

The field surrounding Caipiervell Castle was grazed down for the most part and what was left was cut very short. A little green still dotted the field, but most of it was brown and tan and ready for the coming of winter. An entourage of soldiers and attendants accompanied the princess as she stood and watched the warriors who trained about forty paces from the castle's perimeter wall.

Once again, Josslee and Mir'Karra sparred with staffs, and the girl attentively listened to every word, every command, and adjusted as she was instructed to improve her skill.

Princess Faelon stood about three paces away, her arms folded as she watched the two spar, and her expression betrayed she was not happy with the situation.

Another soldier, one of Caipiervell's knights who wore a tunic in the castle's colors and the royal crest embroidered on the left side of his chest, stood close to the princess as he also watched, his arms folded and his attention fixed on the sparring duo. As the Princess heaved a heavy sigh, his eyes slid to her and he raised his brow. "Not how you envisioned your morning, Highness?"

Faelon never took her eyes from the match as she answered, "Not at all."

"Well," the knight began in a sigh of his own, "she is not the kind of girl to sit about and talk with those her age as they knit, or whatever else it is you do in your spare time."

"You wanted to say gossip," the Princess snarled.

"But I did not," he pointed out.

She glanced at him, and shook her head.

A soldier patrolling the top of the perimeter wall pointed skyward and shouted, "Dragon!"

All stopped and looked where he pointed, and Mir'Karra took the opportunity to swat the girl hard on the backside with her staff.

"Ow!" Josslee shrieked as she dropped her weapon and swung around, rubbing her stinging buttocks.

Mir'Karra smiled and looked toward the approaching dragon.

Falloah swept in fast and stroked her ocher colored wings forward in hard, wind grabbing sweeps, lowering her feet and landing as perfectly as always only fifty paces or so from the humans who were gathered outside of the wall. She trotted off the last of her speed and stopped about twenty paces away, her eyes finding first the Princess, then Josslee, and she said without polite greeting, "I need you." She looked to the Princess and added, "And I need a change of clothes."

Faelon's brow arched and she asked, "A change of clothes?"

The scarlet dragoness crouched down and laid to her belly, instructing, "On my back. We have somewhere to go."

Josslee looked to Mir'Karra and appeared indecisive.

Raising her brow, the Zondaen stared back at the girl and said, "I'd do as she says."

Faelon strode forward with quick steps, her attention on the dragoness as she called, "Falloah! How else can I help?"

"Just the change of clothes," the dragoness assured. "Thank you. I'm sorry I haven't much time to talk."

"It is quite all right," the Princess assured. "Cenna will be back in a moment with the clothes you requested. I will not bother you with why you need them, but please return and let me know if everything turns out all right."

"I will," Falloah agreed. She turned her eyes to Josslee again and urged, "Well, come along. On my back. We have to go."

**

Only about an hour later, they arrived at the same cliffside on the same island they had visited the day before, and the dragoness set down gently. Josslee, still on the dragoness' back and hugging a blue fabric bundle to her, watched the ground to one side as they landed. She was settled in between two of Falloah's dorsal scales, right at the base of her neck where the scales were large. As the dragoness settled to the ground and dropped to all fours, the dorsal scale that held the girl firmly to her neck lifted up, as did all of the scales on Falloah's neck, and once the girl was released, she threw her leg over and slid over red scales to the dragoness' waiting arm, landing on the arm with both feet before hopping do the ground. "That was amazing!" she declared. "I so wish Farg would let me ride on him that way!"

Falloah stood and looked to the cliff side, strain in her eyes as she seemed to be trying to see through it to ensure the village was clear. Her chest swelled as she drew a soothing breath, and finally she sat catlike and wrapped her tail around her on the ground.

Looking up at the dragoness, Josslee asked, "So, am I supposed to change clothes for some reason? What's wrong with what I have on?"

"They aren't for you," the dragoness informed. She drew another deep breath, then forced it out through her nose, closed her eyes and turned her head down, and she mumbled some words that the girl could not make out.

Before Josslee's widening eyes, the dragoness was enveloped in an emerald shimmer and her form grew smaller and smaller, even as she stood, and the dragon she was changed into something quite unexpected. In only a few seconds, the dragoness no longer stood before the girl, but a statuesque red-haired woman did, one who was lean and muscular and perfectly built, and appeared to be in her early twenties—and stark naked but for the gold chain around her neck that suspended a small, golden dragon's talons which gripped an emerald sphere.

Falloah opened her eyes, human eyes, and stared at the cliffside for long seconds more before she ordered, "I'm going to need those clothes now. The air is a bit cold."

Hesitantly, and with small steps, Josslee approached the woman, and she held the bundle to her with both hands.

Falloah took the bundle and untied it, shaking out the dress and seeing that a white undershirt fell from the skirts, and she bent down to pick it up. "I'll be less conspicuous this way, especially if Terrwrathgrawr decides to visit your village while we are there."

Josslee watched Falloah get dressed, and she observed, "You're afraid of him, aren't you?"

"I am," Falloah confirmed as she smoothed out the shirt, then pulled the skirt, which resembled coveralls over her chest and belly, over her head. Now fully dressed, she combed her hands through her long, red hair, then she leaned her head back to shake it out and try to bring it under some control. "I don't know how you can live with such fur on your head all the time."

Finally stepping up to her, Josslee reached to Falloah's hair and said, "I suppose you get used to it. Turn around and hold still. I'll try and do something with it."

Falloah did as she was told, and grumbled, "As long as Ralligor does not find out what we're doing—"

"He likely knows by now," and older man informed as he strode to them from the cliffside.

Josslee shrieked and spun around, seeing an old man in the green and white robes of a wizard striding toward them, robes that were belted at the waist with a few pouches hanging from the belt. He had a long white beard, long white hair coming from beneath the woolen hood he wore, and bushy white eyebrows. His walking stick was a simple one and from the look of it, very old. It was worn on the bottom and almost black where he had grasped it for so long. Otherwise, there was nothing really remarkable about him, but for his expression, which was one of almost fatherly concern.

Falloah froze as she saw him, then her brow lowered and she snarled, "You really need to announce your approach, Leedon."

A little smile curled his mouth. "So much more entertaining to just appear, dragoness. I see you have adopted human form again."

"This is none of your concern," Falloah spat.

"Nor Ralligor's, either, I hear," he countered. Stopping only a pace away from her, he leaned heavily on his walking staff as he grasped it with both hands, staring into her amber eyes as he raised his brow. "You do not wish for him to know, and yet you use his magic to transform."

She slowly reached to her chest and grasped the amulet she wore with two fingers, her eyes widening slightly.

"As soon as you used that power," the old wizard informed, "he knew." He leaned his head slightly. "Not like you to keep secrets from him."

"So I've been told," Falloah grumbled as she looked away. "Where is he now?"

The wizard raised his brow again. "Last I heard he was going to patrol Agarxus' border west of here."

She nodded. "So, he's asleep in his cave."

"Most likely."

She huffed a hard breath and nodded again, staring past him, then she announced, "We don't have much time, then. Josslee and I need to get to her village."

"Indeed," the wizard said. "I thought I might come with you."

"We do not need you along," Falloah informed harshly.

"Really," he almost laughed. "Tell me. How do you intend to travel from this island to her village?"

Falloah dumbly stared back, then she turned her eyes down.

Josslee took a step toward them and said, "Sometimes the fishermen will come here to catch perch."

The wizard smiled and looked to her. "There is a boat here already, dear girl. Not to worry. How are your parents these days?"

The girl was stunned for long seconds, then her eyes widened with recognition and she drew a gasp. "You've been to our village before!"

"Many times," he confirmed. "I was friends with your grandfather for many seasons. I know his passing was a great loss to your family."

Falloah heaved a heavy breath and asked, "Is there anyone you don't know?"

"There are many I don't know," he replied, "and many I do. I am known in that village, so perhaps I can help to abate any suspicion of you when we visit there." He raised his eyebrows again. "Shall we go? I have arranged for a boat."

Giving him a long, hard stare, Falloah finally rubbed her eyes, then stormed past him, angling to a path that ran right around the cliffside, only pausing to turn and bid, "Are you coming?"

**

Piers jetted out from every side of the island, all of them timbers and some as far as fifty paces out into the lake. Not wanting to draw attention to themselves, the three recent arrivals had disembarked on the closest, longest pier of the island that faced them and walked at a casual pace toward the island itself. Many of the piers were covered with wood and grass roofs, but this one was not. The sun was out and lent just a little comfort from the chill in the air. This pier was only about three paces wide and there was not much activity here, but the covered piers to each side were wider and bustling with fishermen bringing in fish, boats being loaded or unloaded, and a few people who simply dropped lines or nets in the water to see what they could bring up.

Only Falloah glanced about her, seeing this place from this perspective for the first time. Leedon watched the activity on the pier to the right. Josslee had seen this her entire life and the routine of what was going on was so familiar as to not interest her at all.

They all moved over as a couple of fishermen walked past, giving them long, suspicious stares. Josslee was walking between Falloah and the wizard and turned her face away from them, fearing she would be recognized and quite probably get into trouble for returning home.

Finally nearing the shore where there were more wooden and stone structures and a lot of activity and commerce taking place, Falloah swept the shoreline and a little snarl took her lip as she shook her head.

"Not the cleanest place in the land," the red-haired woman observed.

Josslee glanced at her. "What would a dragon know about clean?"

"How do you take the smell here?" Falloah grumbled. "I like fish, but..." She shook her head.

"You get used to it," Josslee assured.

Falloah mumbled, "If you say so."

Near the end of the pier, where it finally met the stone of the shoreline, it emptied into a road that was just wide enough for a horse and carriage or a few people walking abreast of one another. Lining the other side of the road were many shops and houses made of stone and planks and timbers, most of which appeared to have been there for many decades. Most of the village area was very drab with grays and browns and tans everywhere, but some colorful signs in blues and reds and greens could be seen hanging over the doors of some of the shops. There seemed to be no houses where people lived here, rather just thatchers and other businesses related to boats or collecting fish.

They reached the end of the pier and finally found themselves walking on the well-kept gravel pathway between the water and the first row of structures that lined the shoreline. This was a large island with a fairly large population of people who came and went, but the pathway and shops were not uncomfortably crowded by any means.

With the pathway about six paces wide, just wide enough to accommodate both pedestrians and wagons drawn by horse, there was plenty of room to walk even when a carriage or wagon would happen by.

They passed a group of men, a couple of them appearing to be rather young, and Josslee raised her hand to wave and called, "Hello, Pord!"

All of the men gave her a hard stare and the young man she addressed, hesitantly waggled his fingers at her in greeting.

Falloah grabbed onto the girl's arm and pulled her in close, hissing through clenched teeth, "We are trying not to be noticed, remember?"

Josslee cringed and offered, "Sorry," in a low voice.

Leedon raised his brow and corrected, "Oh, I don't know. Perhaps that is just what we need." When they both looked to him, he looked back and smiled before directing his attention forward again. "We are not here as sightseers, we have a specific task to perform, and we cannot do that as spectators."

Falloah demanded in a low voice, "Do you even know what that task is?"

He leaned his head slightly as he looked back at her. "Do you?"

She found she could not answer and just turned her eyes ahead as they walked.

Slowly, they were rounding to the south side of the island and the path wound further away from the water, then closer, then around a formation of stone that had been carved into a statue, then closer to the water again.

As they trekked around the south side of the island village, they drew many looks from the people who came and went, some looks of curiosity, looks of fear and recognition, others of alarm.

Falloah finally grumbled as she glanced around at those who watched them pass, "I don't like this. There are too many eyes on us."

Leedon smiled and nodded to a couple of middle-aged ladies who stared as they strode by. "What does a dragon have to fear in this place?"

"She is not currently dragon," Falloah growled.

He glanced at her and a little laugh escaped under his breath. "One would never know."

Josslee pointed ahead of them and declared, "There! Master Haddock's stand! He has the best crab wraps on the whole island!"

Falloah raised a hand toward the girl and barked, "Joss... Wait!"

"Let the girl go," the wizard advised. "Besides. She's right." He looked to the tall woman as she looked to him. "Master Haddock does have the best crab wraps."

Josslee ran the whole way to the sizeable structure of stone and timber that had but a large, very wide, open window and polished timber bar at the front and its shutter swung upward providing shade and shelter over the bar, a straw roof and smoke pouring from the stone chimney at the rear. Three aged wooden tables were distributed in front of the window and bar. She ran past the tables and right up to the bar which rose just to the bottom of her chest, and she slammed her hands down onto it, calling, "Master Haddock!"

A middle-aged man with a cleanly combed black and gray beard and short cut black hair emerged from somewhere in the back, his sharp eyes finding the girl and a smile finding his lips as he approached, and he leaned his forearms on the bar as he regarded the girl with an almost fatherly expression. "Well look who has finally returned. Did you happen to bring a bucket of crabs with you?"

"Not today," she admitted, "but I hope soon."

He nodded. "I'd heard that you and your dragon brother were banished, and I'd hoped it was not true."

She regrettably nodded. "It was true. We have come to fix things." She half turned and looked to the red-haired woman and wizard who had finally caught up to her, then back to him. "We've come to find a solution to this problem."

"I'm sure you have," Haddock said straightly, his eyes finding the wizard. "And I'm sure you have some thoughts on this situation."

"I do," Leedon assured. "Josslee has been bragging about your crab wraps. We thought we might sample them for ourselves."

Haddock leaned heavier on his elbows and nodded. "You know, she has never actually paid for one. She always bartered." His eyes slid to the girl and a little smile found his lips. "I don't see any crabs for barter, little girl."

Leedon reached into a pouch hanging on the belt he wore around his robes. "I'm afraid today you will just have to settle for silver."

With a laugh, Master Haddock took the coins from the wizard and conceded, "Oh, I suppose I can manage that." After he dropped the coins into a box under the bar, hard eyes found the wizard and he informed, "Take care, my friend. All of you. The elders will not look favorably upon her return, especially with all of the destruction that dragon has brought us over the last few days."

Leedon nodded, and as he was handed a leaf wrapped seasoned crab meat with herbs and cheese, his eyes on this hand-held meal he, assured, "Oh, I would not worry over Terrwrathgrawr. His day is coming sooner than you think."

They took their leave and continued on their way, and as they munched away on their meals, Falloah raised her brow and nodded. "This is really good."

Josslee smiled. "I knew you would like it."

They all stopped and looked ahead of them.

Much of the west side of the village was in ruins and smoking timbers still stood from the rubble of structures that had been smashed and burned. Many houses were gone, as were many barns and sheds where fish could be smoked and dried for the long winter ahead. Food stores were gone, and in the distance, at the end of one of the piers that was once lined by many fishing boats, half a dozen boats were being launched with the dead from the dragon's last attack. Three of the boats had family members, two or three lying side by side atop dry scrap wood and covered with linens soaked with lamp oil.

Seeing this, Josslee ran toward them, through the crowd that was gathered at the water's edge. She pushed through the people there and stopped just in front of them as the boats were pushed from the pier and set adrift into the wind.

The girl breathed, "No," as she recognized one of the boats, one painted white and green and sporting brass rings for two sets of oars.

Falloah took her side and grasped her shoulder. "What is it?"

Josslee found that breaths entered her with some difficulty and tears blurred her vision as she watched the boats drift away, and slowly she shook her head and replied in a low voice, "I know all of them and their families. That boat closest to us... He was an old warrior who taught me to fight with a staff. He was always so kind to me. He was like family."

Falloah's mouth tightened to a tight slid and she squeezed the girl's shoulder. "I can assure you that revenge will be swift and brutal."

Archers on another pier, those dressed like anyone else in the village, held the tips of their arrows to torches before them, then they took careful aim and waited.

A who was much better dressed than the others, wearing a black jerkin and a clean dark gray wool shirt and black trousers, raised his hand, and after a brief pause, shouted, "Loose!"

The arrows flew almost simultaneously, and as they struck the boats, the boats exploded into flames.

They all watched for long moments as the burning boats drifted away, and slowly the crowds began to break up as people resumed their lives, many returning to their work cleaning up the shattered and burned swaths of their village.

Leedon had taken the girl's other side without notice and informed, "None of this was your fault, or Farrigrall's."

Josslee could only nod, and she reached up to wipe a tear from her cheek. She turned to walk away, back toward her home, and she stopped suddenly as she saw five men all dressed in brown trousers, black boots, and dingy yellow shirts with black vests all striding toward them, and she mumbled, "Uh, oh."

Leedon and Falloah turned and saw them, and the wizard nodded.

The girl mumbled, "I thought this might be a bad idea."

"Nonsense," the wizard declared as he strode toward the approaching men. "They are here to escort us to your elders."

Falloah and Josslee looked to each other, then they followed the wizard.

Leedon extended his arms and greeted, "Gentlemen! So good to see you all again."

The five men stopped and all recognized the wizard, then several exchanged glances before one, the man in the center of the group, finally spoke.

"Wizard Leedon," he greeted in return. "What brings you to visit our village this fall?"

Leedon strode right up to him and patted his shoulder. "Good to see you as well. How is the family?"

"We've been better," the man informed, his eyes finding Josslee. "I suppose you've come about this kerfuffle regarding the dragon that has attacked here."

"I have indeed," Leedon confirmed. "Any chance the village elders are assembled already?"

Another of the men, on the far left, replied, "As if they expected your arrival." He raised his chin to Josslee and informed, "That girl was banished with Farrigrall, but I assume you already know this."

"Of course, I do," the wizard answered. "Banished not by this visiting dragon, I think, but by her own youth and lack of experience in diplomacy. I doubt the dragon who plagues you even knows of her existence." He extended his hand toward them." Perhaps you would be kind enough to lead the way. We have much to discuss, and we've already had lunch, so no need for such pleasantries."

The men looked to each other again, then to the man in the middle who was clearly their leader.

"In sooth," the leader admitted, "We were coming here to arrest the girl."

Falloah took a step toward him, her brow low over her eyes as she snarled, "That would be a mistake!"

Leedon raised a hand in front of her, not looking her way but silencing her with that simple gesture, and he smiled and assured, "Another who is young and not well versed in the art of diplomacy. No need to arrest Josslee today. We would speak with your elders, and if it is decided, then we will be on our way and we will take the girl to her new life elsewhere. Shall we?"

It was clear to Josslee that the wizard was in complete control and she followed as the five village policemen turned to lead the way to the great hall where the elders awaited them.

One of the men slowed his pace and the girl moved aside to allow him to come abreast of the wizard.

Subtly clearing his throat, the man asked in a low voice, "Can you rid us of this dragon forever? You can do this, can't you?"

Leedon glanced at him and that friendly, confident smile curled his old lips. "No, I will not intervene with the dragon. Only a fool among our kind will do battle with a beast such as this."

The man grumbled, "You must do something! More people die each time he and his minions come here!"

Falloah's eyes widened slightly and she raised her chin.

Leedon looked fully to him and raised his brow. "Minions? He did not come here alone?"

"Three others came with him," the man replied in a low voice, still not looking directly at the wizard. "Two much smaller and a larger, dark colored one that seemed to act as his lieutenant."

"The smaller ones are likely females," Leedon informed.

"They are," Falloah snarled.

Leedon nudged her with his elbow, then assured, "They will be attended to, my friend."

Anger was in the man's voice as he spat, "But not by you?"

"Not by me," the wizard confirmed. "This is not an affair I can attend to personally, but I know someone who will."

Falloah grabbed onto his arm and hissed, "He cannot know about this!"

Patting her hand, Leedon assured, "He must, Falloah. Sooner or later, he must."

She lowered her eyes and tried to respond, but could not.

The village hall was the largest structure in the village. Located close to the village center, it actually backed up to the mountain that rose suddenly from the island and seemed to be built right into it. It was stone all the way to the heavy timber slate roof and was more than thirty paces across the front, almost twice that deep, and the steep roof was about four men's heights tall at its peak.

The heavy timber doors were opened before them and all but the leader of their escorts waited outside as the three were led within, past the seven rows of plank benches that still sat in place from the last village meeting. At the far end was a long table about seven paces long and draped with a black cloth. Stone pitchers and wooden and metal mugs sat before the five people on the other side of it, all five of whom raised their eyes as the four people entered. These were four older men, all with white and silver beards, and one woman with long white hair worn in a bun behind her head. They were all dressed in white robes each with a different color drape over the shoulders. The man on the left wore yellow, the man on his right, blue. The man in the middle, the foreman of the council, wore black, the woman, red, and the man on the right, a gnome, not a human, wore green. All wore strain on their faces, and all seemed almost relieved as they saw the wizard striding toward them, and all stood.

Leedon smiled and extended his arms, greeting, "Good morrow, all." He lowered his arms and stopped about three paces away from the table, his three companions stopping just behind him. "I hear you are having difficulties with a dragon."

"Four," the man in the blue drape confirmed. "I am hoping you are here to rid us of this..." He stopped speaking as he saw the girl who stood beside the wizard. Rising from his seat, he walked around the table and strode right to Josslee, and as he reached her, he took her shoulders and pulled her to him, embracing her as tightly as he could.

She slid her arms around him and hugged him back, burying her face in his neck.

The foreman, wearing the black drape, watched the scene, then looked back to Leedon with strained eyes and said, "I hope you have an answer for these dragons, Leedon." He lowered his eyes and loosed a hard breath before he spoke again. "They have killed many, eaten our stores of food and demand more when they return." He shook his head. "We have no way to attend to such things, and with winter coming and our food gone... "

The man in the yellow drape took his seat and looked to the table. "The big one demanded that we have food awaiting them each time they return or they will start eating our people. Homes are destroyed and many are already dead."

The woman added, "They burned many of the drying huts. It could take us months just to repair the damage they have done. Leedon, if you do not have an answer then this could be the end of us. Most of Shoreline has already fled, we do not know where. We have nowhere else to go, and the dragons will find us if we do run."

Leedon raised his bushy eyebrows. "Well then. It seems these dragons will have to be dealt with, doesn't it?"

Falloah stepped up to him and said in a tone of warning, "Leedon... "

He silenced her with a gesture, not looking at her as he continued, "This is an affair of dragons, and should be handled as such. How goes the fishing of late?"

The man hugging Josslee pulled away from her and returned to his seat, saying as he did so, "Not well, old friend. With Farrigrall gone, many of the crocodiles have returned, especially the big ones." He reached his place and took his seat, looking to the mug before him. "If you do not have the answer we need, then we are doomed."

Leedon nodded and turned his eyes down. "The answer will not be what you think it needs to be. It will be part of the natural order." He looked to the council, his eyes sweeping them from left to right, then right to left. "Something has gone out of balance, and that is why those dragons have come here. Once this balance is restored..." He shrugged.

"How do we restore balance?" the woman asked.

With a smile, the wizard replied, "You leave that to the dragons."

CHAPTER 9

"What do you mean she left?" Farrigrall roared as he sat catlike inside the perimeter wall, Kyshira standing beside him and his attention fixed on Princess Faelon.

Faelon tugged on her finger, sheepishly looking up at the dragon as she answered, "Falloah came and said she had to take her somewhere."

"Where?" the black dragon growled.

Looking back to her Zondaen bodyguard, the Enulam warrior with her, and the two attendants in white who were about her age, she swallowed hard and returned her attention to the dragon, admitting, "She did not say. She did say they would return here, though."

Farrigrall turned his eyes away and snorted, then he looked back to the small human before him. His brow was still low over his eyes, but his eyes softened. "Don't worry, I don't blame you or anyone here." He forced a hard breath from him and considered, then he announced, "I'll be back tonight or tomorrow. If she returns then tell her I said to remain here until I get back."

With a near frantic nod, the princess assured, "I will, and I will keep her under guard until you return."

The dragon nodded back to her, then he stood, turned, and opened his wings.

Aloft over the forest again, the young drake stared blankly forward as he flew without destination.

Kyshira took his side and looked fully to him. "What now?"

"I don't know," he grumbled. "That girl has been a thorn in my side since she was born."

"I mean what would you like to do?" the young dragoness clarified.

He glanced at her. "Oh. I suppose... I don't know."

She stared back at him, then looked away and considered. With a little wickedness in her eyes, she angled upward and flew directly over him, turning her head to look down on him. "Revillee taught me a game. Do you want to play?"

He glanced up at her. "What game?"

"It's called tag."

Farrigrall leaned his head to direct an eye up to her. "I'm familiar with it. The children back home play it."

"Well good," she commended. Reaching down, she poked his head right between his eyes and gleefully declared, "You're it!"

Before the drake could react, she swept her wings forward and slowed almost to a stall, then turned hard to the right and dove, gaining speed as she swept her wings and flew hard away from him.

"Just what I need," he grumbled, banking hard to the right to give chase.

Farrigrall was not interested in playing games and he certainly did not want to expend all of that energy chasing a young dragoness who seemed more interested in garnering his attention than helping him with the issues at hand. Still, chase her he did, and for the first time in his life he found his flight skills truly put to the test. Seasons ago he had done battle with a wyvern, another fast and nimble opponent, but he'd had the fortune of catching it on the ground and that was where the battle stayed. Now, as they swept through fathomless seas of air and clouds, climbing so high the air itself was thin and very cold, he found a purposeful strength within him, within wings that were used far too seldom, and instinct and reflex overtook conscious thought about how he moved. For many seasons he found himself too big to be very agile on the ground, but aloft, he was discovering that his size was no longer such an obstacle. Even the remaining tinges of pain in his still injured side would not slow him.

The young dragoness he pursued was far more nimble than he was, able to turn in tighter circles, and each time he was nearly close enough to touch her, she whipped the other way, arching her body as a cat would, and stroked her wings to change direction far quicker than one would have thought she could. The two young dragons forgot about the passing of time and were simply lost in the game.

The sun moved past its highest point before the two dragons tired enough to abandon their game, and Kyshira led the way toward the lake where the drake had first been found. They landed side by side about fifty paces from the water and trotted to a stop, folding their wings as they strode to the edge of the lake to get a drink. The young dragoness mirrored his movements as best she could and took long, quick strides to keep pace with him.

Nearing the shore, she paused and lowered her body and head, her eyes fixed on the crocodile that sunned itself right at the water's edge, and a little growl rolled from her. This was one of the larger ones that inhabited the lake and the dragoness knew even at this distance that it was larger than she was, stronger, and waiting for something like her to happen by.

Farrigrall had no fear of this crocodile and did not break stride, but instead angled toward the other predator with a thunderous growl of his own, also lowering his body with the expectation to meet an old foe in battle, mostly as a secret ploy to impress the young dragoness who was with him.

The young drake was clearly spoiling for a fight, but the crocodile had no such ambitions and nobody about that he wished to impress, so before the dragon could get into striking range he abruptly whipped his head toward the lake and scrambled as fast as it could into the water with a violent splash and swept its tail as hard as it could as it retreated toward open water.

Stomping into the water after the crocodile, Farrigrall only advanced until the water was about knee high before he stopped, and with bared teeth, he roared at the retreating predator in a clear warning not to return.

Kyshira cringed slightly as the drake roared, and her eyes were wide and locked on the black dragon, not with fear, but more infatuation.

He half turned and looked to the little dragoness, and with a grunt, he motioned with his head for her to approach and get herself a drink, and she was not hesitant as she did so, keeping her attention locked on him as she strode to him and keeping her head low and her arms drawn to her.

Side by side, they both crouched down to drink, and she glanced at him a few times as they quenched their thirst. Farrigrall finished first and waited for the dragoness, then they both turned and waded to the shore.

Once to the tall stalks of grasses that had since turned to tan and amber, Farrigrall laid to his belly and stared blankly ahead of him, toward the north where he had expected to find Josslee, and he soon found himself anxious with worry.

Kyshira laid down beside him, her full attention on him as she asked, "What are you thinking so hard about?"

He glanced at her and found he had no answer.

"I wish I could chase big crocodiles away like you do," she went on. "Big ones like that just aren't afraid of me. I always think they'll eat me so I just stay away from them. What do you want to do now? It seems that if the Scarlet is not about then we can do whatever we want to, but you seem very distracted by something."

His eyes slid to her again.

She stared back almost anxiously.

Farrigrall loosed a hard breath and laid his head down. "I'm the guardian of my village and I am not there to protect them. I promised Mother I would watch after Josslee, and now I have no idea where she is." A deep growl rolled from him. "I don't know what I'm supposed to do now."

"More a grand question than you know, my boy," the wizard said loudly as he approached from the dragon's side.

Farrigrall lifted his head and turned his attention that way, raising his brow as he called, "Leedon?"

With a smile, the wizard stopped only ten paces away, leaning heavily on his walking stick as he continued, "That is a question we all must ask ourselves and more often than we'd like. What do I do now? What is my purpose?" He leaned his head slightly. "We often find that what was once thought our calling was merely a journey to get us to where we needed to be all along."

"How did you find me?" the young drake asked.

"The ways of a wizard," Leedon replied. "I'll not burden your already troubled mind with that. I'd heard of a mighty battle that did not go well for you."

Looking to the north again, Farrigrall grumbled, "That is the mother of all understatements. I failed my whole village, and now I can never go home."

"Is a dragon meant to live with my kind?" the wizard posed. "Perhaps this was an unpleasant part of a journey you've needed to take for some time."

Kyshira pushed herself up and sat catlike, looking over the drake's back to see the wizard, and she leaned her head as she asked, "Just how many humans do you have?"

Leedon looked to her and smiled, laughing under his breath.

"He's not my human," Farrigrall answered. "He visits the village and everyone knows him, I think." Looking back to the wizard, the dragon asked, "Do you know where Josslee is?"

"Indeed, I do," Leedon assured. "Not to worry, mighty Farrigrall. She is safe and in good hands, so that is one less burden for you to carry."

"You have many answers," the drake observed, "so perhaps you can tell me how I can defeat this Terrwrathgrawr and rid my village of him once and for all."

Raising his brow, the wizard replied, "That is beyond my realm of expertise, I'm afraid. Perhaps you just need time to grow, and grow you will. A few decades from now you will have doubled in size and be as formidable as any dragon."

"I don't have many decades," the dragon snarled.

"Well then," the wizard said with a nod, "perhaps another dragon should attend this problem."

"It's my problem to attend to," Farrigrall insisted.

"Is it?" the wizard countered. "You have come to an important crossroads and from my perspective, you have two choices: You may follow your pride and pursue the defeat of a new enemy, one who will likely dispatch you in one more glorious battle."

Farrigrall growled angrily and looked away.

"Or," Leedon went on, "you can take the other road, learn about the ways of your kind and allow yourself to be a dragon." He shrugged. "Your choice, of course, but I'd say you are well on the way down that second path."

The dragon forced another hard breath from him, and looked down to the wizard again. "How does that second path protect my village?"

Leedon smiled, then turned and started to walk away. "It is possible that two roads end up in the same place, my boy, but the road you know may end up impassible, and the other may wind through unforeseen adventures that could bring you strength you'd never foreseen."

Farrigrall looked to the north again as the wizard's words struck his heart as none ever had. When he looked back, the wizard was gone and only a settling mist remained.

Kyshira stood and backed away a step, shrieking, "Where did he go? He was just there!"

Farrigrall also stood and looked toward the north again. "He's right. Perhaps it's time."

"For what?" the little dragoness asked. "And what happened to the human? He was just there!"

He reached for his side, no longer feeling the sharp pain left by the injuries he sustained in his battle with Terrwrathgrawr, and when he looked down to it, he found not even a scar remained. Raising his eyes, he could only surmise that he had been unknowingly healed by the wizard. "It's time for me to learn all there is to know about our kind."

**

Deep in the forest was a field that had been the site of a great battle in the spring, but the dragons who landed in its center had no way to know.

Farrigrall trotted off the last of his speed, then he folded his wings to him and turned to the blue dragoness who had landed behind him and was just folding her own wings. "So, it's not that far removed from what humans do, their hierarchies."

Staring back at him, Kyshira leaned her head and blinked. "I do not know what humans do, but our ways are very simple. A landmaster controls a vast territory and allows other dragons hunting ranges within his territory, mostly females but a few drakes who will act as his *subordinares.*"

"His what?"

"Smaller drakes who will help to defend his territory. Females will also help, but if another landmaster crosses the border it is expected that our landmaster will fight him personally."

He nodded in slight motions. "Still sounds like what humans do."

"I do not know what humans do," Kyshira repeated. "I spent most of my life avoiding them."

"Why would you avoid them?"

She turned her eyes down. "When I was much younger and striking out to hunt for myself, a group of humans tried to kill me. They had all manner of weapons and chased me away from some sheep I was hunting. I was only about as big as their horses at the time and I did not try to fight back. I just ran away and took to the wing to get away from them. Everywhere I went it was much the same, so I just stayed away from them completely my whole life. And then I came here where there seems to be some kind of friendship with humans and unicorns and dragons." She shook her head. "It does not make sense to me, but I do not question what bigger dragons do."

"Sounds wise," Farrigrall said. "So, you've avoided humans your entire life."

"Humans and anything bigger than me," she replied. "Unless Mettegrawr summoned me for something, I also stayed away from other dragons. Sometimes, when hunting is not so good, bigger dragons will eat smaller dragons."

"So, I've heard," he confirmed. "You don't seem to be that afraid here."

She glanced away, then turned her eyes up to his. "Not so much. Revillee was supposed to kill me when I first came here, but she refused because she thought we could be friends instead and her landmaster allowed me to stay. I'm terrified of him, but he has told me to stay close by in case he wants to send me on some errand, which he seems to do a lot, mostly to give a message to one of the other dragons who live here. Sometimes if a bigger dragon has left a kill behind, I can eat some of it." She lowered her eyes. "Mostly, I just stay out of the way and I try not to be noticed."

He found himself staring at her, and there was a familiar ache in his chest. She was clearly not very old, and not a large dragon by any means. It would be easy for another dragon or a wyvern or crocodile to take a meal from her, and he was beginning to see that it likely happened often. "Are you hungry?" he heard himself ask.

She turned her eyes away and fluttered her wings, and finally, shyly replied, "I suppose I am."

**

Having spent very little time around dragonkind, young Farrigrall simply did not know the implications of his offer of food to a dragoness who was clearly interested in more than friendship with him. He had never taken down a grawrdox before, but a lifetime of battle with large crocodiles had made him very strong and formidable, very skilled at the kill, and the lumbering grawrdox he selected, not a full-grown bull but a half-grown cow, barely knew what hit it when he attacked.

Later, lying side by side in a field of tan and light brown grass with the remains of the slaughtered and mostly eaten beast nearby, two dragons were near slumber in the midday sunlight as their meal digested in their stomachs.

Farrigrall's eyes were on the carcass as he drew a heavy breath and said, "So that was grawrdox. I like it."

Kyshira smiled, her full attention on him as she gently laid her head to the ground.

He continued, "I've spent my entire life eating fish and crocodiles, and one wyvern, but this was really good. I suppose in the future I'll be eating more of them." He looked down to her. "It wasn't all that hard to take down, either."

Her eyes were closed and she was slumbering peacefully.

He could only stare back at her for a moment, and a little smile curled his scaly lips. Drawing another breath, he laid his head down beside hers and closed his eyes.

CHAPTER 10

Something, some sound or movement, alerted the young blue dragoness and in an instant her head was up as she was torn from a deep sleep. Wide eyes scanned the tree line in the distance, nearly a half a league away, and there she saw black smoke settle to the ground just under the first of the trees there. A cold wash swept through her and she slowly turned her eyes to the black drake at her side. Part of her wished he would awaken, and most of her hoped he would not.

Slowly and quietly, she pushed herself up, keeping her eyes on the slumbering dragon as she stepped as quietly as she could away from him. Opening her wings, she took to the sky and flew in the direction of the settling smoke, seeing it gone but noticing a trail of it ahead of her that was in a straight line, and a careful order for her to follow.

A few leagues away, she landed in a small field where the forest had yielded to the flat stone that had risen from the ground, stone that was dotted with mosses and grass grew in the cracks that had formed in it. Settling gently with broad strokes of her wings, she lowered herself to all fours and looked around her, folding her wings to her back and sides as her heart thundered at what she knew to expect, and what she knew had to be waiting for her somewhere.

Long, clawed fingers protruding from a powerful wing grasped her neck and forced her all the way to the ground and a clawed foot slammed onto her back and crushed her to the stone she now lay on. Kyshira's wide eyes could make out the black smoke settling all around her and she crooned ever so softly, a fearful croon of what was to come.

There was a growl right beside and behind her head, right in her ear and that sinister voice observed, "You are getting very friendly with that black drake."

Drawing a broken breath, she reminded, "You told me to get close so I am."

"What of him?" the wyvern demanded. "How is he important?"

She swallowed hard, her eyes darting about, and finally she answered, "He is of no consequence, just a drake."

"With whom you are very friendly," the wyvern hissed. "Are you hoping his loyalty will find Mettegrawr when you are returned home? Will he betray the Tyrant to be at your side?"

Her brow lowered and she informed, "He is not one of Agarxus' *subordinares*. He came from the west."

"And?"

She had to answer truthfully, but carefully. "He, um... He was driven this way by Terrwathgrawr. I do not think he is loyal to any landmaster."

"And you are very friendly with him," the wyvern observed. "Very friendly. Do you have your own plans for him? Will he help you betray us?"

"No!" she whined as his foot crushed down on her harder. "You told me I would have more time."

"Your time is almost up," the wyvern hissed. "In the time you were generously gifted you have produced nothing but excuses, and I feel I am wasting my time with you, as does Mettegrawr. We feel you have outlived your usefulness."

"I haven't!" she assured desperately. Thinking quickly, she reported, "Terrwrathgrawr has crossed the border to the west and may have brought others with him. He occupies the land to a lake well within this realm and seems to mean to seize it. Agarxus will have to respond with his strongest *subordinares* and he might have to go attend to this problem himself."

The wyvern took his foot from her back and drew his head away, nodding as he commended, "Finally, something useful from you. I suppose this information will win you another day of life." He leaned his head as she sheepishly looked up at him. "Another gesture will, perhaps, win you many more. Might even win you a safe return home."

With a tiny voice, she asked, "What gesture?"

"You will be told in time," was all he would say. "Return to your little friend and disclose nothing to him." His eyes narrowed. "Nothing. I will be watching and I will be about when you think I am not." He stood fully on his feet and wing knuckles, demonstrating his full size to her. "Find out more, and you will let us know when the Tyrant ventures to the west to meet Terrwrathgrawr." He glanced aside. "And, lure your little friend toward the north. Show him the splendor of the Dark Mountains, and summon your little burgundy friend as well."

She gasped. "Revillee?"

"I do not care what her name is," the wyvern growled. He turned and opened his wings. "Before nightfall, or you will be a wonderful breakfast for me come the morrow."

She watched him take flight and turn toward the north, and noticed something very important.

Farrigrall was noticeably bigger.

Still, fear would keep such hopes at bay. She pushed herself up, sitting catlike as she turned her attention to the ground before her and just stared for a time. What the smoke wyvern and Mettegrawr's minions had planned for her was a mystery, but dragging Revillee into this web... Perhaps that was the test they had in store for her. Perhaps they wanted Revillee to abandon what she knew in Agarxus' territory and go north with her. And what about Farrigrall? What did they have planned for him?

It was too much for such a young mind to ponder all at once. All she could sort from it was her growing feelings for a young drake she had just met, a young drake who seemed to want to protect her, and for the first time in her life, she did not feel like she was in the way of a larger and more powerful dragon. For the first time, she felt the stirrings any young dragoness would feel.

Looking over her shoulder, she knew that someone would have to be betrayed.

CHAPTER 11

The house in which Josslee had grown up seemed to anchor one of the piers to the shore and stood on old timber stilts out into the lake. Many houses were like this and it was one of those on this side of the island that had survived the fiery attacks of the invading dragons. Walking with Falloah still at her side, Josslee quickened her pace as she saw the old black wood slat roof of her house and her heart jumped a little as she approached.

It was a simple wooden structure of solid construction that had been there for a long time, at least three generations of her family. Rather large for the area, it housed her entire family including her surviving grandmother, her parents, and two brothers, one older and one younger. It was a simple rectangle on the outside with vertical wooden slats covering it and shutters flanking the many windows. Smoke poured from the one chimney which told her someone was cooking in there, and seeing her family, especially her parents, after being away for so long sent surges of excitement through her and a little smile curled her mouth as she neared.

Falloah kept pace easily, but felt more uneasy about meeting strangers than excited to meet the girl's parents. Her eyes kept straying to the sky, darting about as if she sensed that something was amiss, though she was not entirely sure what it was that had her so alerted.

The crushed stone path on which they walked crunched beneath their feet and only that could be heard by the girl as she reached the house in which she had been born and grown up.

Someone looked out a window, then retreated back inside. The door facing the island burst open and a plump woman in a blue dress with a white apron over it rushed out and hurried to the girl. Graying brown hair was worn in a bun behind her head and her eyes were wide with surprise and relief at seeing the girl. As best she could, she hurried to the girl with outstretched arms. Josslee ran into the woman's arms and wrapped her own around the woman, and buried her face between the woman's neck and shoulder. She was only slightly shorter than the woman, who was also tall for her gender, but melted like a little girl as they embraced.

Falloah's approach was a slow one and she did not need anyone to tell her that the woman was the girl's mother. A strange ache weighed on her heart. She stopped a couple of paces away, her attention on the exchange of affection before her.

The woman whispered to her, "Your Papa and I have been so worried about you."

Nearly brought to tears, the girl replied, "I've worried about you, too. I saw the funeral boats and feared the worst."

A tall and rather husky man emerged from the house, leaning heavily on a cane as he stopped just outside. His gaze found the two and stayed on them for long seconds, then he started forward with heavy steps on big, leather boots. Wearing a dirty white shirt with long sleeves rolled back to his elbows, a brown pocketed vest, and brown trousers, he was a big man with big arms and a big belly, a black and silver beard and long black hair.

As he reached the women, he dropped the cane and wrapped his arms around both of them.

Falloah drew a deep breath and finally looked away from them, folding her arms as she found herself becoming impatient and just wanting to continue with her mission here.

Josslee finally pulled away from her parents, still clinging to them as she looked from one to the other and found herself unable to speak.

Looking the girl up and down, she smiled and observed, "You are far removed from the pretty dresses you always wore."

"Ya lookin' like a warrior woman," her father commented. "Had you some adventures out there, I see."

"I got to train with a Zondaen," the girl gleefully reported, "and she gave me these clothes so that I could move better! I also met the Princess of Caipiervell and I met other dragons!" She glanced back at Falloah. "One of them is really mean to him but the others seem nice."

Falloah's brow lowered and a little snarl curled her lips.

"How is our Farrigrall?" the mother asked, concern in her voice.

Josslee reported, "He finally ate something and made sure I was taken care of like he always does." She heaved a hard breath and turned her eyes down. "I wish he had not been banished at all."

"Or you," her father added.

Falloah cut in, "Leedon has spoken to your village elders and remedied that, but we still have the issue of Farrigrall to attend."

All three turned toward her and Josslee's parents looked on her with some suspicion.

"Oh!" Josslee declared. "This is Falloah. Falloah, these are my parents, my Papa Eston and my Mother, Ucira."

They nodded to the dragon-woman, and she simply nodded back.

It was Eston who asked, "How did Josslee come to be in your company?"

Without hesitating, Falloah replied, "I'd heard of a problem you are having with a dragon and came to investigate."

His eyes narrowed slightly and he nodded. "Of what interest is this problem to you?"

His wife scolded under her breath, "Eston!"

Raising her brow slightly, Falloah folded her arms and answered, "The affairs of dragons affect us all, and if there is to be conflict then we will need to know so that we can act accordingly. Your elders mentioned several dragons that have come here."

"Yes," he confirmed. "The larger one drove Farg away, and a few days after that another swam from just north of Shoreline Village and attacked us again."

Falloah glanced at Josslee. "Swam? It did not fly?"

"It did not have wings," Eston confirmed. "The large one returned a couple days after that with three others, but the smaller one has returned almost every day since. Shoreline has been abandoned and they left nothing for it to eat there, so it comes here, and now we have no Farg to defend us from it or the many crocodiles that seem to know of his departure."

Her eyes sliding to Josslee, Falloah recalled, "Your elders did not mention anything about a swimming dragon, nor one that is coming here almost every day. And if it is big enough to not worry over crocodiles when it swims... "

Josslee guessed, "Perhaps it was watching all this time and would not approach with Farg among us."

Falloah nodded. "Terra dragons will not generally approach larger predators, especially larger dragons that will kill them on sight."

Eston raised his chin to Falloah and there was some disdain in his voice as he asked, "You some kind of expert on dragons?"

"Yes," Falloah answered.

Josslee quickly interjected, "She came with me from Caipiervell to investigate. She, uh... She's the royal—"

"I need to see where it comes ashore," Falloah interrupted, looking past them. "Terra dragons quickly become creatures of habit and it will not stray far from a path where it knows it can easily find food, and I'll wager it does not lair far from here." She turned her eyes to Eston. "Why did your people not evacuate when it started attacking your village?"

With hard words, he countered, "And go where?"

Josslee pulled away from her parents and took Falloah's arm, pulling her along as she said, "Come on. We should see where it comes ashore."

Eston picked up his cane and ordered his wife back into the house with a gesture, then followed as best he could. "It's nearly high sun, and if those other dragons do not come this way it will visit soon. We need to get inside."

Glancing back at him as the girl led the way, Falloah informed, "If it is big enough to not worry over crocodiles then it will tear through your flimsy houses to get to you."

With some effort, Eston caught up to them and demanded, "What do you think we can do about it? We have no weapons that can deal with such a beast!"

Falloah glanced at him again and corrected, "You may have one."

They began to pass people who were in a hurry the other direction and Eston stopped one of them, demanding, "What are you running from?"

"It's coming," the thin man frantically reported as he pulled away. "Get yourselves to cover!"

Falloah strode on, following the road that circled around the island's west side, and Josslee and Eston followed.

"Woman!" Eston scolded. "You are going to get yourself killed!"

Ignoring him, Falloah strode on, saying as if to herself, "If this terra dragon is so comfortable visiting here when..." She stopped suddenly, raising her chin as she stared out into the water, and she mumbled, "Oh. He *is* big."

About a hundred paces from the shore and swimming like some great monitor lizard, the terra dragon approached without fear, and with almost casual movements of its body, and it clearly did not fear any crocodiles with which it might be sharing the water.

Falloah looked around her, seeing that many houses had already been destroyed and she could not tell if it was damage from the terra dragon or caused by visits by Terrwrathgrawr and his minions. No time to think about it. Setting her hands on her hips, she focused on the approaching terra dragon and her eyes narrowed. "Any caves around here?"

"No caves," Eston replied, "only the stone quarry dug into the hill in the center of the island."

"Then that is where we go," Falloah informed as she watched the terra dragon near the shore only thirty paces away. "Lead the way."

They turned and retreated at a pace that Eston could maintain, but a pace that did not seem to be fast enough to outrun the beast that pursued them.

Josslee looked over her shoulder, her wide eyes filling with the image of the terra dragon as it clamored ashore.

Heavily built with an armored back, it was dark gray in color for the most part, but the armor plates on its back were black fading to a dark brown on its sides. Thick, gray hide covered its legs and most of its head and its build was that of a giant monitor lizard. Small but piercing eyes swept the island before it and fixed on the trio who fled from it a hundred paces away. It moved much like the giant lizard it was and with hungry, intense purpose.

The girl's heart jumped and she realized that they would never arrive at the quarry before it caught them. Looking ahead of them, she saw the opening in the old mountain peak that was a height and a half tall and two paces across, mostly square but clearly it was just clumsily bored into the stone with the simple tools with which the people here had to work. Looking behind them again, she saw the dragon closing the gap too quickly for them to escape.

Eston took Falloah's shoulder and pushed her along, ordering, "You girls to ahead. I'll catch up."

"Papa!" Josslee protested.

"Go!" he shouted. "Get my daughter to safety!"

Josslee's attention fell to a path that crossed the one they were on, and the mostly stone building that looked nice and sturdy, and without warning, she broke away from her small group and sprinted that way.

"Josslee!" her father cried.

She ignored him and after a hard sprint she arrived at the far corner of the structure and stopped there, spinning around to see the terra dragon still in pursuit of Falloah and her father. Waving her arms, she yelled, "Hey! Over here!"

The dragon hesitated and turned his full attention on her. At this point it was only about forty paces away from her and could catch her easily, but still she held her ground.

Her heart sank a little as it turned its attention back to her father and Falloah, and she heaved a frustrated breath. Waving her arms again, she shouted, "Over here! Come on, a nice, tender girl to eat!"

This time, less than twenty paces away, it stopped and turned its head to look fully at her.

Josslee finally got a good scale of how big it was, and as she faced it down, she mumbled, "Oh, bugga," as it turned fully on her. Her eyes darted about and she retreated a few steps, and finally saw the open window shutters on the stone building's west wall. With a defiant look at the terra dragon, she crouched down to pick up a large stone, never taking her eyes from the beast as it stood there and just seemed to study her.

Indecision racked the beast and it looked back to the fleeing woman and man, and as it did, the stone struck the side of its head near its eye. A growl escaped it as it bared its teeth and swung its attention back to the girl.

Josslee finally realized that this creature was not quite as large as Farrigrall and a little bit of fear seeped away from her as she bent down to pick up another stone. Standing back up, she raised her chin and shouted to the terra dragon, "You aren't so scary!"

It charged!

She dropped the stone and turned to flee, shrieking, "Yes you are!"

Always an athletic girl, she jumped into the window and scrambled through it, falling to the stone floor within the building. She managed to get back to her feet and flee deeper into it before she stopped and wheeled around.

Three of the terra dragon's black claws hooked onto the wooden window ledge and with seemingly little effort it pulled the lower part of the wall away, widening the opening of the window almost all the way to the ground.

Josslee backpedaled, her wide eyes fixed on the nose of the dragon as it pushed into the hole it had made in the wall. She was barely award of nets and benches and wooden tables all around her, the large wooden double doors to her left, the overturned wooden boat that lay near the doors, and all of the other fishing and boating implements that hung from the timbers overhead and lay on tables. A pile of nets that lay on one of the larger tables in the center of the room.

The dragon sniffed loudly, then again. It knew she was in there and pushed harder against the wall, its nose felling more stones around the ever-widening hole. It withdrew its nose and turned its head, directing an eye inside that found the girl with quick focus.

She swallowed hard and slowly backed away more. Looking around her, she found a sharp gaffe pole, much like a pike with a sharp end and a hook, and darted to it, and as soon as she moved, the dragon growled and clawed at the hole it had made to widen it further. Josslee picked up the gaffe, which was a man's height and a half long. She gripped it firmly with both hands, holding it with the sharp point toward the dragon, and her wide eyes locked on the claws that ripped away more of the wall.

When it stuck its nose inside to sniff again, she ran toward it and thrust the gaffe as hard as she could, ramming the metal point right between its nostrils. The point barely penetrated, but the dragon roared in anger and withdrew.

Watching through the hole in the wall, Josslee could see it backing away, then she retreated herself as it charged forward and rammed its nose and head into the hole and this time got most of its head inside. She screamed and hurled the gaffe pole at its head before she turned and fled again.

Another wooden door was on the far end, a door just big enough for someone to walk comfortably through, and she slammed her palms into it as she reached it, as the dragon pushed further into the sturdy building. Looking behind her, her eyes widened further as she saw it stopped by its own shoulders, but it continued to push into the hole, and the wall continued to crumble around it. The roof began to buckle and it was clear that the building she was in was beginning to succumb to the terra dragon's strength.

Turning back to the door, she grabbed the wooden bolt that was slid into its place on the wall and pulled it back, but it stopped, and she found herself trying to force it open. With a quick glance back at the ever-closing dragon, she pulled back against the wooden bolt with all her weight and jerked as hard as she could. It came loose and opened and she tumbled to the floor again.

The dragon was nearly all the way inside now and as the girl scrambled to her feet, she found an oar leaning against the wall, took it, and hurled it at the dragon's head before she turned and raced out the open door

Some kind of safety was to be had pressing her back against the stone wall on the other side near the still open door, and when she looked that way and saw the door still open, she pulled against it to close it. This gave her just a smidgen of reassurance that the terra dragon would not get her. Drawing a breath to calm herself, she looked ahead of her and saw the entrance to the stone mine where others waited in safety, still more than a hundred paces away.

Then, a chilling realization. The dragon within the building she had just left was suddenly quiet.

Calling on all her remaining courage, she pushed the door back open and peered inside, seeing the destruction it had left, but no terra dragon. Her mouth fell open and she managed, "Oh, this is just not good in any way."

Behind her, black claws grabbed on to the stone corner of the building with loud clacks, and she turned around as it gaped its jaws and roared at her through long, murderous teeth.

Josslee screamed and ran the other way, tripped over a log that was half sunk into the ground to serve as a border for the gravel walkway, and fell to her belly. She tried hard and quickly to scramble away, but looked over her shoulder to see the gaping jaws of the terra dragon three paces away from her, and she screamed anew, feeling the painful inevitability of her death a second away.

The scarlet dragon's murderous teeth and jaws clamped onto the terra dragon's head and she pulled it away from the girl with a deep growl. The terra dragon fought to free its head from its rival's jaws, but was instead hurled ten paces away where it rolled to a stop nearly to the next structure.

Falloah looked down to the girl who lay on her side staring back at her with wide eyes, and the dragoness scolded, "That was stupid!"

Josslee defended, "Well, it worked!"

The dragoness growled and turned fully back to the terra dragon as it rolled to its feet and pivoted to face her. She was slightly larger, and as she stood fully over it and half spread her wings, she looked larger yet, baring teeth some of which were twice the length of a man's hand. Her eyes bored fearlessly into the terra dragon and a growl rumbled from her.

The terra dragon did not see a dragon trying to protect a village. It could only see a rival posturing for new territory, new hunting grounds, and in the moment, it was not interested in backing down. Thick, scaly lips slid away from hand sized teeth and it hissed back, opening its jaws ever so slightly.

Falloah stomped forward, just one step, and the terra dragon flinched. The dragoness did not wish to fight, nor would she back down if this ground dwelling predator forced the issue, and she meant that it should know this in no uncertain terms. Her jaws swung open and she roared a mighty challenge to the terra dragon, and it took a step back, responding with a roar of its own.

A standoff ensued for just a moment as each stared the other down, exchanging growls and snarls in a brief game of intimidation, a game that could not last.

The villagers peered out of their hiding places all over to watch the outcome, some hoping for an epic battle, some hoping both dragons would just go away, and others still fearful that the victor would simply try to eat anyone it could find.

Patience would be tested, and the patience of the terra dragon would faulter first. A rear foot slid slightly forward, claws dug into the ground, and its back end tensed as its thrashing tail was suddenly still. This could mean only one thing.

And Falloah knew it.

Even before it could spring toward her, she had a plan, and as it launched itself, she twisted aside and slammed her claws hard into the side of its head as it passed. Turning fully, she watched the terra dragon stumble, lose its footing and crash head first into the stone structure it had damaged before, and this time the wall held firm.

Slightly stunned, the terra dragon scrambled back up and turned on the dragoness again, this time with his jaws gaping wide, but the nimble scarlet was much faster than she appeared, and dodged out of range. Teeth clacked together finding only air and Falloah pounced with ripping claws, and her teeth found the back of its neck. Her jaws could not quite drive her teeth through its armor here, but they could crush down on its neck and drive it to the ground. Her hands slammed down on its snout and back and one foot raked her claws across its armor and upper leg.

This struggle lasted a moment with each trying to out power the other and tails thrashing violently. The terra dragon was clearly very strong and growled and hissed as it pushed back against the dragoness, and as she tired, it eventually was able to wriggle free of her grip.

Falloah released it and backed away, her jaws still open half a man's height and her teeth bared as she stood ready to receive the terra dragon when it charged again. The terra dragon turned toward her, also baring its teeth as it raised its head, and each stood ready to defend themselves, and for long seconds neither would advance.

The dragoness gaped her jaws fully and roared a brief, loud roar, taking a single, stomping step toward her opponent. The terra dragon flinched, but did not retreat.

In a clear demonstration of her superior maneuverability, Falloah sidestepped and tried to flank the terra dragon, knowing it would turn to keep facing her. A game of patience could not last and the dragoness knew time was not in her favor. This had to end.

During this struggle, Josslee had made her way to the entrance to the mine where many people stood both inside and outside to watch the outcome. As she took her father's side, he took her under his arm and pulled her close to him, his attention fully on the stalemate outside.

Once again, patience would abandon the terra dragon first and it roared and charged with gaping jaws, this time rearing up on its hind legs with the claws of its hands splayed out. Falloah tried to dodge aside, but she could not avoid the one hand that grasped her arm and pulled her off balance. The two tumbled to the ground in a succession of mighty thumps and this time the terra dragon ended up on top of her.

Falloah knew that its back and down its flanks were armored, but its belly was not. She drew a foot in, between her and the terra dragon, and this time claws found their mark as she kicked back against it and left three rips in its hide from its belly to its side armor and managed to get it off of her just long enough to roll free and get her feet and hands under her. Not stunned nor deterred, the terra dragon roared in anger and charged with open jaws again, and this time the dragoness responded in kind. Her jaws clamped down on its shoulder and the terra dragon's found her nape and both wrenched their heads violently back and forth to drive teeth into hide.

Falloah's teeth won the battle first and it was the terra dragon that retreated, wrenching his shoulder free and backing away before he released her with his own jaws and roared. The dragoness bit at its face, connecting a few times as she advanced only a couple of steps, and it shied away and retreated faster.

The two entered another stand-off, and this time Falloah remained on all fours, staying ready for another charge as she opened her jaws and teeth and bored into her opponent with wide eyes and a low brow.

Still unwilling to yield, the terra dragon darted toward her side and tried to get a bite in there, but the dragoness pivoted and managed to get her jaws around its head and neck, and this time she drove forward with all her strength to try and topple the beast she fought. Skill was clearly winning this fight, and while the terra dragon seemed to have a slight advantage in strength, it could not match her speed or experience. Sidestepping to keep its balance, it roared again and tried to turn its head to bite back, snapping its jaws on air instead of dragon. Falloah's claws did their work on its side as she drove her teeth into its thick hide, her lower teeth finally sinking into flesh and drawing blood.

With a shriek, the terra dragon turned away and tore his neck and head from the dragoness' grip, and this time he did not turn back toward her. He did not run, but he just walked away, back toward the water and back the way he had come.

Falloah did not advance this time and just watched the terra dragon retreat, and her chest and flanks heaved as she struggled to catch her breath. Though clearly able to fight on, she was weary from this bout and appeared to be glad it was over. As the terra dragon reached the water, strode in and began to swim to the shore across the lake, the dragoness lowered her nose and closed her eyes, drawing a few deep breaths to calm her body and nerves.

Only one human approached, a tall girl in the garb of a Zondaen.

Josslee just stared up at the dragoness for a moment, then she folded her arms and asked, "Are you going to go finish it off?"

Her eyes opening with her brow low between them, Falloah just stared at the ground before her for long seconds, then slowly turned her attention to the girl.

Fearlessly raising her brow, Josslee informed, "Farg would have killed it."

Falloah snarled, "Bully for Farg." She pushed herself up and, once standing, grasped the nape of her neck, then she looked down at her hand to see there was a little blood present. The terra dragon had managed to bite through her hide, and she did not seem happy about this. She turned her eyes skyward, then looked down to the quarry and called to Eston, "I'm going to need that dress." Turning her eyes up, she scanned the cloud dotted sky only once, then looked down to the man who approached her with the bundle of material in his arms. She placed a hand low on her neck and grasped there, then closed her eyes and mouthed the words.

As before, she was overtaken by a shimmering emerald light and shrank quickly to human form, and in half a moment was standing naked before all of the onlookers of the village who had witnessed the battle. Seemingly without modesty, she took the dress from Eston and worked with it for a few seconds to position it to pull on over her head as she had before, unaware of the many eyes on her as she dressed herself.

Josslee rubbed her eyes and mumbled, "You couldn't do that in private?"

Falloah finished dressing and looked around her at the many people who watched from the crowd that had gathered, then she raised a hand to her nape and rubbed it there where it was clearly still sore.

"Your wound is gone," Josslee observed.

"Injuries do not follow when one changes form," Falloah explained. "If I stay like this long enough before I change back then it will be as if it never was."

A tall, very muscular and amazingly handsome man with bronze skin, deeply chiseled features and long, shiny black hair pushed his way through the crowd of humans and scolded, "Perhaps that injury should come back to remind you of foolish decisions!" He wore only a white shirt that was open across his broad chest, black trousers and no shoes or boots, though the gravel road did not seem to bother him. A gold chain hung around his neck suspending a small golden dragon's talon with an emerald sphere in its grip.

Falloah looked that way, then rolled her eyes from him and faced Eston again. "I need to speak to your elders again and—"

The tall, black haired man interrupted as he reached her, "You need to get yourself home!"

She wheeled back to him, her brow low over her eyes as she barked, "Stay out of this, Vinton! None of this concerns you!"

"Since when do dragons keep such secrets?" he demanded. When she huffed a hard breath and tried to walk past him, he grabbed her arm and stopped her, spinning her to face him. "Answer me, Falloah!"

She jerked her arm from his grip and turned her eyes down. "Just leave it alone."

"We both know I am not going to do that. I suppose Ralligor still does not know, either? Do you think you can use his magic and keep secrets from him?"

Falloah tried to respond, oblivious to all around her, but could not seem to find words.

Vinton took her shoulders and held her firmly before him. "I am proud to call you my friend and would not trade that for anything in the world, and when I see you engaging in such behaviors as deceiving your mate and picking fights with terra dragons you know I will worry and intervene."

Her brow was low over her eyes when she looked back up at him. "I am not Shahly."

"At the moment, I see little difference." He slid his hands over her shoulders and to her neck, grasping her there as he demanded, "Tell me what you are doing and what is so important that you would risk your life and what this other dragon has to do with it all. Tell me!"

Tears glossed her eyes as she stared back at him.

Vinton's eyes widened slightly and he raised his chin, then he blinked and his lips parted.

Falloah pulled away from him again and backed away, then she walked past and insisted, "I must see the elders." She stopped abruptly as another man appeared before her, her eyes wide with surprise and recognition.

Leedon stared back at her with his brow high over his eyes.

Taking a step back, Falloah pointed to Vinton and barked, "Are you responsible for this?"

Leedon smiled. "Of course not. Your mate is. I simply held onto his amulet for him in the event he might need it again."

"Then I suppose you know as well," she spat. "Did you tell Ralligor, too?"

The wizard shook his head in slight motions. "That is not my place, dragoness."

Falloah's hair flailed as she whipped her head around to Vinton, and she snarled, "Nor yours!"

Leedon gently took her shoulder and said, "It is difficult to feel cornered by friends, I think more so than it would be to feel cornered by enemies." When she looked to him, he continued, "Falloah, perhaps what you fear the most will not come to fruition unless you force it to do so, or perhaps your trust in those closest to you could stave it off forever."

Once again, she found herself without words and turned her eyes down, then her lips tightened to thin slits and she looked around her. "These people are very important to him and he already feels as if he has failed them."

Josslee scolded, "What do you care about Farg's feelings? You've been nothing but mean to him!"

Leedon raised a hand to the girl, then he looked to Vinton and suggested, "We need to talk to the village elders, and I will be along to help."

Vinton's eyes narrowed and he folded his arms. "This little conspiracy has a huge chance of going horribly wrong, Leedon." His eyes found Falloah. "Your landmaster needs to be the one to take care of this problem, not you, not this other dragon, not Ralligor."

Leedon smiled and assured, "And attend to it he shall."

CHAPTER 12

Once again, Farrigrall opened his eyes, turned them upward and found the little blue dragoness staring down at him. He blinked, then asked, "How long have you been staring at me like that?"

She just shrugged.

He heaved a breath, trying not to be annoyed with the little dragoness, then pushed himself up, arched his neck backward and roared a little as he stretched. Sitting catlike before her, he looked down at her and asked, "So, dinner is taken care of. What now?"

"You choose," she answered. Glancing aside, she suggested, "Do you want to find Revillee and see the Dark Mountains?"

"I suppose we can," he sighed. "Falloah was insistent that we stay near the lake, but I don't see what a tour of these dark mountains can hurt." His eyes narrowed. "Will that other dragon be there? That Lornoxez?"

"I don't know," she replied. "He is supposed to be patrolling the norther border and he usually does not have her along if he strays too far to the east, something about other dragons, she said. We can see if she is about and then go and see the Dark Mountains unless there is something else you'd like to do."

"No current plans," he grumbled, looking away from her. "Why do you want to go see mountains?"

She shrugged and replied, "I just do, and you've never seen them. I thought it would be a fun thing to do."

He looked at the mostly eaten grawrdox carcass. "What about that?"

"We can always finish it later," she suggested, "or we could leave it for the scavengers. They would likely welcome a large and easy meal."

His attention returned to her. "You seem to be trying to keep my mind off of something, and I appreciate it."

She smiled at him.

**

A short time later they were flying north and Farrigrall could see the snow-capped mountain peaks in the distance.

Kyshira constantly scanned the sky around them, then finally looked to her left, gaped her jaws and trumpeted a long call.

In the distance, another dragon answered in the unmistakable voice of a female. Other creatures would not be able to tell male from female, but it was easy for Farrigrall and he looked that way to see a winged burgundy form approaching them.

Revillee swept behind them and turned sharply to take Farrigrall's other side, flying just off of his wingtip.

They turned and Kyshira took the lead as they flew parallel to the Dark Mountains and only about three leagues from them. This could be considered dangerously close to the border with Mettegrawr, but subordinares would often fly this close on routine patrols to watch for mischief from the other side.

Moments after being joined by Revillee, Kyshira saw something in a field below, something obviously missed by the other two, and her eyes locked forward in a flustered stare, and she drew a deep breath as that horrible crawl returned to her belly. As they flew on and the field yielded to forest again, she looked about and found another clearing in the trees that was just large enough to land, one half a league to the right, and she veered toward it and began to descend.

She landed ahead of the other two near the far side of the clearing which was mostly circular but more in the shape of an egg that was nearly a third of a league at its longest point. Farrigrall landed at her side. Revillee stumbled when she landed but managed to regain her balance and trotted off the last of her speed about twenty paces beyond the other two dragons.

Farrigrall watched the young burgundy dragoness fold her wings and turn toward him, then he raised his brow and asked, "Have you thought about landing slower?"

She snarled at him and grumbled, "Yes, I have."

Kyshira looked behind them, clearly trying to hide the strain on her face, then she looked to the other dragoness and said, "Revillee, I have something I need to show you, something I saw when we were flying in." Turning her eyes to Farrigrall, she continued, "We'll be right back. I just want to show Revillee something."

He met Revillee's eyes, seeing that she was as perplexed as he was, then he shrugged and watched as the two dragonesses opened their wings again and took flight, and he kept watch as they circled back the way from which they had come and soared over the tall trees behind him. His eyes narrowed. Something seemed amiss, and he knew in his gut something was terribly wrong. There was only one clearing so close where she could have seen something, where they could land, and it was surrounded by very large trees that were fairly well spaced out.

Farrigrall opened his wings, ran into the wind and swept himself into the sky, turning sharply to follow the dragonesses. He could easily see them in the distance about a league or a little more in front of him. He flew low, near the treetops to avoid being seen, but he knew that dragons were apex predators, the top hunters in the land, and they would have no reason to fear anything that might be trying to catch them.

Their flight was not a long one and they descended quickly, sweeping their wings forward to land in a broad field they had passed over before. This was a problem. Turning his attention down, he quickly realized there was nowhere for him to land, and a little growl escaped him as he scanned the forest below. Turning toward the north to avoid flying right over them, his eyes swept back and forth, and finally he saw something he thought he could use. It was a long path cut through the trees, not a road built by humans, but a game trail, a big one. Grawrdoxen like the one he had killed to eat earlier frequented the grazing in the fields and meadows, and often hid among the trees from their top predators: Dragons.

Turning hard to come parallel to the path, he set his attention on a wide spot ahead of him, and realized that it was nowhere near wide enough to allow him to land. Thinking quickly, he descended until his wings brushed the treetops on both sides, then he pulled his wings to him and quickly arched his body forward to bring his feet down, and he ended up dropping like a stone for more than seventeen men's heights.

He hit the trail much harder than he had anticipated he would and ended up slamming to his belly. His head hit last and his eyes were tightly closed as his jaw slammed onto the ground, and he quickly slid to a stop. The trail was about eight paces wide, offering more than enough room for him to move and appeared to be plenty of room for the grawrdoxen to move comfortably, if single file.

He lay there motionless for a moment before he finally opened his eyes and stared forward at nothing. Slowly, he pulled his hand under him and pushed himself up, and a growl escaped him. "Not my best landing." Once he was standing fully, he turned his attention ahead of him, and his eyes narrowed. Lowering his body to bring it nearly parallel to the ground, he started forward, slowly at first, then he accelerating to a trot.

Hiding in the shadows of the forest, a small herd of grawrdox watched as he simply ran by them. Forest creatures fled into the deep of the forest. A dragon running through the forest like this had never been seen before and none of the inhabitants seemed to know how to respond to it.

Hearing something ahead, Farrigrall slowed to a walk, and as he neared the clearing ahead, took softer and slower steps, and he turned his head slightly as he listened harder. There were voices ahead, one he recognized as Kyshira, but the other was male, one he did not know, and it did not sound dragon. A few more, slow steps, and he stopped and looked down, raising a foot, and a snarl took his scaly lips as he realized he had stepped into a large pile of grawrdox dung.

"That's just great," he growled as he shook his foot.

Somewhere in the distance, Kyshira cried, "You can't ask me to do this!"

Farrigrall's attention snapped that way, his brow low between his eyes.

The other voice, deep and raspy and hissing, spat back, "I am not asking! If you want to prove your loyalty to the Master then you will kill her! Now!"

The black dragon crept forward, poking his nose between a couple of trees to see into the field, and his eyes widened!

Out there near the center of the field, and only about sixty paces away, Kyshira crouched nearly on her belly, her head low, her tail flat against the ground as she stared down the large smoke wyvern that held the burgundy dragoness firmly to the ground, the fingers of this wing grasping her neck right behind her head while his foot was planted on the center of her back. Her limbs were sprawled and she appeared to be barely conscious.

The wyvern tightened his fingers around her neck and a pitiful croon escaped her as she tried weakly to struggle away from his grip.

With a hiss, the wyvern growled, "Kill her. Kill her now."

Kyshira's eyes fixed on her friend, and slowly she shook her head. "I won't do this. I won't."

The wyvern screeched, "She will die by you or she will die horribly by me. By you she may die swiftly, but she dies this day nonetheless." His eyes narrowed as they bored into the little blue. "Perhaps you both can die today."

Farrigrall had heard enough. He recognized this threat as a big wyvern, and while he was unaware that wyverns could even talk, he would not be deterred. With a loud growl, he pushed his way through tree limbs and crashed into the clearing with loud stomps, and when all looked his way, his jaws gaped and he roared a nightmarish challenge. He did not want to give the Wyvern time to react to him and opened his wings, springing forward as he stroked his wings, covering the sixty paces between them with only a few bounds and far too quickly for the wyvern to be able to react.

The wyvern had managed to leap from the burgundy dragoness and fully face the charging dragon, and he screeched a reply right before the black dragon slammed into him.

One of Farrigrall's hands gripped the wyvern's throat, just below his jaw, and he slammed his teeth shut around the base of the wyvern's neck, plunging them deep through thick, scaly hide and into muscle. The wyvern screeched and tried to retreat, but the dragon simply drove him backward, slashing the claws of his free hand across wing and belly and chest. Deep wounds were opened quickly on the wyvern and he fought to return the favor, struggling to wrench his head free of the dragon's grip, even as Farrigrall's claws dug in deeper.

Revillee struggled to all fours and backed away, her wide eyes on the battle before her. This dragon she had really met only once had left her with the impression that he was a very even-tempered drake, but now she was seeing him as a dragon that was as fierce as she had ever seen.

Farrigrall knew that he dare not release the wyvern's head, as he knew this creature had a venomous bite, and he also knew that this fight would have to end quickly. The wyvern rose up and managed to rake the claws of one foot down the dragon's belly, but he could not penetrate the black dragon's scales, and this maneuver threw him off balance. Wrenching his head back and forth, the dragon worked his teeth deeper into the wyvern's flesh, burying them all the way to the gums, and as he could taste the wyvern's blood in his mouth, he growled a thunderous growl, sidestepped, and threw his opponent sideways, slamming him hard onto the ground. His teeth were ripped from the wyvern's neck and he lost his grip on his head, but dared to just stand there and watched as the wyvern crumpled to the ground and rolled to a stop a few paces away.

All things considered, Farrigrall had already decided to deny this wyvern a fair fight. It was larger and stronger than both dragonesses, but could not hope to match the black dragon's size, weight, or power. Just as long from nose to tail, it was built leaner than the dragon, and as it struggled to rise up on its feet and the knuckles of its wings to turn quickly and retaliate, it soon learned that the dragon's superior weight and bulk would act against it.

The spines running down the wyvern's back and all the way down its tail stood erect for battle, but the black dragon's foot slammed onto the middle of its back anyway, laying flat most of the spines, breaking some off, and a few penetrated the bottom of his foot. He was not concerned with the pain this caused and crushed the wyvern to the ground with all of his weight, leaning forward with gaping jaws and braving the wyvern's dorsal spines again as he this time slammed his jaws shut right behind the wyvern's head. He drove his teeth through armor and flesh as he bit down with all the force he could muster, and even over the wyvern's screech, one could hear the crunching of bone in its neck.

With his foe's neck in his jaws, Farrigrall drew back and wrenched his head aside, and his teeth did their final, horrible work on the wyvern with a loud crunch.

The wyvern went limp and all of it collapsed limply to the ground with the end of its neck hitting the ground last and sloshing blood for nearly seven paces when it hit.

Still holding the wyvern's disembodied head by a short length of its neck in his jaws, Farrigrall looked down at his vanquished foe, relishing the flavor of blood in his mouth. He growled with each deep breath, then a grunt escaped him as he stepped off of the wyvern's carcass and opened his jaws to allow its head to drop nearly four men's heights to the ground. Perhaps by instinct or perhaps by some tremendous sense of accomplishment, he threw his head back and roared as if to broadcast news of his victory to all the land and give notice to all other challengers that he was more than a force to be reckoned with.

The dragonesses watched his victorious display in silence, and with wide eyes.

His roar faded into the distance and he closed his jaws and looked to the dragonesses in turn, and finally asked, "Someone going to tell me what that was all about?"

Revillee bared her teeth and looked to the little blue, growling, "It was about betrayal." She suddenly roared, "I thought we were friends!"

Kyshira lowered her head and meekly offered, "I didn't know. I'm sorry. I was just so afraid."

"Afraid!" Revillee shouted. "So afraid that you delivered me to that creature that wanted to kill me! No, wanted *you* to kill me!"

"I did not know," the little blue cried. "He just told me to bring you here."

"So, now you take orders from a wyvern?" Revillee looked to the black dragon, then to Kyshira, and stomped toward her. "I should save Agarxus the trouble of killing you and do it myself!"

Farrigrall finally stepped forward and grasped the burgundy dragoness' shoulder, stopping her as he ordered, "That's enough. There will be no more killing today."

She looked up at him and bared her teeth. "You have no authority here, outlander, and—"

Baring his own teeth, Farrigrall raised his head far above the dragoness he glared at and roared, "I said enough!" Only rarely in his life did he use his size to assert himself over another, and this would prove to be a necessary opportunity to do it again.

Revillee knew to back down and backed away, turning angry eyes to the little blue as she did.

Kyshira stared back at her for a moment, then she turned her eyes down and said, "I did not want to betray anyone."

Movement to the north caught the young drake's eyes and he turned them that way, barely moving his head. To any but a dragon, they would be but five dots against the clouds and the blue of the sky, but to Farrigrall, who squinted slightly to bring them into close focus. "Who else are you expecting?" he suddenly asked.

Both dragonesses looked to him, then they followed his line of sight to the five approaching forms.

Farrigrall's eyes narrowed and he asked, "Anyone know who they are?"

Grimly staring at the approaching forms, Kyshira replied, "They are Mettegrawr's."

Revillee stared back at the four dragons as they neared and she found herself tensing, her dorsal scales slowly growing erect as she grumbled, "We're outnumbered and that drake looks pretty big from here."

Glancing at the burgundy dragoness, the black drake drew a deep breath and ordered, "Revillee, get out of here. Fly south and see if you can find other dragons from this realm that can come and help." Turning his full attention to her when she hesitated, his brow lowered over his eyes and he barked, "Go! Now!"

She stared back at him for long seconds, looked back to the approaching dragons, then she opened her wings and turned, sweeping herself quickly into the sky and south as fast as she could fly.

Standing fully as he turned his attention back to the approaching dragons, Farrigrall slowly opened his wings, stroked them a couple of times, then casually refolded them to his back and sides. Despite an awkward crawl in his belly as he faced what appeared to be a hopeless situation, he stood his ground, raising his head as the first of them landed in the center of the field, and he refused to show any fear at all. All of the females were larger than Kyshira and the drake appeared to be older, but only slightly larger than Farrigrall, but was not as thick with muscle.

"We should have fled," Kyshira whimpered. "They are going to kill us!"

"Just stay close to me," the young drake ordered as he watched the last of the dragons settle to the ground. His eyes were on the drake, and the drake's attention was on him, not Kyshira. With hard eyes still fixed on the invading drake, the black dragon raised a brow and waited for long seconds before he spoke. "Are you eventually going to tell us why you are here?"

A low growl rumbled from the older drake as he regarded Farrigrall with annoyance clear on his face. His gaze shifted to the young blue and he finally replied, "Kyshira knows exactly why we are here."

Looking down to his claws, Farrigrall sighed, "I'm sure she does, but I'd rather hear it from you." His eyes slid back to the older drake and that brow cocked up again. "This is when you should make me an irrefusable offer."

His eyes narrowing, the drake snarled, "Make you an offer?"

"Of course," the black dragon drawled, exasperation in his voice as he looked down to his claws again. "We both know you don't want to fight me." His eyes returned to the older drake with a blink. "That would be suicide."

Another growl rumbled from the older drake and his claws curled inward slightly. "Awfully bold words, young one, but it appears that you were never taught to count. There are five of us, and you do not appear to be so formidable."

Farrigrall cocked an eyebrow up again. "Perhaps your eyes have withered with age, old dragon. I only see one here worth fighting." His eyes darted from one dragoness to the next. "You don't seem so confident, since you seem to need your dragonesses to fight your battles for you."

The old drake narrowed his eyes and growled deeply again, this time sliding his lips away from his long, pointed teeth. Farrigrall's banter was having the desired effect.

"And that," Farrigrall went on, "is why you'd rather make me an offer instead, on behalf of your landmaster, that is."

The old drake turned his head slightly. "You would shift your loyalty from Agarxus to Mettegrawr?"

Farrigrall looked back down to his claws, then inspected the other hand as he casually reported, "I have no loyalty to Agarxus. No bargain has been struck to win that loyalty, so I am what you would call, for hire."

Staring the black dragon down, the old drake's cold expression turned more inquisitive. Glancing at Kyshira, he said, "I have been sent to deal with that one, not strike some bargain with you on behalf of Mettegrawr." He looked to the little blue. "Come along, Kyshira. Your reckoning awaits."

Once again, the black drake's gaze shifted to the older dragon with a blink and he bared his teeth slightly as he informed, "That's going to be a problem. She belongs to me now."

Kyshira's eyes widened and slid to the black dragon.

A growl rolled forth from the older drake. "You dare to claim Mettegrawr's property?"

"She is not in his territory," Farrigrall pointed out, "and if your Mettegrawr wishes her returned then he can come and fetch her from me himself. Now strike your bargain with me on behalf of your master or you are dismissed."

His eyes wide with anger, the old drake drew his head back, another deep growl thundering from him as he rose up, curling his claws inward, then flailing them out in a clear demonstration of his strength and willingness to fight.

Once again, Farrigrall would not give the old drake the satisfaction of even reacting to the threat and simply looked back at him with exasperation in his eyes. "You'll not strike a bargain with me, you'll not grant me an audience with your landmaster, and you've too little courage to face me without your females to do most of the fighting for you. Where I am from that is called cowardice." He waved a hand in dismissal. "Away with you, old timer. Tell your master that you've failed to win my loyalty for him."

The old drake's eyes widened further, rage in them now. "It is time for you to die!"

Farrigrall's brow lowered between his eyes and he rose up. Curling his claws inward as he stomped toward the older dragon with one foot, his dorsal scales stood erect as he bored into the other drake with great challenge in his eyes. "I've spent my entire life killing big crocodiles. *Really* big crocodiles. If you have the courage fight me, then fight me one on one."

One of the females stormed forward, baring her teeth as she roared, "Enough of this! Let's just kill him and..." She fell silent as the older drake's head whipped around and he snarled at her loudly.

The older drake stepped toward his younger foe and the two began to slowly circle.

His teeth bared, the invader glared at his opponent and growled, "Very well, young imbecile. Let's see if your combat prowess is a match for your mindless boasting."

Farrigrall had fought only one other dragon his entire life, but many, many crocodiles. When one fights a crocodile, the form and movements are far different, as this invading drake would soon discover. The older drake would look for an opening to get to his younger opponent's throat, but the young drake would employ his vast experience fighting an entirely different enemy.

Bending his knees, Farrigrall crouched slightly, holding his hands and claws ready as the claws of his feet dug into the ground. His tail whipped fully to one side, something his older foe had never seen before, and without a combative roar, he gaped his jaws and lunged, whipping his tail back for added speed and power. The old drake turned his head and lowered it to protect his throat and found an opening to his opponent's, but unexpectedly, Farrigrall's jaws slammed shut around his head and snout, clamping the older dragon's jaws shut as many teeth plunged through skin and scales and hide and a few of the more robust teeth actually penetrated bone!

Using all his size and weight, the young drake wrenched his head and stepped back, pulling the older drake by the head toward his right side and hurling him toward the ground as the claws from one hand slashed away at the thinner scales of his throat and chest and shoulder.

The older dragon slammed onto the ground and rolled to a stop, stunned and bleeding from four rows of punctures on his head and snout and lower jaw. As he tried to get back to his feet and rejoin the fight, his younger foe was already upon him, one of his feet slamming onto the older dragon's back right between his shoulders. He whipped his head around, jaws gaping, blindly trying to get a bite in, but, once again, Farrigrall's teeth crashed through the skin and scales of his head, this time further back, and one row of teeth crunched against the base of the older dragon's horns.

Farrigrall backed away, wrenching his head back and forth to work his deadly teeth in as far as he could, and he was dragging his enemy by the head toward the middle of the clearing.

The four invading dragonesses backed away in a slightly expanding semicircle as wide eyes watched the battle rage, and not in their drake's favor.

Kyshira still laid on her belly, now more impressed than ever by the black drake as he fought with a savagery that she had never seen before, and with power that the youth of his size had not betrayed until now.

The older drake's claws raked against his foe's armor and finally found a place they could penetrate, a place below his arm where wing webbing met his side and back. Three wounds were opened on the young drake, and a furious roar escaped him. Twisting his body, he hurled the older drake to the ground again, and even before the old drake could settle to the ground, Farrigrall's foot slammed home between his shoulders and drove him down hard.

Barely able to catch his breath and bleeding profusely from the many punctures to his head and jaw, the older drake looked to the four females, bared his teeth and roared, "Kill him!"

Farrigrall raised his eyes to the four dragonesses who were clearly hesitant to be the first to move against the powerful young drake. Blood stained his scaly lips, the blood of his enemy, and he raised a finger to wipe some of it away, then, as he stared at the four dragonesses with a powerful glare, he slowly licked the blood from his finger. His confidence was surging as he looked down at his stunned foe, then back to the dragonesses, and he dared to ask, "Who is next?"

The largest and oldest of the females looked down to the older drake, to the young one who had a foot planted between his shoulders, and her brow lowered, her lips sliding away from her teeth as a challenging growl rolled from her.

This very brief distraction was all the older drake needed and, calling on all his strength, he rolled away from the young drake, got to all fours and turned to face him once again, his teeth bared and parted for battle.

Farrigrall did not seem to react and only stared him down again.

The next bout would have to wait.

Revillee streaked in and crashed talons first into the middle of the line of females, toppling two of them as she tumbled into the third and knocked her over as well.

The commotion drew the attention of the two drakes and Kyshira as the downed dragonesses scrambled to right themselves. The fourth of the invading females turned that way and crouched to leap into battle.

A mountainous form slammed into the ground almost on top of her and the huge, clawed hand of a dragon hit the base of her neck and crushed her to the ground. The smallest invader among the dragonesses turned and let out a loud shriek, then she wheeled around and took to the wing, flapping frantically for speed.

The dragon that had just landed was the biggest Farrigrall had ever seen or even heard of! He was crouched on all fours, pinning the largest female to the ground with ease, and still his head was four men's heights above the ground! For the most part he was very dark green, darkening to black over his back and his massive dorsal scales. The growl that rumbled from him was deep like distant thunder and actually shook the ground. His cruel eyes were first fixed on the dragoness he held down, then they lifted beneath a heavy, scaly brow as scaly lips drew away from very long, very robust pointed teeth. Tusks protruded from his heavy lower jaw about halfway to the top of his snout.

The older drake's eyes were wide and filled with the huge dragon and he hesitated for long seconds, his dorsal scales standing erect as he slowly rose up on his hind legs and held his hands ready for another fight, one that he could not hope to win.

The massive dragon's attention strayed to the older drake, and his eyes narrowed.

Despite the presence of what had to be the biggest dragon in the world, Farrigrall decided that his fight with the old drake was not over. He turned fully and roared at his foe, and before the invading drake could react, he leapt into battle, once again taking careful aim at the drake's head with his teeth.

Kyshira knew that this was her chance, a chance at freedom, and she sprang up and attacked one of the other females that was squaring off with Revillee, leaping onto her back and biting at her neck.

The female beneath the massive dragon's hand crooned and tried to struggle to free herself, but claws dug into her hide and armor, and as she looked away from the fray, the huge dragon lowered his head to hers and his jaws parted.

"No," he thundered. "Look back to your companions and watch them die."

Reluctantly, and purely out of fear, she complied, looking first to the four females who fought, and then to the two drakes.

Farrigrall found himself fighting an opponent of his own caliber for the first time in his life, but three decades of fighting crocodiles had left him vastly experienced in combat with other huge predators, and he found himself enjoying this life and death battle more than any he had ever enjoyed anything. His jaws were, once again, clamped around the head of his opponent, much as he would fight a crocodile, and as the invader struggled and slashed at thick armor, the young drake's hand was clamped around his enemy's neck, his other planted on the ground for balance, and his one foot raked his own claws down the older drake's belly. Squeezing his jaws as hard as he could, he could taste the blood of his foe in his mouth, and he could feel bone beginning to succumb to teeth. The old drake kicked him hard in the thigh and Farrigrall raked his claws catlike down his foe's belly, and finally shifted as they wrestled for position and managed to slash at the thinner hide of the drake's side. Thick skin and scales ripped open under the onslaught as the young drake's claws did their deadly work over and over until blood leeched forth.

This fight had to end and end now. Farrigrall used all of his weight to twist around and throw the older drake off balance, and finally toppled him to his side. Releasing his foe's head for just a second, the black dragon opened his jaws wide and lunged forward, slamming them shut hard around the older drake's head further back. There was a loud snap as one of the drake's horns was broken off, quickly followed by a loud crunch as teeth penetrated skull. The old drake let out a loud cry as the black dragon's jaws clamped down with all the strength he could muster, and the young drake twisted his head hard, pulling against the hand that still clutched the other dragon's neck and now pinned it to the ground. In that motion, another loud crunch was heard and Farrigrall's jaws suddenly drew much closer. Blood spewed forth and the older drake's body went limp and settled to the ground.

Drawing deep breaths to catch his wind, Farrigrall just stood there for a moment, one hand still planted on the ground, his other on the neck of his opponent, and the old drake's crushed head still in his mouth. His eyes strayed to the huge dragon and he opened his jaws and allowed the older dragon's head to fall to the ground.

The massive dragon was staring back at him with no discernable expression, and he still had the largest dragoness pinned to the ground.

Finally hearing the battle of the dragonesses that still raged, Farrigrall looked that way as Revillee was locked in a pitched battle with one, and the other threw Kyshira from her and turned to attack while she was down, foolishly turning her back to the black dragon.

Without acknowledging the huge dragon again, Farrigrall bared his teeth and growled as he charged the female that descended on the little blue, and he did not roar to announce his approach until he was only a few paces away.

She turned with wide eyes as the black drake rammed into her, his jaws finding her head as they had found the old drake and slamming shut with all of the force he could muster. Unlike the now vanquished drake, the female's head succumbed to the power of Farrigrall's jaws almost easily and was crushed by powerful jaws driving those murderous teeth right through the bone.

Farrigrall stepped back and twisted his body again, throwing the dead female from him before turning to the last of the invaders, and this time his bloody jaws opened wide as he announced his intentions.

This female managed to twist away from Revillee and swung her tail, catching the burgundy dragoness on the side with enough force to send her stumbling sideways. Then her wide eyes found the black drake that stared her down from only about twenty-five paces away. He was much larger than she was ready to deal with and she took a step back, glancing at the two dragonesses that turned fully on her also.

Farrigrall's bloody teeth were bared as he growled deeply, and with one heavy step, approached to meet her head-on.

In a panic, she opened her jaws and loosed a burst of fire that hit him square in the chest and rolled upward to singe his throat and head, and he closed his eyes and turned his face away from the flames that lapped away at him, but he did not retreat.

The flames thinned and died, and she slowly closed her jaws, her eyes growing wider as she looked upon the smoking black dragon who had barely reacted to her attack.

Slowly, Farrigrall turned his full attention to her again, his brow low over his eyes and his bloody lips sliding away from red stained teeth.

The dragoness stepped back, then again, and as he roared and charged her again, she turned and opened her wings in a desperate attempt to flee from this now hopeless situation.

Farrigrall was upon her much faster than she had anticipated he could move and just as she had lifted herself from the ground. With the force of all of his weight, he slammed into her back and his jaws slammed shut around the base of her neck. She was crushed to the ground with a loud shriek, her jaw hitting last. The black drake stepped back, dragging her from the ground and again he twisted with all his strength, throwing the much smaller dragoness from him as he spun fully around.

She landed on her side thirty paces away and rolled some ten paces more before she stopped, now bleeding from the fresh rows of punctures from teeth that had plunged right through the thickest armor of her back. Slow to push herself up, she turned her full attention to the black drake and noticed that he was just standing where he had been and was glaring down at her, and for a few brief seconds it seemed that mercy was to find her.

Mercy came as the massive dragon's jaws snapped shut around her neck and shoulders and ribs, and robust, long, sharp teeth and tusks plunged into her body and she let out one anguished cry before blood spewed from her mouth as she threw her head back.

The huge dragon stood and twisted around much as Farrigrall had, hurling the dead female from him, over the largest female who still cringed on the ground and all the way to the trees where she struck the base of one and her body wrapped unnaturally around it. There, she settled to the ground and moved no more.

Farrigrall met the huge dragon's eyes, his own widening slightly under the attention of such a powerful killer, and a little relief washed through him as this largest of dragons turned his attention back to the female still on the ground.

The massive dragon dropped to all fours, his nose approaching to within a pace of the terrified dragoness as he bared his teeth and growled that thunderous growl. "Did you see?" he demanded. "Did you see that fate that awaits invaders in my realm?"

Unable to look at him, she cringed, and was actually trembling under his attention as she meekly admitted, "I saw."

The massive dragon ordered, "Go back to Mettegrawr and give him a message for me. Tell him that the next of his minions who cross the Dark Mountains will suffer horrible deaths at the teeth and claws of my subordinares, if they are lucky enough not to encounter me first." His eyes narrowed. "And once I have dispatched them, I will be coming for him." Scaly lips slid away from those long, murderous teeth and a long growl rolled from him. In a low voice, almost a whisper, he ordered, "Go."

Slowly, hesitantly, she drew her feet and hands under her and pushed herself up, still unable to look toward him as she backed away on all fours. At what seemed to be a safe distance, she rose to her feet and slowly ruffled her wings before opening them, and only then did she dare to look to the huge dragon who watched.

His demeanor changed from bad to worse, from warning to terror and he gaped his jaws and roared, "Go!"

With a shriek, the dragoness wheeled around and stroked her wings as hard as she could, quickly finding flight and flapping hard for speed and height, and barely over the treetops she turned hard toward the north and flew toward home as fast as her wings could take her.

Farrigrall watched her, turning as she retreated north, and he dared to shout after her, "And don't come back!" With that, he turned back toward the massive dragon and offered him a satisfied nod.

The huge dragon just stared at him, again with no readable expression.

Swallowing hard, Farrigrall guessed, "You must be Agarxus. I've heard a lot about you."

Still, only that cold, unblinking stare.

With the situation over, Revillee turned to other matters, baring her teeth as she faced the little blue and cried, "Traitor!"

Swinging around, Farrigrall growled an exasperated growl and shook his head as the burgundy dragoness charged and tackled the little blue, who was just a little smaller than she was. As the two wrestled and Revillee bit at her, and Kyshira crooned and just tried to get away, he stomped over to them, grabbed onto the burgundy's arm and neck and pulled her rather brutally away from the little blue. Once they were separated, and as the burgundy dragoness tried to charge again, he pushed her back by the shoulders and ordered, "That's enough!"

Revillee turned furious eyes to him and roared back, "She's a little traitor! Why would you protect her?"

"That is not for you to decide," he barked back.

With a growl, Revillee angrily pointed out, "She brought me here so that Mettegrawrs dragons could kill me, so that that wyvern could kill me!"

"The wyvern ordered her to kill you," Farrigrall pointed out, "and she refused. Your friendship was worth more than her own life."

Revillee glared back up at him for long seconds, then she turned to the little blue and demanded, "How long have you been some agent of Mettegrawr? How long?"

Kyshira was cringing on all fours, her attention on the ground before her as she meekly whimpered, "I'm not. I was afraid."

"Of what?" the burgundy roared. "How long have they been using you as a spy here? I thought we were friends and I discover you have been under Mettegrawr's control all this time! I could have killed you when I was told to and I didn't! That means nothing to you?"

The little blue finally turned defeated eyes to the burgundy dragoness, and she admitted, "It meant the world to me."

"And yet," Revillee raved on, "you lure me here so that your masters could kill me, so that you could go back to Mettegrawr's territory and they would take you back in!" She turned those furious eyes to Farrigrall. "You heard that wyvern and what he said. You heard him!"

"And I killed him," the black dragon reminded. A thump on the ground behind him drew his attention, and he turned and retreated a few steps as Agarxus approached.

Lowering his head to the little blue, the massive landmaster growled that thunderous growl and demanded, "How long have you been acting under the commands of my enemy?"

She could not look up at him, but answered with fearful words, "The last couple of moons. The smoke wyvern that Farrigrall killed found me and said he would kill me horribly, that he would paralyze me and eat me alive if I did not do what he commanded."

That growl rolled forth from Agarxus and he raised his head, turning his attention to Revillee as he commanded, "Follow the invader to the Dark Mountains and report back to me as soon as she crosses."

Revillee looked fully to him, glared at the little blue and snarled at her, then turned and took to the wing.

The huge Landmaster's eyes slid to the black dragon again, and for long, horrifying seconds he just stared him down again.

Farrigrall just stared back at him as fearlessly as he could, refusing to display the terror that coursed through him.

"I suppose you are Farrigrall," Agarxus assumed. "You are not among my subordinares."

Raising his brow, Farrigrall informed, "I did kill three of your enemies today, one of whom held control over one of your dragonesses. And, if you could use my services, I would gladly offer them. As you can see, I'm quite a formidable dragon."

"That remains to be seen," the Landmaster countered. "From where did you come?"

"Peak Island Lake in the mountains west of here," the young drake replied. "I've lived there my entire life, guarding a village of humans who took me in when I was still in the egg."

The huge drake's brow tensed. "Peak Island Lake? South of the Hard Lands?" He growled inquisitively and turned fully to the young drake. "How long?"

With a shrug, Farrigrall replied, "Thirty seasons."

"That long," Agarxus said in an ominous tone. "Three decades in my territory and only now is anyone becoming aware of you."

"This is the first time I've left home," the black dragon pointed out.

Giving the young dragon a hard stare, the Landmaster finally nodded and almost absently said, "All that time at the southern point of Ralligor's range, and nobody noticed."

"I live a quiet life," Farrigrall assured. "I protect my village, kill crocodiles and other threats to my humans, and otherwise I just do what I do."

With another deep growl, Agarxus lowered his nose to the young drake until they were only about two paces apart, and he demanded, "Do you fear me?"

"To be brutally honest," Farrigrall answered, "I'm very close to relieving myself where I stand and screaming like a little girl as I flee into the woods."

"You fear me that much," the huge landmaster observed, "and yet you stand your ground."

Farrigrall raised a brow. "You may bite me in half today, but I'll clutch my dignity close to me and fight to the end while you do it. The way I see it, you'll either accept me or kill me, and flopping around and screaming like a frightened whisker fish will not help my case at all."

"You are brash," the huge drake snarled, "and there is an arrogance about you, and a certain overconfidence you will have to learn to keep in check. Reminds me of someone else." He raised a scaly eyebrow. "Where are your loyalties?"

Farrigrall's eyes narrowed. "With the highest bidder."

His eyes also narrowing, Agarxus growled, "I could kill you easily, so your continued existence relies entirely upon me."

Giving the massive dragon a hard stare, Farrigrall answered with hard words, "That would make you the highest bidder."

Agarxus' head moved in a slight nod. "Very well, Farrigrall of the Lake." He stood fully, towering over the smaller drake as he regarded him with ultimate authority. "I shall grant you range in my territory, that place you protected for the last thirty seasons. It will extend north to the sands, west to the end of the Hard Lands, South to my border where the river meets the sea, and east to the end of the scrub country." He glanced at Kyshira, then turned to stride away. "You'll return to your range until I summon you, but first you will prove your loyalty to me. Kill the blue and leave her broken carcass here as a reminder to others."

Farrigrall's heart felt like it skipped a beat and he looked to Kyshira with wide eyes, seeing that she was staring back at him with horror in hers for the first time. She seemed to know he had to comply and kill her. She knew he would do this. He had to obey the Landmaster. Perhaps it was a lifetime with humans, being raised by them. Perhaps there was some lingering pity from that lifetime with humans. Perhaps he just could not bring himself to kill one he regarded as an innocent. His brow lowered and he bared his teeth, telling the little blue that her death was a moment away.

"No," he said with loud defiance.

Agarxus stopped and stared at the body of the old drake for long seconds, then he half turned his head, baring his teeth as he demanded, "What?"

"I won't kill her just to prove my loyalty to you," the black dragon answered.

With slow, ominous movements, the massive dragon turned fully on the insolent dragon who dared defy him.

Even as the huge dragon bared his teeth and growled loud enough to shake the ground Farrigrall stood on, he defiantly held his ground, glaring back as he roared, "She has lived her entire life in fear! Her entire life! Even after she came here, she was afraid of everything around her, including the other dragons who were supposed to protect her."

Agarxus stomped toward him, one step, his brow low over his eyes.

Kyshira raised her head, terror in her eyes as she cried, "Farrigrall, don't!"

The Landmaster stomped toward him again, and this was a final warning.

Still, Farrigrall held his ground. "It is not her fault she was intimidated by this wyvern that your enemy controlled, it was yours!" Baring his teeth, he finished, "Perhaps you aren't worthy to be my Landmaster!"

With a deafening roar, Agarxus charged forward and swiped with one hand, sweeping the young drake easily from his feet and sending him fifty paces away where he rolled to a stop.

"No!" Kyshira cried as she sprang forward. Racing past the huge landmaster, she threw herself over the black dragon and clung to him even as he sluggishly pushed himself up and tried to stand. Looking back to the massive dragon, she pled, "Please, Landmaster! He was raised by humans and does not know our ways! Please, just let him go."

Farrigrall pushed her aside and ordered, "Get out of the way!" He glared up at the massive dragon, his dorsal scales erect and his teeth bared as he informed, "You won't be the first landmaster I've tangled with, and even if you're the last, you'll remember me until your final breath! I will fight a battle with you that will haunt your nightmares until you die!"

As Agarxus stomped toward him, Kyshira threw herself on the ground between them and cried, "Farrigrall, just kill me! Just kill me!" Her eyes were closed and her hands covered her eyes. "Please, just be swift. Kill me so that he will spare you."

Both drakes looked down to her, then to each other.

Agarxus boomed, "*That* is loyalty."

"All the more reason she should live," the black drake insisted. "None of this was her fault. None was her doing. She was easily manipulated through fear that nobody here thought to take from her."

The giant landmaster turned his head, eyeing the much smaller drake almost suspiciously as he asked, "You say you fought another landmaster?"

Throwing his arms out to his sides, Farrigrall shouted, "What do you think I'm doing here?" He lowered his arms and continued, "This other dragon attacked my village and I fought him as hard as I could." He looked away. "I failed. He defeated me handily and cast me out of my home. I can never go back." He bared his teeth. "At least not until I can figure out how to defeat him and drive him away." A deep grunt from the Landmaster summoned his attention.

With a snarl on his scaly lip, Agarxus demanded, "Name this other landmaster."

Raising his head, Farrigrall answered, "He calls himself Terrwrathgrawr the Terrible."

His eyes narrowing, Agarxus growled, "And you fought him at Peak Island Lake, *that* far inside my realm."

"Twelve days ago," the black dragon replied. "He has declared that part of the land—"

"Quiet!" the Landmaster ordered.

Taken aback, Farrigrall backed away and assured, "I am shutting up at once!"

The huge dragon turned away and considered, breathing in deep growls, then he turned back to the black dragon, and finally down to the little blue, demanding, "Is this true? You acted out of cowardly fear in your betrayal of me?"

She stared back up at him for a few seconds, then she lowered her eyes, pointing her nose to the ground as she replied in a whimper, "It is true, Landmaster, and I am ashamed."

The huge dragon forced a heavy breath from him as he stared down at her. "Killing you now would be a mercy, and I am not feeling so generous today." He raised his eyes to Farrigrall. "This one is your problem now. Teach her the ways of courage and see to it that she does not betray me again. If she does, you both will pay." His eyes narrowed. "Your insolence will be tolerated only once, Farrigrall of the Lake. Only once. Defy me again and your death will not haunt my nightmares at all, but you will surely linger long enough to know suffering and pain you cannot even imagine now."

With a nod, Farrigrall acknowledged, "I understand, Landmaster."

Another winged form swept in and all looked toward the east to see Lornoxez stroking his wings forward and lowering his feet for a hard landing, and he slammed into the ground only fifty paces away and facing the black dragon.

With his teeth bared, Lornoxez stood fully as he folded his wings, his tail thrashing and his teeth bared as he growled, "Shall I dispatch this intruder, Landmaster?"

Farrigrall's eyes narrowed and he turned fully to the larger dragon, baring his own teeth as he growled in response.

Agarxus turned toward the smaller green dragon and stomped toward him, grabbed his throat right under his jaw and almost lifted him from the ground as he roared, "You can explain why Mettegrawr's minions came so deep into my realm and you did not take notice! Explain this to me!"

Raising a finger, Farrigrall heard himself say, "If I may, Landmaster."

Agarxus turned his head just enough to see the black drake.

Farrigrall continued, "He's only one dragon watching what I can only guess is a vast border. Of course, they were able to slip by him undetected no matter how carefully he watches." When the Landmaster's eyes narrowed, the black drake looked down and he finished in a low voice, "Just pointing that out. It's a lot of border to watch."

Agarxus' full attention returned to Lornoxez and he bared his teeth. "I am not a dragon who tolerates failure, no matter how many other dragons come to defend you." He hurled the smaller dragon to the ground and turned back on Farrigrall. "Return to your range and watch for Terrwrathgrawr."

"I can't go back," Farrigrall informed grimly. "I've been banished."

Lowering his jaws to the black dragon, Agarxus roared, "Did *I* banish you?"

Farrigrall stared back fearfully, then he turned his eyes away and considered only for a second before he ordered, "Come along, Kyshira. We need to get back to Peak Island Lake." He looked back to the Landmaster and half turned to point to the west. "We're going to go, now. By the by, what am I supposed to do when that other dragon shows up? I doubt another fight with him would—"

"You will call," the Landmaster ordered. "I will be nearby for the next few days. Kill any of his minions you wish to kill, but you are not to fight him again. The blue will teach you the summon." He turned and started to open his wings, then he stopped and looked back to Lornoxez. "Return to the Dark Mountains, and see if you can keep your eyes open long enough to see an invader in my realm."

Lornoxez looked away and growled.

"Landmaster!" Kyshira cried as she leapt up. When the massive dragon turned toward her, she fell to all fours again and settled her backside to the ground. "I do not deserve your forgiveness, Landmaster, but still I humbly beg for it."

A deep growl rolled from the massive dragon's throat as he regarded her with disdain, then he turned fully and lowered his head to her, collecting her head almost entirely in between his jaws, all the way to his tusks, and he growled again as she shrieked. He held onto her head for long, terrifying seconds, then he released her and raised his head only slightly as he snarled, "My forgiveness is extended only once. Betray me again and I'll make you wish I had killed you."

"I understand," she assured in a meek voice, staring at the ground. "I shall never again even think of betraying you. I will die the most horrible of deaths before it ever happens again."

Agarxus looked to Lornoxez, to Farrigrall. "See that she is taught this in no uncertain terms. I leave her in your charge." His eyes slid to Lornoxez and narrowed. "All dragons will take her back into my subordinares and see to it her loyalty does not stray again."

Sweeping her wings forward in frantic motions, Revillee was, once again, approaching way too fast to land, lowered her feet and slammed them onto the ground, then crashed onto her belly, rolled to the tree line and was finally stopped by the trees there.

Agarxus just shook his head and growled as he watched her struggle to her feet and turn to limp toward him.

She looked up at him with a high brow and reported, "The invader has gone back over the mountains, Landmaster." Her eyes found the little blue and narrowed as she growled and bared her teeth. A grunt from the Landmaster drew her attention back to him and she looked back up at him, lowering her head as she found disapproval in his eyes.

Agarxus informed, "That one has been forgiven for her part in this matter, and there will be no strife between you two."

Revillee turned her eyes down and snarled, "I understand."

With another look at Farrigrall, Agarxus boomed, "I will be close by."

The four smaller dragons watched him open his wings and somehow get his massive bulk airborne.

When the landmaster was safely out of sight, Lornoxez bared his teeth at the black dragon and growled, "I do not need you speaking up for me, new drake!"

Farrigrall's eyes slid to the other drake and with his voice laced with sarcasm, he assured, "You are so welcome. Glad to help."

His eyes narrowing, Lornoxez growled back at him, then they both looked to Revillee as she strode to the little blue, her brow low over her eyes and her dorsal scales standing erect from between her horns all the way down to the end of her tail. Kyshira finally stood and turned to face her, looking sheepishly back as she lowered her head.

Stopping with her nose less than a pace from the blue dragon's nose, Revillee snarled, "Don't think the words of the Landmaster will change anything, traitor!"

Farrigrall's eyes slid to Lornoxez again and he said, "See if you can get your woman in line." Turning toward the west, he opened his wings and summoned, "Come along, Kyshira. We have somewhere to be."

Lornoxez was clearly perplexed as he mumbled, "My woman?" Shaking his head, he opened his wings and took the lead as Revillee followed him toward the north.

CHAPTER 13

One of the tables outside overlooking the lake seemed like the perfect place to enjoy a little peace and quiet and allow restless minds to calm. And it was. But for the crunching of the crab wrap the wizard was munching on. He sat on one end of the bench furthest from the water they were looking out over and the boats that cruised cautiously looking to catch some fish. Josslee's father sat beside him, Falloah across from him and Josslee beside her. Vinton, still in human form, paced between them and the water, his attention mostly on the rippling surface of the lake, straying from time to time to a boat as he was fearful of the ever-emboldened crocodiles.

The crunching finally wore Falloah's nerves thin and she shot a glare at the wizard, who was just finishing.

He paused and stared back at her, then he raised his brow and reminded, "I offered to buy you one, too."

She ground her teeth and looked out over the lake again.

Taking advantage of the break in the silence, Eston finally looked to the red-haired woman and asked, "What happens now? We need protection against the crocodiles and we need someone to attend to these dragons. You are the only one who can."

Vinton stopped his pacing and folded his arms as he stared over the lake, and he corrected, "No, she is not. She should not even be here."

Rubbing her eyes, Falloah assured, "Vinton, I am working on it. Something has to be figured out, some way to restore this balance and drive Terrwrathgrawr back over the border for good."

"You know what has to be done," Vinton informed with harsh words.

As the three others at the table watched, Falloah abruptly, almost violently stood stepped over the bench and turned toward the village, walking a few steps before she halted and set her hands on her hips.

Leedon, who stared at her almost too calmly, raised his bushy eyebrows and stuffed the last of the crab wrap into his mouth, chewing loudly, almost intentionally.

Vinton finally turned and strode to the table, leaning on it where she had been sitting, and he eyed her for long seconds before he spoke. "There is no need to be so secretive. I'm sure all will work out fine once you—"

"It won't!" she shouted. She drew and released several hard breaths, then bowed her head and rubbed her eyes again. "You just don't understand. Our ways and yours are so different."

Josslee's mother hesitantly strode to the table and placed her hands on her husband's shoulders, and he reached up to grasp one of hers. Her eyes darted from one to the next, and finally fell on her daughter. "Pardon the interruption, but will your friends be staying the night?"

Leedon looked over his shoulder to her and assured, "We do not want to be any trouble."

"None at all," she assured, forcing a smile. "You've helped our village through hard times before, Leedon. You were there when the village discovered that I had a baby dragon in my house and you helped them to understand that he was not a threat to anyone."

Falloah abruptly raised her head, then she wheeled around and stormed back to the table, slamming her hands down on it as she stared wide-eyed at the wizard.

He looked back at her, and once again raised his bushy eyebrows.

Her stare lasted only a moment, and only until she realized that everyone's eyes were on her, and she backed away.

Leedon looked past her, then back to her and informed, "I hope you have it figured out, Falloah. I think they are ready for answers." He raised his chin to the group that was approaching from one of the gravel roads.

Falloah turned as everyone else looked to see the village elders only about ten paces away. All eyes were on the dragoness in human form.

The foreman, still in his black robe and silver embroidered drape, strode right to Falloah and stopped only a pace away, the rest of the elders stopping behind him, and he raised his chin to her.

Among them this time was a gnome who wore a dark brown robe and the traditional pointed hat of his people, laid down almost to one shoulder. His beard was long and white and his dark eyes were on the path before him, and it was he who spoke first. "This dragon has banished Farrigrall, but he has not banished you. You are the only one who can stand against him, you and Leedon."

Falloah's lips parted to answer, but she was stopped as the wizard began to laugh, and she turned and looked to him.

Still enjoying a jolly laugh, Leedon raised his hands to them and shook his head, eventually offering, "Sorry! Sorry. Just thought of something amusing. Never mind me. What was it you were saying?"

Shaking her head, Falloah looked back to the foreman, then to the gnome and corrected, "There is no way I can stand against a dragon of Terrwrathgrawr's power, not even with Leedon helping me."

Vinton finally turned around and loudly added, "But we both know someone who can."

Falloah wheeled around and barked, "Vinton!"

He finally strode to her, his dark eyes fixed on her as he shouted back, "And why not, Falloah? Is it not his duty to defend this territory from invaders?"

"Do not start this again!" the dragoness roared.

"Is the suffering of these people worth guarding this secret so closely?" Vinton demanded as he reached her.

She raised a finger and growled, "I'm warning you... "

The roar of a dragon drew everyone's attention, and collective gasps were drawn as the winged form swept in from the east and descended toward the docks.

"Oh, no," Falloah breathed as she watched Farrigrall sweep his wings forward and land perfectly on the longest pier.

The black dragon did not fold his wings all the way to him and he did not even look at the collection of people a few hundred paces away on the shore. His eyes were fixed on one of the fishing boats, and he opened his jaws and roared at them, then pointed beyond.

The three men in the boat looked to where he pointed, then two of them got on the oars and pulled on them as hard as they could to turn the boat and get to shore as fast as they could.

All looked to where the dragon had pointed, and all could see the massive crocodile that had surface only thirty paces from the boat. Though much of it was still submerged, all could tell that it was huge, and was close to making a meal of the three men in the boat.

Baring his teeth, Farrigrall leapt from the pier and opened his wings, lifting himself about six men's heights into the air as he charged toward the invading predator, then he pulled his wings back, opened his jaws and dove on the big crocodile, slamming teeth-first into it as he plunged into the water and drove the huge beast fully under the surface.

Dragon and crocodile disappeared beneath the surface in a mighty splash. The dragon's black and red tail broke the surface, then submerged again. The water was violently disturbed by something unseen. The crocodile's tail swept up from below and splashed back down.

A moment passed and nothing else broke the surface, and all of the humans watched anxiously and wide eyed, all but Leedon, Josslee, and Eston, who almost seemed to smile.

Much closer to shore, and only about fifty paces out from where the group was, Farrigrall broke the surface, the crocodile held by the head in his jaws. While a very large beast, the crocodile did not match the black dragon in size or length, and as the dragon strode into shallower and shallower water, it hung limply in his powerful jaws, its head crushed by murderous teeth driven into its skull by those unimaginably powerful jaws.

Farrigrall waded ashore and took the crocodile almost all the way to the table where he stopped and dropped his prize, staring at it only for a few seconds before he turned less than pleased eyes to Josslee. With his brow low over his eyes, he roared, "I have been worried sick about you!"

She stood and turned on him, setting her hands on her hips as she countered, "No more than I worried over you, you big lummox!"

He growled, then he turned his attention to Eston and Ucira, and his chest seemed to puff out as he announced, "Mother, Papa, I have brought home dinner."

Falloah shouted to him, "What are you doing back here?"

His eyes shifted to her and narrowed. "I seem to know that voice, but I do not recognize you."

Leedon explained, "You know her, all right, just in a different form. This is Falloah, the Scarlet."

The black dragon blinked, glanced at Josslee, glanced at the wizard, and finally asked, "What?"

"It's me," the dragoness explained. "It's Falloah." She folded her arms. "And you were supposed to remain in Abtont like I told you!"

He just stared at her for long seconds, then he bent forward and closed the distance to her with a few steps. Butting her with his nose, he sniffed, then grimaced and drew away. "Falloah's a human. Why is Falloah a human?" He stood fully and his eyes slid to Leedon.

The wizard waved his hands and assured, "Not my doing, my friend."

The council foreman stepped forward, looking up at the dragon as he loudly informed, "Farrigrall, you were banished! You know what that other dragon will do to this village if he finds you here! You must go at once!"

The black dragon's brow lowered over his eyes as he regarded the foreman with an authority nobody had ever seen from him before. "I'm afraid things have changed, and Terrwrathgrawr has no power to banish anyone." Looking back to his human parents, he backed away and fell to his belly, holding his head low to see them better as he ranted, "Oh, I have such stories to tell you! I've seen the land far to the east of here and it's wonderful and lush and there's another big lake. I met other dragons! Oh, speaking of which... " He raised his head and looked to the mountain peak in the center of the island, then his jaws opened and he trumpeted loud enough for his voice to actually echo off of the stone of the mountain and surrounding buildings, a sound no one in the village had ever heard him make before.

Falloah spun around and looked up, her mouth falling open as she leaned her head and mumbled, "Oh, why is this happening?"

Kyshira had been watching from the safety of the mountain peak, but now, summoned by the black dragon, she opened her wings and leapt off, gliding down to where the big drake lay, and the village elders fled toward the lake as she swept in and landed gently about ten paces behind where they had been. She folded her wings, glancing about at the humans who looked on, then her eyes found the black drake and there seemed to be a need for reassurance there.

Farrigrall introduced, "Mother. Papa. This is Kyshira."

They were not sure what to make of her for a few seconds, but Ucira smiled and looked to the big drake, leaning her head as she asked, "Did you finally find that special girl?"

The black dragon smiled a strained smile and looked away from her.

The foreman dared to approach the black dragon, his eyes shifting to the little blue and back. "Farrigrall, does this mean you are bringing others to fight this threat? She looks awfully small."

Barely moving his head, the drake eyed the foreman for long seconds before he informed, "Falloah and Kyshira will not be fighting anyone."

Falloah loudly added, "Nor will you!"

He seemed to ignore her and pushed himself up, looking to the long bridge that connected the island to the land beyond. "I did not see any movement over at Shoreline. Have they all left?"

The foreman answered, "They fled days ago. Shoreline is abandoned and now—"

"Good," Farrigrall interrupted. "More room to maneuver over there." His eyes slid to the little blue and a deep growl rolled from him, then he motioned to the top of the mountain on which she had been perched before.

Appearing to follow his command, the little blue stood and wheeled around, opened her wings and lifted herself effortlessly into the sky.

Falloah set her hands on her hips and looked to Shoreline herself, and it was clear that she felt as if she were losing control of the situation. Forcing a heavy breath from her, she returned her attention to the black drake and ordered, "You need to get yourself back to Abtont like I already told you. You and Kyshira both need to go!"

His focus still on Shoreline, the black dragon countered, "Afraid not. This ends today."

Falloah shouted back, "What ends today is this foolishness! Get Kyshira and return to Abtont! Now!"

Once again, Farrigrall seemed to ignore her and instead turned his attention to Eston. "When this starts, everyone should get inside or otherwise to shelter. I think the mine would be a good place for most people to go if they don't have a sturdy house."

It was clear that he was simply not going to take Falloah seriously so long as she was in human form, and finally she yelled, "Oh, enough of this!" as she reached over her head and grabbed onto the back of the dress.

Most people watched her with great interest as she stripped her clothing off, and Josslee's mother mumbled, "Oh, my!" as she finally averted her gaze from the now naked red-haired woman.

Falloah wheeled around, grasped the amulet and whispered the incantation as she strode angrily away from the group of humans. Her transformation was violent and swift, and in a few seconds, the scarlet dragon whipped back toward the black drake, baring her teeth as she roared, "You will do as I say!"

It soon became abundantly clear that Farrigrall was no longer intimidated by her in any way, especially now that he was back on his home turf. Almost as an act of defiance, he stood, towing over her, and a low growl rolled from deep within him. His eyes slid to the west, to the mountains beyond Shoreline, and he turned that way, opened his jaws, and roared a mighty challenge.

All of the humans nearby covered their ears against the air splitting roar that echoed off of the mountain of the island and every structure. It lasted for long seconds and he finally, slowly closed his jaws as it abated.

Falloah strode to him and the humans still in her path fled as she approached, and she reached up and clamped a hand over his snout, hissing, "What are you doing?"

With another growl, he pushed her hand away from him and turned fully on her as he roared, "This is my range and I intend to defend it!"

Her jaws fell open and she barely managed, "Your... Your *range*?"

An answer echoed from somewhere beyond the mountains, a deep, almost gravely roar, the roar of an older, larger dragon, and the black drake turned his attention that way. His eyes narrowed, and he turned his head slightly toward the mountain top that stood in the center of the island, and the little blue dragon who was still perched there. With a low grunt, he nodded, then motioned with his head toward the east.

Without hesitating, the little blue opened her wings and leapt from the peak, turned, and headed out over the lake.

Farrigrall looked down to the village elders, to the foreman, and he ordered, "Get everyone to safety. The siege of Terrwrathgrawr ends today." Turning his eyes to Falloah, he added, "Get back to Abtont." Without waiting for a response, he turned toward the lake, opened his wings and swept himself into the air, and once he was high enough, he banked hard and stroked his wings hard as he flew toward the open shore of the other side of the lake.

Ucira watched as he soared toward the main shore of the lake, toward the abandoned town of Shoreline and the wheat field that was now plowed under, and she shook her head. "What does he think he's doing? That bigger dragon nearly killed him the last time."

Falloah forced a breath from her in a snort and growled, "Something happened while I was away from Abtont, and I need answers." She strode toward the lake, careful not to step on the fleeing humans, and she opened her wings and jumped into the air, following the path the younger dragon had.

Vinton's eyes followed her as she flew toward Shoreline, and he asked for everyone to hear, "What is the quickest way to get over there?"

CHAPTER 14

The field that ran almost up to the shore of the lake and nearly to the mountain that stood to the west was freshly plowed and still disturbed from the last battle of dragons that had been fought there days before. About fifty paces from the shore of the lake, the black dragon slammed onto the ground and dropped to all fours, kicking up dust all around him as he opened his jaws, bared his teeth and repeated his challenge as loudly as his lungs would allow. His tail thrashed behind him and it appeared that he was a young dragon who was spoiling for a fight.

Pushing himself up, Farrigrall scanned the mountains in the distance, and his eyes fixed on the largest of them, right in front of him. The smaller mountains beyond formed a line of peaks that did not reach quite as high.

Something cut through the air behind him and he turned his head only slightly, his eyes sliding that way as the scarlet settled gently to the ground beside him and about twenty paces away. Instead of turning to her, he scanned the mountain tops again, and a low growl rumbled from him.

"He won't come right away," Falloah informed. "The dragon that answered you was not even him. It was one of his subordinares."

"Then I'll kill this subordinare first," Farrigrall snarled.

"One dragon will not come to answer you," she said flatly, also scanning the mountains. "They will all come. Terrwrathgrawr knows not to come here alone."

"He did the first time," Farrigrall corrected.

"He likely had subordinares watching from the mountains. He knows if the wrong dragon catches him on this side of the border again and he is alone then things will not go well." Falloah raised her brow. "If your villagers are correct and he only brought two females and one of his male subordinares then things will go badly for him, anyway."

The young drake grunted. "I intend for this to be the worst day of his life, and hopefully the end of his miserable life."

The two dragons looked to each other.

"You aren't going to order me back to Abtont?"

She just stared back at him for long seconds, then she looked past him, toward the north. "Your mind is set and you are too stubborn to hear anything else I have to say, so I'll not waste the words on you."

Farrigrall also looked toward the north, wondering if she thought they would come from that way, then he looked to the highest mountain peak, to the left and right of it. This was where the dragon had come before, and he was sure that he would come from there again.

Falloah raised her nose and trumpeted in a higher pitch than one would expect from a dragon her size. This done, she sat catlike beside him and looked to the west again.

The young drake leered at her and suggested, "You should go."

"No," she sighed. "I think I'll stay here and see if you are as mighty as you think you are."

"Funny," he snarled. "What was that call about?"

She glanced at him as he sat beside her and wrapped his tail around himself on the ground. "It was hopefully not a huge mistake. Of course, all of this is a huge mistake, so I could not possibly make it any worse."

"Not as much a mistake as you think," he countered.

"What happened to make you come back here?" she asked in an almost motherly tone.

He glanced at her again and growled a sigh. "I'll tell you when this is all over."

A little smile touched her mouth. "Mighty, stubborn, and now mysterious. You remind me so much of another."

"So, I keep hearing," he grumbled. He abruptly raised his head as a brown and gold form in the distance soared around the mountain and found an outcropping to land on, and his eyes narrowed. His heart was now thundering behind his chest. The moment of truth was at hand, and he slowly stood, his hands curling inward, his brow low over his eyes as he bared his teeth. This was the dragon he sought, and this day, timing would be crucial. As the big dragon, a very dark brown and copper in the distance, crouched on the outcropping and stared back at him, Farrigrall opened his jaws and roared his challenge yet again.

Falloah did not rise, and just stared back at an old enemy with wide eyes. Her claws dug into the ground as she nervously braced for flight, and somehow fought off the instinct to flee. She looked to the north again, then turned her attention to the big form that watched from the mountain almost a league away.

Terrwrathgrawr seemed to be waiting for something, and he appeared to be alone.

Falloah's eyes danced about and she mumbled, "Something is wrong."

"You should go," Farrigrall suggested.

Her gaze slid to him. "You're up to something."

He raised a brow.

Terrwrathgrawr leapt from the mountain and opened his wings, soaring toward the two dragons who awaited him. As he approached, it was clear that he was a big dragon, one who was used to combat. His belly and throat were almost a metallic gold ringed in black where the gold met the dark brown of his sides and back. Spines of black jetted outward from his lower jaw and swept toward the back of his head, the same black that his horns were. Claws were a bronze color and the webbing of his wings was the same gold as his belly. Orange eyes regarded the two dragons he approached almost with amusement. This was a lean dragon, though larger than those he approached and very well-muscled. His tail seemed thin for his size and swept with the wind to give him direction as he lowered his feet and slammed them onto the ground about ninety paces away.

The landmaster approached with slow steps, casually folding his wings to his back and sides as he extended his arms, and he almost seemed to smile as he said in a deep, bellow of a voice, "I must say, I am surprised to see you back here. I thought I made my wishes to you perfectly clear." One of his scaly, spiny eyebrows cocked up. "Still, you have a brash courage. I admire that."

Farrigrall countered, "No more brash than you to think you can take my territory and I'll just peacefully comply with your demand that I leave." He looked down to his claws, raising his eyebrows as he suggested, "Might be time for you to go back the way you came." His eyes hardened as they turned on the much larger dragon again. "And don't ever return."

More of a smile curled the big dragon's scaly lips. "Oh, to be so young and arrogant again. I am sure, had you lived past today, you would one day find yourself a landmaster in your own right."

"The day is still young," Farrigrall pointed out, looking down to his claws again.

Terrwrathgrawr glanced upward. "It is past high sun." He looked past the young dragon, toward Peak Island Village. "I get the impression those humans on the island mean something to you."

Farrigrall did not look up from his claws as he said, "What they mean to me is none of your business."

"Very well," the big dragon sighed. Finally turning his eyes to the scarlet, he leaned his head and offered, "My apologies, Falloah. I did not mean to be so rude and just ignore you so."

She did not answer and just stared back at him, trying to mask the fear in within her.

"Have you decided to return home?" the landmaster asked.

"I am home," she replied with hard words.

"I see," Terrwrathgrawr accepted with gentle words. "If you will not live in the home from which you emerged, then you will die in this one."

The only warning was a couple of seconds of wings cutting the air behind them and they did not even have the time to turn toward the threat that swooped in on them before two other dragons collided with them at high speed. Both were larger than Farrigrall, both were drakes, and one pinned Falloah to the ground, holding onto the back of her neck with a hand clamped down between her horns and the other hand and a foot solidly on her back. The other toppled Farrigrall and both of them rolled to a stop about thirty paces away.

Farrigrall was stunned by the swift attack but quickly forced his wits back to him as he scrambled to all fours and faced the older drake that was facing him, and he bared his teeth. This older drake was clearly very old and silver tipped his dark green scales, horns, and the nearly black spines that seemed to grow from his jaw. Silver dorsal scales stood erect and his thrashing tail was flanked by sharp, pointed scales that stood out from both sides.

The dragon holding Falloah down was a dark yellow with a lighter yellow belly and black claws. This one was scarred and one horn had been broken halfway to the point. He was rough looking with one scar that ran from behind his left eye all the way to his throat, a scar that was gray and stood out plainly. The webbing of his wings was also torn in places and there were holes in the webbing that betrayed many seasons of battle. His nose and lower jaw were not pointed or round like most dragons, rather his snout was almost square and blunt and his mouth was filled with robust, sharp teeth. Yellow eyes were wide and wild and hinted that he barely clung to sanity. This one looked to the landmaster and asked in that deep, gravely voice that had answered Farrigrall's challenge, "May I kill her, Master? I want to taste her flesh between my teeth and feel her bones snap!"

"Patience," Terrwrathgrawr ordered. He turned slightly and regarded the young drake with calm, conceited eyes, and his head leaned over slightly as two smaller dragons, both females, landed at his sides, one a dark orange and the other, a rather small female about the size of Kyshira or Revillee, a light brown, almost a gold color, with darker brown dorsal scales and horns and a pale brown belly. This dragoness appeared to be uncomfortable and glanced about rather than focusing on her landmaster's intended victim.

Farrigrall looked back to see Falloah pinned down with a dragon a third larger than he was lowering his head, his jaws to her, and tasting her with a forked tongue, and he knew she dare not move. He glanced at the green and silver drake that had toppled him, his eyes danced back and forth between the two females, and finally landed on the big landmaster, and he dared to stand and look up at him with bared teeth, a low brow and defiance in his eyes. "Of course, you would call in others," he chided. "You're too much a coward to face me alone."

Raising his brow, Terrwrathgrawr answered back, "Am I, now? You have a short memory, young one." He spread his arms and his hands, and the dragonesses backed away, as did the old green. "If battle with me is what you want, then I shall surely oblige. Every condemned dragon is entitled to a final request." He turned his head to the side and slightly behind him, focusing on the big yellow dragon. "See to it she watches him die."

Farrigrall did not wait for him to finish his order before he leapt forward and opened his jaws, aiming for the big dragon's head as he always did. Stroking his wings, he held his claws out and was ready to slash through his foe's armor, but Terrwrathgrawr was far swifter than the young drake had anticipated and swung hard with his open hand.

Claws collided with the side of the young drake's head, snapping it over and sending him careening to the ground twenty paces away where he rolled into a dusty heap and came to rest on his belly. Farrigrall's head and face bled from four long gashes and he was slow to push himself up.

With a little smile, Terrwrathgrawr folded his arms and raised his brow as his smaller opponent struggled back to his feet. "Do you think you are the only dragon I have ever fought? No, my brash young friend. You will just be one of many that I have killed, and in a few seasons, I doubt I will even remember your name."

Blood dripped from the side of the young drake's head and his brow was low over his eyes as he growled back, "My name is Farrigrall." This time, he did not charge right in, but he backed away a step, angling toward the direction from which he had first charged.

The big landmaster did not otherwise move, but followed the brash young dragon with his eyes.

Slobber dripped onto Falloah's head, then her neck, and the yellow dragon lowered his head to her and sniffed, then he opened his jaws and bit her shoulder, and she crooned as his teeth plunged through her armor and into her flesh.

He released her and a growl rumbled from him as he moved his jaws close to the side of her head, and he hissed, "Your flesh is sweet, Falloah the Scarlet. Watch him die, and then perhaps the Master will allow you the privilege of being my next meal."

Though there were only a few clouds overhead, the soft roll of thunder boomed from the north.

Falloah dared to turn her head and leer at the dragon who held her, and she raised an eyebrow as she countered, "No, I think the privilege will be watching *you* die."

Thunder sounded in a deafening clap and lightning burst from thin air only a hundred paces away. The very air burst into a ring of boiling fire and lightning that quickly expanded outward until it was a ring of flames more than thirty paces across.

And a black, winged form burst through the flames like something from a nightmare, and all of the dragons turned toward the north as this new arrival slammed onto the ground hard enough to shake the very earth on which they stood.

Black scales reflected jade green and midnight blue as the sunlight hit them just right. Black horns swept back from behind pale blue eyes that had a heavy brow held low over them. An emerald jewel the size of a human's fist sparkled in his forehead. Heavy armor of these black scales encased bulging muscles of frightful power and long black claws curled as he charged forward with heavy steps. As the fire behind them quickly burned out, his jaws gaped, revealing stout, sword sized white teeth as he roared a nightmarish roar, his full attention fixed on the startled landmaster.

Faster than he appeared, the black dragon veered to his left and lunged with gaping jaws, and even as the yellow dragon screeched and retreated, the black dragon's jaws slammed shut around his neck and head, breaking his horns off and plunging through hide and scales and bone and flesh. Wrenching his head the other direction as his sword sized teeth did their murderous work, the big dragon, a third larger than the yellow, tore the yellow dragon's head from his neck and hurled it away from him. Turning quickly as the yellow's body slumped over Falloah, he raised a hand to the green and a bright emerald light burst forth, impacting the green dragon's chest and exploding with enough force to blast him from his feet and almost a hundred sixty paces backward where he slammed onto the ground and rolled to a stop twenty paces more.

The gold and brown dragon screeched and wheeled around, opening her wings and fleeing into the air as fast as she could. The other female backed away, her wide eyes locked on the black dragon, and she turned and followed suit.

Directing his other hand to the landmaster, the black dragon sent another burst of that green light toward him and hit him squarely in the chest, blowing him from his feet and back about thirty paces where he landed on his back and raised a could of dust around him.

Farrigrall's eyes widened as the big black dragon turned on him next, and he raised his palms to the much larger dragon. The huge black dragon regarded him coldly, angrily, and his lips slid away from those murderous teeth again as his jaws parted and a thunderous growl rolled from him.

Falloah drew a sharp gasp as she sprang up, pushed the yellow dragon's body from her, and rushed toward the larger black dragon, and she cried, "Ralligor, wait! He is one of us!"

Even as she reached him, the huge black dragon glared at the young drake with an expression of rage and seemed to want to kill him, but as Falloah rubbed the side of her mouth along his throat, he seemed to calm, and he looked down to her.

The dragoness repeated, "He is one of us."

Ralligor looked back to him and raised a brow, then movement caught his eye and he turned his head and attention to the green who was struggling to push himself back up even as the scales on his chest still smoldered in small glowing orange spots where ribbons of smoke rose. His eyes slid back to the young drake and he motioned to the green with his head, then he turned fully on the landmaster who had rolled to his side, then to his belly, and was trying to push himself back up.

Fortunes had changed in less than a moment. One invading drake was dead, one was struggling to get his wits about him, the two females had wisely retreated, and the big, powerful landmaster was down and very slowly trying to get back to his feet. Delaying his foe for the landmaster to deal with was suddenly not even on the young drake's mind, and his eyes narrowed as he slowly turned on the other drake and strode toward him with heavy steps. No longer outnumbered and outmatched, Farrigrall's confidence soared. He had finally met this elusive Ralligor.

The larger green dragon still did not seem to have his wits about him as he finally stood on unsteady legs and faced the young drake, and he no longer seemed so confident in his ability to fight.

Farrigrall stopped twenty paces away and folded his arms. This would be an easy kill for a young dragon looking to prove himself. Too easy. With a subtle movement of his head, he motioned toward the west, clearly giving his foe the opportunity to flee rather than fight.

The larger dragon looked beyond the young drake to the much bigger black dragon, and, even with his landmaster present, he did not want to do battle any longer, not with Ralligor on the field. His eyes slid to Farrigrall, he nodded in a slight motion, then turned, opened his wings, and took to the air.

Terrwrathgrawr had gotten to his feet and his gaze quickly found the last of his *subordinares* in retreat, and a snarl found his lip. The smaller black dragon turned toward him, but simply sat catlike to watch the outcome, as did the scarlet dragoness. This landmaster would face the fearsome Ralligor alone, and now he felt confident that he could turn his full attention to the slightly smaller dragon. Looking him up and down, he observed, "You've grown."

The black dragon snarled back, "You haven't." He turned his claws upward and his entire hand was engulfed in a bright emerald flame.

Already knowing fear of Ralligor's power, a power he had not faced from this dragon before, Terrwrathgrawr fixed his gaze on the flaming hand of the black dragon, then looked to his face with narrow eyes, baring his teeth only slightly as he said, "Put away your new found power and face me as a dragon should, if you have the courage."

Ralligor never took his eyes from Terrwrathgrawr's, but he turned his hand over and swept it to the side, and the flames were extinguished easily. "I do prefer it this way. It will be much more personal to rip the life out of you with my claws and teeth."

Farrigrall raised his brow and seemed to be enjoying the banter between these dragons.

Ralligor was poised for battle and slowly closed on his old enemy with heavy, ground shaking steps, and a glare in his eyes that was nothing less than animal hatred for the old landmaster. Terrwrathgrawr did not advance, but instead lowered his body and held his claws ready to receive the mighty black dragon as he stood his ground with bared teeth and slightly open jaws.

Agarxus slammed onto the ground near the water's edge, dropped to all fours and roared a deep, air splitting roar through bared teeth that the young drake could feel all the way to his bones.

Though the black dragon was a clear threat to Terrwrathgrawr, the mountainous Tyrant was more of a nightmare, and the invading landmaster spun around, his eyes filling with an old enemy who had threatened to kill him on more than one occasion. This was one of those occasions where the difficult choice of cowardice was the only means of survival, and before the huge dragon could advance on him, Terrwrathgrawr wheeled around, opened his wings and stroked them hard as he ran to the west, lifting himself into the sky with frantic sweeps of his wings for more height and speed.

Ralligor watched the invader retreat, then he turned and faced his own landmaster with bared teeth and a growl, and he grumbled, "I could have killed him this time."

His eyes still on the retreating landmaster, Agarxus casually folded his wings and stood fully, towering over all as he countered, "We've talked about this, Desert Lord. You are not ready to face the consequences of killing him."

The black dragon roared, "You don't know that!"

Slowly, the landmaster's attention turned on his subordinate, and his brow was low over his eyes. His scaly lips slid away from his massive, pointed teeth and he growled in a clear tone of warning, "You will mind your place, Ralligor!"

The black dragon dared to advance on his massive landmaster a few steps and his voice was still loud and laced with anger as he countered, "My place is defending the western border, which is exactly what I was doing!"

Agarxus turned fully and advanced on his subordinare, who was just over half his size, and at only twenty paces away, he roared, "Your place is to do what I tell you to, not to challenge other landmasters! If Terrwrathgrawr is to be killed, it will be *my* place to do so!"

Farrigrall's wide eyes danced from one to the next, and he was so involved with the confrontation that he did not even notice that Falloah had approached him until he felt the backs of her fingers push against his arm. As the two big dragons stared each other down, he finally tore his gaze from them and looked to her. She was staring back at him, and she appeared to be terrified. Kyshira swept in and landed behind her, just beyond the length of the scarlet's tail, but her attention was on the confrontation closer to the water.

"Go," Falloah ordered in a low voice. "Just go. Return to Abtont near my lair and stay there until I arrive."

His attention strayed back to the bigger dragons. "I want to see how this comes out."

"Quit being difficult!" she hissed.

Ralligor growled deeply as he glared up at his landmaster, then he half turned and pointed to the west. "Mark my words, Agarxus, if he ever crosses that border again—"

The landmaster roared, "Where were you when he crossed here twelve days ago?"

The black dragon was frozen where he stood and stared back at the massive dragon before him for long seconds before he lowered his hand, and he could only manage to say, "What?"

Agarxus slowly advanced on him, lowering his nose to bring it only a pace from his subordinare's. "Where have you been for the last thirty seasons? It was not here. It was not guarding this southern tip of your range as you were supposed to be."

Ralligor's brow tensed. "What makes you think that?"

His eyes narrowing as a thunderous growl rolled from him, Agarxus turned his attention to the dragonesses and ordred, "Falloah. Follow Terrwrathgrawr and see that he crosses the Territhan Mountain Range. Tell me when he does, and tell me if that is as far as he goes." His eyes flitted to Kyshira. "Take the blue with you. Go."

Her jaws were parted and she stared back at him with wide eyes, and gave the young drake a fearful glance.

Without awaiting a response, the landmaster looked back to the black dragon and ordered, "Fly to the north, to the neutral place in the Dark Mountains, and call to Mettegrawr. Tell him I will be there in three days to have words with him, and take a couple of my subordinares with you." His eyes narrowed again. "And be careful not to challenge him. You will leave that to me."

Ralligor turned his eyes down and nodded in subtle motions. Looking over his shoulder to the other black dragon, he raised a brow and turned back to the landmaster.

Agarxus raised his nose slightly. "From south of the Hard Lands to my southern border, to the western borders and to the edge of the scrub country is his range now."

Ralligor growled. "You are just giving away another chunk of my range."

"Your range," the landmaster snarled. "He has been here for thirty seasons and you did not take notice."

The black dragon's eyes flitted away, toward the abandoned town.

"All that time," Agarxus went on, "and you did not come this way even once. This has not been a part of your range all that time."

Still staring toward the abandoned town, Ralligor nodded and agreed, "I suppose it will be less to patrol." He glanced back at Farrigrall again. "You going to be here once I have summoned Mettegrawr?"

"A couple of days," the landmaster replied. "I hear there are crocodiles here." His eyes slid to the smaller black dragon. "And I hear they are quite tasty."

A disturbance at the water's edge drew their attention and they both looked to see the bay unicorn wading from the water.

Vinton trotted to them and stopped about twenty paces away, and he shook himself violently to clear some of the water from his mane and hair. This done, he looked up to Ralligor, then Agarxus, and he reported, "The bridge broke under me halfway across and I fell through and had to swim the rest of the way."

Ralligor stared down at him for long seconds, and a slight smile curled his mouth. "That is the most delightful thing I've heard in a long time."

Vinton glared up at him and snorted.

Agarxus returned his attention to the black dragon. "Go, and take Farrigrall of the Lake with you. See about returning here before nightfall." Looking to Falloah, his eyes narrowed, and he was clearly annoyed that she had not yet departed.

Falloah stared back at him, still wide eyed, for only a couple of seconds before she opened her wings and ordered, "Come along, Kyshira." Her eyes found the young drake as she strode by and she snarled, "Behave."

He regarded her with a tense brow as he watched her take flight with the young blue right behind her. With a snort, he turned toward the other two drakes and strode to them, and once there, he quickly realized he was the smallest dragon in the area, and the two dragons with him were immensely more powerful than he was. Still, he finally had the feeling that he was among friends and had no fear of them, and confidently stood among them even as they both looked down at him.

His attention shifting from one to the other, to the unicorn, then back to the landmaster, Farrigrall finally asked, "So, what's the plan? Is there another epic battle awaiting us?"

The two bigger drakes glanced at each other, and the black dragon informed, "We have a message to deliver."

CHAPTER 15

Farrigrall was not sure how long or how far they flew in silence. He stayed to the big black dragon's left, his wingtip a few paces behind the wingtip of his much larger companion, and he glanced at him often. While he craved conversation, he could also feel that this dragon was annoyed, and any dragon that was willing to stand his ground against the mountainous landmaster was a dragon to be feared. So, he just flew along in silence.

And it seemed like an eternity.

The big black dragon finally looked back at him with an expression that could not be read. This was not a long stare, just a quick look, almost as if to make certain that he was still there. A moment later he asked, "Any idea what this meeting is about?"

Finally! It was time to sound authoritative and dignified, and he answered, "It seems that Mettegrawr sent some of his agents over the border, and they got caught."

"Not the first time he's done that," Ralligor informed, his eyes forward and on the mountains in the distance that drew reluctantly closer. "Who discovered this?"

"I did," the young drake replied proudly.

The Desert Lord's brow tensed. "You discovered this from that far south."

"No," Farrigrall answered, "I was near the Dark Mountains when I found all this out. I killed the wyvern that was found spying and then I had to fight and kill one of his lieutenants and one of his females. That was after the landmaster arrived."

"Really."

"I'm sure Agarxus would have attended to them himself, but this other dragon had already made the issue personal."

"I see."

Farrigrall glanced at the much larger black dragon. "So, I've heard a lot about you."

With a leisurely glance back at his smaller companion, Ralligor dryly grumbled, "And yet, I have heard not a thing about you."

The young drake raised his brow. "Not surprising. Until recently I had never strayed far from my village, not until that other landmaster arrived and drove me out." His brow lowered and he growled. "I wish Agarxus had allowed you to kill him."

A growling breath rumbled from the larger drake and he agreed, "We both do."

"Seems like it would have just been easier," the younger dragon went on. "That's how humans seem to do it. One ruler overthrows another and expands his lands and wealth. Seems like dragons work the same way."

Ralligor glanced back at him. "Perhaps Agarxus does not want his territory any bigger."

"Why wouldn't he?" the young drake asked.

They flew in silence for a moment, and the Desert Lord finally replied, "You have no idea how big this territory already is, do you?"

"I do not," Farrigrall admitted.

With a grunt, the big black dragon shook his head.

"You know at some point he'll just come back and challenge the border again," Farrigrall informed. "From what I hear, he seems to do it all the time."

His brow tense and low over his eyes, Ralligor observed, "You talk a lot."

The young drake forced a hard breath from him and offered, "Sorry. This is my first time dealing with my own kind. I was raised by humans my whole life and only in the last few days did I get to spend any time with other dragons." He glanced at the big drake. "So, what do you know about Falloah?"

Ralligor's eyes narrowed and he clenched his jaw, then slowly he turned his head and leered at the smaller dragon. With bared teeth, he deeply growled, "What of her?"

Farrigrall did not see the bigger dragon's expression and he went on, "When she found me by the lake, she did not want other dragons too close to me, and she was determined that I stay out of sight. She seemed protective, but she's extremely bossy and she acts like I've offended her somehow. I asked about it and she said I had not, but still she treats me like an enemy. I just don't know what to think of her."

Looking forward again, Ralligor snarled, "Then don't."

The young drake continued, "Kyshira and Revillee behave completely different toward me."

"They are young and foolish," the Desert Lord pointed out. "Like you."

Farrigrall raised a brow and leered at the bigger dragon for long seconds. "I haven't seen other dragons my entire thirty seasons, and it seems that the only ones I have to learn from are too young to teach me much, those who want to kill me, and those who just don't care if I learn about our kind or not, like you and Falloah."

Ralligor's brow tensed as he stared forward in silence for a moment. "Thirty seasons?" he finally asked.

"Thirty seasons," the young drake replied. "I was raised by humans that whole time and made quite a name for myself as a crocodile killer."

"You were raised there," the Desert Lord guessed.

"Hatched there, I hear," Farrigrall confirmed. "The woman I've called my mother all this time found me as an egg and took me home. The village eventually embraced a dragon living among them and that's how I was raised." He raised an eyebrow. "It's a fishing village so you can imagine how delighted they were when I was big enough to fight off the large crocodiles that have been eating them for so many seasons."

Ralligor was quiet a moment more, then he suddenly veered to the right and descended toward a large clearing in the forest below. The dark mountains were well within sight, but still he felt the need to land, and his young companion followed apprehensively.

The big dragon swept his wings forward right before his feet hit the ground, kicking up a hurricane of dust and fallen leaves as he landed, and he trotted off the last of his speed. Farrigrall landed about fifty paces behind him and as gently as he could, his eyes fixed on his larger travelling companion as he slowly, almost absently, folded his wings to his back and sides. Ralligor's wings folded slowly as he stared across the clearing with hard eyes.

Farrigrall did not approach for a moment and instead just watched the big dragon as he stood there staring into nothingness. Finally, with a little growl, he closed half of the distance between them and demanded, "What did I say to annoy you this time?"

Ralligor turned his head slightly as if to see the smaller drake, but he did not look back at him.

Leedon emerged from the forest to the Desert Lord's right with the bay unicorn right behind him, and he loudly asked, "What indeed, mighty Farrigrall. What, indeed." His eyes were on the black dragon and he stopped and leaned heavily on his walking stick as Ralligor slowly turned his head to look down at him.

Vinton stopped beside the wizard, his attention also fully on the big dragon with no readable expression.

Falloah's unmistakable trumpet sounded from behind the dragons and they turned fully as she descended toward them, and moving a little too fast to land.

The scarlet dragoness veered away before colliding with Farrigrall, lowered her feet and landed a little too hard, stumbled, ran into her momentum as she stroked her wings forward with all her might, and finally fell to all fours and slid to a stop. She was out of breath and her nose was directed to the ground as she panted to regain her wind.

Ralligor's brow tensed as he stared at her, and finally he commented, "You are supposed to be teaching Revillee *not* to do that."

Still staring at the ground, she gasped, "I... I've been trying... Trying to catch up to you."

The big black dragon turned fully to the dragoness, then looked to the young drake who approached a couple of hesitant steps.

She seemed very irritated as she raised her head and looked to the Desert Lord. Finally catching her breath, she snarled, "And I do *not* land like Revillee!"

Ralligor watched as she pushed herself up and stood, and his eyes narrowed as her gaze found the wizard and unicorn, causing her to pause. "Why, exactly, were you in such a rush to catch up to us?"

Vinton whinnied to him, "Because she has something very important to tell you!"

This clearly annoyed the dragoness anew as she barked, "Thank you... Vinton!"

The Desert Lord had hard eyes for the scarlet as he took a couple of steps toward her and bent forward, bringing his head down and closer to hers as he demanded, "Does it have anything to do with this drake who now occupies my southern range?"

She could only stare back at him with wide eyes and her jaws slightly ajar. Her eyes flitted to Farrigrall, and she backed away a step.

The young drake closed the distance with only three steps and also demanded, "I think we both would like answers!" He stopped where he was as one of Ralligor's hands clamped around his snout, and he knew to remain still even as his now wide eyes strayed to the bigger dragon.

Regarding him with an expression of irritation, the big drake bared his teeth and growled a single warning, and the smaller drake backed away, pulling his nose from the larger dragon's grip.

Still, Farrigrall's gaze found the scarlet and it was clear that he was eager for an answer.

Ralligor's attention fell on his small mate again, and his teeth were still bared as he ordered, "Answer!"

Her fearful eyes strayed and found the wizard and unicorn, who also stared at her and waited a secret truth from her. She finally looked down, finally admitted, "*Unisponsus*, he is your son."

For once, the mighty Desert Lord found himself without a thing to say, no sharp words, no witty comment that would break the tension and put him somehow in control. He only stared at the scarlet, and his eyes followed her as she strode away from him, toward the edge of the field, and nearly to the trees where she sank to the ground and settled on her belly.

Farrigrall and Ralligor looked to each other.

And finally, the Desert Lord found his voice. "Well," he began, "I suppose that would explain your good looks." He turned his head and looked back to Falloah. "Still doesn't explain how you came to be raised by humans."

Leedon and Vinton had approached unnoticed and the wizard laughed and said, "There is an easy way to answer your questions, mighty friend. All she needs is an understanding ear and the support of her new family." Looking to the unicorn, he announced, "Come along, my friend. I do believe we have somewhere to be."

Vinton watched the wizard turn and stride with casual steps toward the trees, then he looked up at the dragon and informed, "Looks like we've both been blessed with a family. Yours just came a little faster than mine." He glanced at Farrigrall, then turned to follow the wizard. "Makes me wish my own stallion was already here."

Ralligor watched after him, and before Vinton could reach the trees, he called after him, "I'll wager you're having a mare!"

Vinton stopped and looked over his shoulder, smiling as his attention fell on the black dragon. "Perhaps. Either way, I expect it to be the most challenging and rewarding part of my life, and I face the time with greater anticipation with each passing day."

Farrigrall watched the unicorn disappear into the shadows of the forest, then he looked up at the big dragon and raised his brow.

Ralligor just grunted at him before he turned back to the scarlet and strode to her, unaware that the young drake was hesitantly following. The big dragon fell to all fours at her side and also settled down to his belly, staring ahead of him much as she did. The smaller drake stopped behind them and sat catlike, his attention fixed on the Desert Lord, then on the smaller scarlet.

Silence thickened the very air around them but for the wind in the trees and the few birds who chirped from them, those that were brave enough to share this area with three dragons.

Finally, Ralligor reminded with as gentle a tone as he could muster, "Terrwrathgrawr killed our first clutch."

Falloah's nose lowered toward the ground and she just nodded.

"Go on," the big dragon ordered.

The dragoness drew a deep, shaky breath, and she shook her head, closing her eyes. "I tried to defend them. I tried. I could not defend my own babies." A tear slipped from one eye. "I thought if I could save just one... When you attacked him and told me to flee, I took one in my mouth and did what you said. If only I could have saved just one."

Ralligor finally turned his full attention to her.

She just stared at the ground as she continued, "I flew it away from the fight and hid it in the grass along the lake. I thought it was well hidden, but when I returned..." She shook her head. "I did not think I was away long enough for anything to find it, and it was gone when I returned. When you and Agarxus drove Terrwrathgrawr and his minions away, I went back and I looked and I looked, and I began to doubt that I remembered where it was left."

"Losing that clutch upset you for months," the Desert Lord recalled.

Falloah closed her eyes. "It upsets me still, *Unisponsus*. I thought if I could save just one..."

"You did," Farrigrall assured.

Ralligor turned his head and looked back at the smaller drake.

Farrigrall stood and dared to approach the dragoness, and he laid down to his belly on her other side. His attention was fixed on her and he drew his nose in close, leaning his head, and finally butted her gently below the horn with his nose. "You saved one, and I'll always be grateful that you did."

She finally, slowly turned her eyes to him.

"You did save one," Farrigrall repeated. He turned his eyes up, meeting those of the Desert Lord, his father, and he explained, "The battle you fought drew the attention of those who lived near the lake. My... The woman who found me was just a little girl at the time and was looking for crabs along that shoreline and found a really big egg instead." He looked to Falloah. "She had no way to know that my mother would return for me, and she did not want to just leave that egg to its fate, so she took it home. I hatched sometime later. She raised me all that time as if I were her own and I was eventually accepted by the village. In the last ten seasons or so I've come to protect them and I've saved many of the villagers' lives from crocodiles and invaders. But for what you did thirty seasons ago, many more of them would no longer be here." He raised his brow. "Your act of kindness is one that have many, many people in your debt, human and gnome, and now dragon."

For a quiet moment the dragoness just stared at the young drake, her eyes glossed by tears, and finally she closed her eyes and leaned toward him, gently rubbing the side of her nose against his.

Ralligor watched this, and while he was unaccustomed to seeing his mate show such affection toward another dragon, he did not seem to mind. There was a connection to this young drake. Still, he grunted and drew their attention, and he looked to the younger drake and informed, "By now, I would have expected you to hunt on your own and strike out to start your own life."

"I have," Farrigrall assured. "I even have my own range in the landmaster's territory."

Ralligor's eyes narrowed. "You have part of *my* range."

Farrigrall's eyes also narrowed. "It's my range now, Father."

The Desert Lord grunted again, then he pushed himself up and stood, looking down to the smaller scarlet as he ordered, "Catch your wind and then return to the lake. We will be along after Agarxus' message is delivered.

Still lying on her belly, she only stared up at him, and her answer was but a nod.

Farrigrall also stood, facing the larger black dragon as he asked, "Shouldn't she come with us? He said something about a show of force."

Ralligor growled and shook his head, turning away as he opened his wings and strode into the wind. "I will explain why that is such an idiotic idea on the way."

The young drake snorted at him, then he looked down to the scarlet and offered a little smile. "We'll be back as soon as we can." He leaned his head and finished, "Mother."

She beamed a big smile back to him and watched as he followed her big mate into the air, and she pushed herself up and sat catlike, her attention fixed on the two dragons as they turned north and stroked their wings to gain height. Another tear slipped from her eye and she said in a wisp of a voice, "I will see you soon, my son."

**

A couple of leagues passed behind them in silence as it seemed the big dragon was trying to process these new events. Farrigrall would not interrupt this silence and flew off of Ralligor's left wingtip and a little behind him.

About ten leagues from the first slopes of the Dark Mountains, where forest yielded to the crumbling, dark gray slate that made up much of this range, the Desert Lord turned his attention to the north, opened his jaws, and trumpeted an air splitting call, and within this trumpet, Farrigrall could make out the name Lornoxez. Apparently, more of a show of force would be summoned for this mission.

A subtle growl escaped the young black drake and he grumbled, "There is one dragon who does not seem to care for me. I've done everything I can to get along with him, but he's just... Spiteful."

Surprisingly, Ralligor raised his brow and replied, "He does not seem to care for anyone beyond Revillee. He's young and brash and goes too far at times to prove himself a formidable drake."

"Well," Farrigrall sighed, "he seems to draw the ire of the Landmaster rather easily, I dare say even easier than you do."

"It helps to know where the line is that should never be crossed with him."

"I came really close today," the young drake reported. "I thought he was going to kill me, but he seemed to change his mind in an instant.

Ralligor glanced at him. "He has subtle ways of testing your loyalty, and some that are not so subtle."

"You've known him a long time."

The big dragon glanced at his smaller companion. "Since I was about your age, I think, about a hundred and ten seasons or so."

Farrigrall's eyes widened. "That's a long time!"

They flew in silence a few more moments as the young drake worked up his courage, and finally with a hard stroke of his wings to bring him more parallel to his travelling companion, he finally managed, "Do you mind if I ask a favor?"

"You can ask," the Desert Lord assured.

"Well," the young dragon went on, "as you know, I've been with humans my entire life. I was raised by humans. I never knew how to be human, but there was no one to teach me how to be dragon." He looked fully to the larger drake. "I can think of nobody better to teach me about our kind than you."

Ralligor's eyes slid to his son. "You seem to know what you're doing."

"There is so much more I want to know. Like, do we really breathe fire, or is that just something of stories?"

His brow tensing, Ralligor just gave the younger drake a hard stare.

CHAPTER 16

There was thankfully an open space on the west side of the island where a dragoness could lie sprawled in the late season sun and stare longingly at the shoreline beyond. This meant blocking part of a road, but the human inhabitants of Peak Lake Island did not seem to mind. It was as if a dragon being in the way was common place.

Falloah stared ahead of her and focused on nothing, really. The big landmaster slumbered in the sunshine, laying sprawled on his belly as big dragons often do as if he was there to guard the battleground where his territory had been defended once again. The wind created little sparkling ripples on top of the water and the village behind her seemed to be trying to resume something that resembled their normal lives. Once in a while a fishing boat with its sails bloated with wind would cruise by, but she barely took notice. Her heart and her mind seemed to be willing to reconcile the recent event of a young dragon from her first clutch that had somehow survived. This made her happy, but her heard weighed heavy at the thought that she had missed thirty seasons of his life and only now, when he was grown, did she get to know anything about him.

The humans of the village kept their distance, but many stopped to fill their eyes with the sight of the lovely scarlet dragoness who was in their village. Even some of the gnomes who inhabited the caves and mines of the mountain would come into the daylight to marvel over her despite the presence of a dragon in their village for thirty seasons.

One human did approach, but drew little more than Falloah's awareness of her, even as she stopped only a few paces away from the dragoness' head. Silence thickened the air between them, and finally the dragoness asked, "Was he happy growing up here?"

Ucira just stared at her for a moment, then she nodded in subtle motions as she replied, "He was very happy here. With few exceptions, he was always happy." She turned and stared at the shoreline a league and a half away. "I worried over him much of his life. We all did. But then, he got big enough to start dealing with the crocodiles that have plagued us since this village was founded. It gave him a sense of purpose and made everyone here regard him as a hero."

Falloah just stared, and she drew a deep breath. "I suppose I should thank you for being his mother when I could not."

Ucira smiled and shook her head. "I was never his mother. I wanted to be and he came to call me mother because I cared for him, but I always knew that there was only one in the world who could ever truly be his mother. I am glad you happened this way, and I am glad for the opportunity to make your acquaintance."

"It gives me some peace to know that he had someone like you to care for him in those early seasons," the dragoness informed. "So many others would have just killed him outright, just because he is dragon."

Raising her brow, Ucira said, "Oh, early on, when the village found out about him, there was such talk. Everyone was afraid of having a dragon about."

"And you changed their minds?" Falloah asked.

"No," Ucira assured. "Farg did. He won them over himself. When he was big enough, he even helped bring in fish. When he was only five seasons old, he was already nearly twice the size of a man, and when bandits would come to raid our village or Shoreline, he would fiercely run them off, and as he got bigger, he would see to any threat that would approach the village." She motioned toward the mountain behind them with her head. "He eventually got so big that he would have to spend winter nights in the mine, and the gnomes who live in there would build fires to help keep him warm."

A little smile finally curled the dragoness' mouth. "So, he ended up sleeping in a cave."

Ucira laughed under her breath. "The gnomes and village recently quarried it out more to make it bigger for him so that he would fit. He spends the summers sleeping on the piers or sometimes right here. A couple of seasons ago he would sleep here one night and at Shoreline the next, just to make certain that crocodiles and bandits knew not to come too close. To be honest, I don't know how any village gets along without a dragon about to protect them."

Falloah's eyes slid to the woman. "You may have to get used to having two about." When Ucira raised her brow and looked to the dragoness, Falloah smiled slightly and went on, "Kyshira is very smitten with him, and it seems that he feels the same, and from what I understand, she has been ordered by Agarxus to remain here with him."

Ucira grinned. "So, how long until we have the patter of little dragons about?"

Looking back across the lake, Falloah replied, "She is still very young and will likely not even go into season for some time, but it's hard to say. I was just a few seasons older than her when I laid that first clutch."

"Have you any other children?" Ucira asked.

The dragoness longingly whispered, "No."

"Maybe soon," Ucira suggested.

Falloah shrugged. "Maybe." She raised her eyes as something aloft caught her attention, then she lifted her head as she watched Kyshira soar in and sweep her wings forward to land.

The little blue lowered her feet and settled easily to the ground about halfway between Falloah and the water, then she crouched down and lowered herself to all fours, laying to her belly as she turned and looked behind her.

Josslee slid from the base of the blue dragoness' neck to her shoulder and finally hopped down to the ground, and as she did, Kyshira stood and turned toward the scarlet with the girl walking at her side at a brisk pace.

"I just don't understand it!" Josslee complained as she looked up at the dragoness at her side. "It just seems easier than just holding me with his hands the way he does."

Kyshira raised her brow and shrugged. "I don't know. It seems easier to me, but then that would be a question for him."

Looking forward, Josslee saw her mother, smiled, and sprinted that way, calling, "Mama!" Reaching her, the girl took the woman's hands and ranted, "You won't believe where we've been! We followed the shore all the way to the south end of the lake and all the way to the waterfall! It was amazing! We even flew over the forest beyond it and saw all kinds of things. There is the ruin of an old castle down there that we want to go back and explore!"

"Um..." Ucira stammered, "uh, perhaps another time." She looked up to the blue dragoness and raised her brow.

Kyshira regarded her calmly and looked down to Falloah, leaning her head as she asked, "They aren't back yet?"

"No," the scarlet replied.

Drawing her head back, the little blue observed, "You seem concerned. Do you think Mettegrawr wanted to fight them?"

"I doubt it," Falloah answered, staring across the lake again. "His last bout with Ralligor did not end so well for him."

Ucira looked to the dragoness and said, "Well something beyond the events of the day is on your mind."

Falloah just stared, and nodded in slight motions.

Almost as if summoned by the conversation, the deep roar of a large male dragon ripped though the land and all looked up and back over the mountain as a huge black form swept right over it.

Ralligor turned slightly as he got over the water, then whipped his tail forward and banked hard as he suddenly changed direction and seemed to stop right over the shore of the lake and about twenty paces from the ground. He drew his wings in and dropped straight down, slamming into the ground and falling to all fours. His attention was still on the sky and he reared up again and roared through gaping jaws.

Wide eyed, Josslee backed up into her mother and demanded, "What is happening?"

Farrigrall swept in from the north, angling toward the larger black dragon as his jaws gaped and he roared a mighty response. He lowered his feet and swept his wings forward, holding his hands ready to attack and collided with the Desert Lord with brutal force. Ralligor spun and easily threw the smaller dragon into his momentum and sent him rolling across the field in a dusty heap. The young dragon quickly scrambled back up and lunged at his much larger opponent again with another mighty roar.

As the two dragons collided again, Ucira wrapped her arms around her daughter and pulled her close as she asked in a loud voice, "What happened? Why are they fighting?"

Falloah slowly pushed herself up and sat catlike where she was, her eyes fixed on the fray before her, and a little smile curled her mouth as she absently reported, "They're playing."

Josslee and Ucira looked up at the dragoness, then back to the violent scene before them.

The scarlet watched a moment longer before she said, "I haven't seen him play like that for a long time."

The humans watched with a mix of interest and horror as the two black dragons tumbled to the ground and appeared to be biting at each other.

The commotion had roused the huge landmaster and he casually raised his head and looked that way, watching for a moment with half-hearted interest before he settled his head back down and closed his eyes.

That strange little smile lit Falloah's face as she watched the two black dragons wrestle and she was taken by pride and relief. She drew a deep breath and shook her head slightly. "I was so afraid he would not accept his son after so long, and more that Agarxus would reject him and kill him." She turned her eyes to Kyshira. "I suppose he did not need anyone's help to make a name for himself, or to be accepted by other dragons."

The young blue looked back to the fray as the two drakes squared off again, and she raised her nose slightly and trumpeted a rather high-pitched call.

Stopping where they were, the black dragons looked toward the island, to each other, then the young drake grunted to his father and turned, trotting toward the water as he opened his wings and took to the wind. With ease, he glided over the choppy water of the lake, only stroking his wings a few times on his approach, and as he did this, Ralligor turned and strode toward his landmaster, a deep growl rolling from him as he neared.

Farrigrall lowered his feet and slammed them onto the ground right at the water's edge, folding his wings as he trotted toward the group who watched him. As he arrived, he lowered his body nearly parallel to the ground, looking first to his human mother, then his dragon mother, then to Josslee, and with an enthusiasm that it seems only the young can feel, he shouted, "You should have seen it! He called in a couple of other drakes and once we were all assembled, he led the way to this place in the mountains where it looks like a mountain top was sheered off, a big, flat place where we all could land. He roared to the north and brought other dragons led by this Mettegrawr and he announced what the law was in no uncertain terms. I thought that bigger, copper and bronze colored dragon wanted to fight, but he sure did not seem interested in tangling with the mighty Desert Lord! Not today!"

Falloah and Ucira exchanged quick looks.

The young drake continued, "He delivered the Landmaster's message and sent him on his way and then we all left the mountains. Lornoxez and that other drake went different directions and we ended up going to the southeast. Father showed me so many things, so much that we can do!" He raised his head and bade, "Watch this!" Turning his head, he gaped his jaws and took a deep breath, his chest and neck swelling, and he loosed a long burst of fire toward the sky, one that boiled ever upward and finally dissipated aloft.

The humans on the ground could feel the heat of the flames and tried to shield their faces with their hands.

Ending his long burst of fire, Farrigrall looked down to Josslee and shouted, "I told you we could do that! It wasn't just stories! Dragons can breathe fire!"

The girl folded her arms and looked away, snarling, "Whatever, Farg."

He looked back to Ucira and went on, "Kyshira can also do that. Nobody will even think about attacking the village now! Oh! And I found out that my range is much larger than I always thought it was! I have to patrol the western border every day or two to make sure other dragons don't try to cross and I'm also supposed to fly as far south as the sea to keep things in check there!" He raised his nose slightly as he wore a proud little smile. "You always wanted me to find my place in the world and now I have. I'm a *subordinare* of the most powerful dragon in the land!"

Ralligor slammed feet first into the ground about forty paces behind Farrigrall and sent tremors that everyone present could feel beneath them. As he folded his wings and strode toward the small group, Falloah pushed herself all the way up and stood, Kyshira wheeled around and raised her nose, and the young drake casually turned to face his approaching father.

"Another question," Farrigrall began. "Why exactly do you do that?"

Sitting catlike in front of his son, the Desert Lord countered, "Do what?"

"Land so hard like that," the young drake clarified.

"It's a show of dominance," Ralligor explained. "As the biggest dragon on the island, I demonstrate my strength to other dragons when I land."

Farrigrall nodded. "That's why you don't do that around Agarxus."

"That's why."

Drawing his head back, Farrigrall announced, "So, I should start doing that."

Ralligor raised a scaly eyebrow.

"When you aren't about," the young drake added.

The Desert Lord confirmed this with a slow nod. The big dragon turned his eyes to Falloah, to Kyshira, then back to the young drake. "I'll return in the morning and we can fly the perimeter of your range."

"I would like that," Farrigrall said in a low voice.

Ralligor looked to the scarlet and asked, "You staying here for a while or returning to your lair?"

Falloah looked to the young drake and replied, "I'll stay for a while." Her attention returned to the Desert Lord and she cocked up an eyebrow. "Then, perhaps, I'll end up at *your* lair."

He also cocked an eyebrow up, then he looked to his son and ordered, "Keep your humans from disturbing Agarxus. I think he wants to stay for a few days as a statement to Terrwrathgrawr and his minions. I'll see you sometime in the morning."

Farrigrall watched as the big black dragon turned and swept himself into the sky, his eyes on him as he turned and turned north, and he said under his breath, "I shall eagerly await your return, Father."

CHAPTER 17

Days passed. Terrwrathgrawr and his minions did not return, and in fact, did not even approach the Territhan range again. Agarxus eventually left, apparently to attend to his meeting with his northern rival, and Falloah departed only hours later. With the crisis over, the people of Shoreline began to return to their village. Peak Village was well underway rebuilding and repairing the damage left by the invading dragons and it seemed as if life was finally returning to normal, but for one important detail.

Kyshira still found herself apprehensive about living on an island inhabited by humans and surrounded by crocodiles. While she felt safe at her drake's side, she always seemed anxious in his absence and would, more often than not, perch atop the mountain in the center of the island until his return. This day found him departing early with the powerful Desert Lord, his father, to patrol the edge of his range and perhaps learn more about things that only an older drake could teach a young drake, and the young blue laid on the top of the mountain in the center of the island as she scanned the sky and the land and lake all around, clearly anxious for his return. There was a large flat spot, formerly a lookout, some kind of post where sentries could see for miles and watch for incoming danger. A few artifacts remained—an old firepit for colder weather, what had been some kind of shelter and was now a collapsed pile of ancient wood—such signs that humans had once spent time up there. Now, it was a perch for dragons that was about ten paces across at its widest.

Unbeknownst to the young dragoness, there was a trail that led to the top of the mountain, one that twisted and turned along ledges and corkscrewed ever higher until it reached the peak, and a teenage girl made the long, exhausting trek toward the top.

Josslee found the Zondaen attire she had been given at Caipiervell not only fit her very well but offered better protection against the chill that was brought by the winds of mid-autumn. This attire was also better for moving and especially climbing, and she reached the top of the mountain and the dragoness in short order, a little out of breath and feeling good about finally arriving.

Sitting catlike as she scanned the horizon, Kyshira heard the approach of the girl and slowly turned her head and eyes as she approached, and wore no readable expression.

Josslee set her hands on her hips as she raised her brow and looked up to the little dragoness. "You spend an awful lot of time up here when Farg is away."

Kyshira just stared back at her for long seconds, then she turned her head to look down on the village.

"You also don't seem very comfortable when he's gone," the girl added.

Releasing a hard breath through her nose, the young dragoness turned her eyes down.

"Many in the village are growing concerned about you."

Kyshira's gaze strayed to the girl, and finally she confessed, "No, I'm not comfortable down there without him."

Glancing about, Josslee found a large block of stone and strode to it, sat down facing the dragoness, and looked up at her again. "Are you comfortable with me?"

The dragoness responded with a little shrug. "I suppose so."

"You flew me around the lake," Josslee reminded. "I like to think we're friends. You're involved with my brother, so I'd like us to be."

"It's odd you call him your brother," Kyshira said.

"To many people it is," Josslee agreed, "but I've never known a time without him, and I hope I never will."

"I hope I'll never be without him, too," the dragoness confessed.

Josslee smiled. "You really like him, don't you?"

Kyshira looked away again.

A broader smile took the girl's mouth and she nodded. "I thought so."

"He's the first drake... The first dragon to ever stand up for me, and he was willing to even stand against the Landmaster for me." Kyshira's eyes slid back to the girl and just the hint of a smile curled her mouth. "I suppose I felt something for him even before that."

Josslee laughed. "You have yet to realize what a huge pain in the backside he can be!"

"Certain I will in time," the dragoness assured. "The humans here seem very fond of him."

"He's one of us," Josslee confirmed. "He's family. For as long as I can remember he has always helped the village, bringing in fish, building things and mostly defending us from crocodiles and bandits and invaders. The other villages even call on him for help from time to time."

Kyshira turned her eyes down. "It must be good for him to know he has such an important place in his life."

Leaning her head slightly, Josslee observed, "You seem to not know about your own."

The dragoness glanced at her. "I've spent a lifetime running away from things and being afraid of everything. Even humans tried to kill me, especially when I was young and much smaller."

"No more running away," Josslee insisted. "This is your home and you will always be welcome."

The little dragoness shrugged again. "I suppose."

"And," Josslee added, "you and Farg are the only dragons here. There is nothing else for you to be afraid of."

"I'm afraid of big crocodiles," Kyshira mumbled, "and we seem to be surrounded by them."

"Just like everyone else," Josslee confirmed. "Except Farg. I don't think he's afraid of anything."

"All the more reason I'm so uncomfortable when he's gone," the little dragoness admitted.

Josslee stared back at the small dragoness—and understood what she was feeling. She pushed herself up and dusted off her backside, then she approached the dragoness, realizing that, sitting, she appeared to be just over half of Farrigrall's size, and she ordered, "Come on. Let's go down to the village. I want to introduce you to people."

Kyshira glanced at her again. "I don't know. They seem busy with things."

"They're rebuilding the drying huts and some houses." Josslee raised her brow. "Maybe we can help them. My father's already down there helping put the timbers up on one of the drying huts, and we have little time until winter arrives."

Looking fully down to the village, Kyshira heaved another heavy breath, then she lowered herself to her belly and grumbled, "Oh, come on."

Kyshira landed near the water and about thirty paces from where much of the village was trying to complete a drying hut. Its stone walls were in place and now several men from the village were struggling to get the timbers for the high-pitched roof in place. They were rather large and cut square, about the size a man's thigh, for the most part, and were clearly quite heavy. Another, thicker timber was held in place by these structures on each end and a rope was thrown over to help pull the next toward it. Half of them were in place to form rafters in the shape of an A and the next was going up with some difficulty. Three men pushed from below, two stood atop the wall to steady it, and three others pulled the rope from the other side.

A notch about half a man's height from the lower end of the timber would seat atop a straight timber laid along the top of the wall, and it was less than half a height from sliding into place when a man on the other side shouted, "Watch out! Rope's fraying!"

"Damn!" one of the men pushing from below swore. "Get ready to run, boys! That rope goes and we'll have us a problem."

"We don't need no more delays!" another barked. "Get it in place!"

Without further warning, the rope snapped and all of the weight was suddenly flung toward the inside of the structure to cause untold damage and mayhem, and men all around fled.

Before the timber fell half way, it impacted the waiting hand of the little blue dragoness and she stopped it cold. Studying the rest of the structure only briefly, she lifted it upward, her eyes on the top main beam which was just half a height over her head, and she carefully maneuvered it into place and set the notch down perfectly on the wall.

All of the men grew silent.

The little dragoness' eyes danced from one man to the next.

One of the men, a brawny, bearded fellow, stepped toward her and pointed a thick finger up at her as he shouted, "Lass, you help us finish this roof before dark and me next day's catch is yours!"

All of the other men cheered.

Kyshira looked down to Josslee and appeared to smile.

Raising her brow, Josslee informed, "I never said they would not put us to work."

Eight more such timbers were needing to be secured to complete the structure of the roof and, with Kyshira's help, they were all up in just over half an hour. Pegs were hammered in as quickly as she could raise the timbers. And before long, flat slats were being put in place by men on ladders as well as the dragoness. A young dragon was helping to build the future of this village once again!

No ladders were needed for lifting supplies to the men on the roof who were finishing their tasks as Kyshira handed slats, timbers, and boards one by one. She was just tall enough to get them up to the men awaiting them and wore a little smile as they made her feel more and more helpful.

Turning her head as she handed a slat to a waiting carpenter, she took many quick sniffs, then looked to the man and asked, "What am I smelling? It smells wonderful!"

He took the slat and passed it on. "That's yesterday's catch drying in the sun. We get this smokehouse done and we'll be ready to preserve it so that we won't starve come winter."

She reached down and picked up the next slat, her eyes on it as she said, "Well, it smells good as it is. I'll bet the wind carries it..." Her eyes widened and she raised her head, then she wheeled around and looked to the A-frames that were lining the road that led to the water, the many poles between them that suspended the drying fish, and she whispered, "The wind." Backing away, she looked around her, her eyes darting about, and she raised her nose as another scent reached her.

Everyone stopped and looked to her, and suddenly all was quiet.

Kyshira backed away, opened her wings, and swept herself into the air, stroking them harder and harder to go higher, and once she was well aloft, she began to circle the village, her eyes sweeping the lake around them. Once she was high enough, she could see the ripples on the water forming three Vs, and heading toward the shore. From this high up, she could see how large they were, could see that all three of them were far larger than she was. Looking to the people who had gathered to watch, the humans who had taken her in and accepted her, she knew that a terrible threat was approaching, one that they had, themselves, unwittingly summoned with their drying fish and the guts and bones of them thrown into the lake.

Movement at the shore of the mainland caught her eyes and she turned fully that way just as the terra dragon that had visited before was sliding into the water. It was larger than even the crocodiles, and she watched it swim right toward the village. Feeling near panic, she raised her nose and trumpeted a loud call for help that echoed throughout the land.

On the ground with the other people, Josslee watched her, her eyes narrowed slightly as she heard the call, one that she had never heard from Farrigrall. She grasped one of the carpenter's shoulders and mumbled, "Something's wrong."

Kyshira spiraled down and landed in the middle of the widest road, quickly folding her wings as she trotted back to the structure she was helping to build.

Josslee ran toward her, and both stopped about four paces apart.

The dragoness looked beyond her to the people who were still gathered beyond and watching, then she frantically advised, "Everyone needs to go hide! Predators are coming!"

"What is coming?" Josslee demanded.

Looking toward the water in the direction of the docks, Kyshira answered, "Crocodiles from that way." She turned her head and looked toward Shoreline. "Terra dragon is coming from that way. They smell the fish that were hung to dry and they are coming for it!"

One of the men shouted, "What can we do?"

A woman who was looking on glanced around her, then looked to the dragoness and yelled to her, "You must stop them, as Farrigrall does!"

Kyshira turned her eyes toward Shoreline and raised her head, still unable to see the approaching terra dragon over the tops of the buildings. She heaved a heavy breath, then she looked down to the girl and admitted, "I am not a match for any one of them, especially that terra dragon. Everyone needs to get to a good hiding place."

Josslee looked around her, and her eyes fixed on her father as he approached. Turning to him, she insisted, "Everyone needs to get to cover. Papa, we need to get the people inside!"

He looked up to Kyshira and asked, "How far out is the terra dragon? How long do we have?"

"Moments," the dragoness replied grimly.

He looked toward the docks. "The crocodiles will stop when they reach the fish." Shaking his head, he added, "That terra dragon is going to be a problem."

Kyshira looked that way, then back to the humans who had accepted her into their population. Heaving a heavy breath, she looked toward Shoreline and ordered, "Get everyone into hiding. I will see if I can occupy it." Without waiting for a response, she opened her wings and swept herself into the air.

Josslee shouted, "Kyshira!"

The dragoness looked back at her and cried, "Get to hiding!"

She circled and veered toward the mountain, stroking her wings to go higher and higher and finally reached the top, and she landed quickly, raised her nose and trumpeted for help as loudly as she could. Scrambling to the west side, she drew a loud gasp as she saw the terra dragon already scrambling ashore, and there were people running to get out of its way who would not escape it in time. These people had accepted her where most of her own kind had not—and she was tired of running and being afraid. Her brow lowered over her eyes and she raised her nose, trumpeted her call for help once more, then she opened her wings and leapt from the mountain top.

The Terra dragon, walking as a giant monitor lizard would, tested the air with its long, forked tongue, then its eyes locked on the fleeing humans before it, those who would never reach the flimsy buildings that would likely not keep them safe, anyway. With a growl, it launched itself into a fast pursuit with open jaws and bared teeth to snare the first meal it overtook.

Only fifty paces away from its intended victims, the blue dragoness slammed onto the ground only ten paces in front of it, dropped to all fours, and gaped her jaws as she roared a mighty challenge through bared teeth.

The terra dragon stopped suddenly and raised its head, wide eyes finding this new challenger. It remembered the last, and quickly realized that this one was much smaller. It snarled, bared its teeth, then opened its jaws and roared and mighty reply.

Kyshira scrambled a few steps back, then she craned her neck around and looked behind her. Many of the people still fleeing were slow moving, perhaps older, and they needed time to get to safety. Looking back to the terra dragon, she knew she was just no match for it, but she stood a better chance against it than the humans it meant to eat. They needed time, and she was sure she could distract it long enough to allow the people to get to somewhere safe. Her eyes narrowed, and for the first time in her life, it was time to go into battle.

Rearing up to make herself seem as large as possible, she half opened her wings, held her claws ready and roared at the terra dragon again. When it started to advance, she stomped toward it and roared still again, and it hesitated. She only needed the standoff to last a couple of moments.

The terra dragon seemed confused as it stared back at its little foe, and it leaned its head almost inquisitively. Surely this little dragon did not mean to fight. Surely! Another growl rolled from it as it hesitantly started forward, and it paused again as the dragoness stomped toward it a second time. Now out of patience, it opened its jaws and lunged!

Kyshira screeched and stroked her wings hard as she leapt over it, and she raised her feet to her as it reared up and tried to bite her as she passed over. She hit the ground and wheeled around fast, sweeping her tail as it turned to face her, and this time she backed away.

It charged and she retreated as it slammed its jaws shut only three paces away, and she continued to scramble backward as it pursued her ever faster, lunging and snapping its jaws each time it thought it was close enough. The dreadful truth finally got through to the dragoness: She was its next intended meal!

Stroking her wings hard as she leapt backward, Kyshira roared at the terra dragon again, drawing its attention to her and back toward the direction from which it had arrived. Having never fought one of these before, she was not sure how to even begin or what to expect from it, but she was determined to keep its attention and give Farrigrall's humans as much time as they needed.

It lunged with gaping jaws and she screeched and darted away from it, veering to one side. It lunged again and snapped its jaws at her and almost got her. She dropped to all fours and scrambled backward, hissing back at the terra dragon as she retreated. It charged and she stroked her wings and leapt backward in retreat, and this time underestimated its speed. As she came down and scrambled backward again, it was upon her and she darted aside, and its jaws closed around her upper wing. She screeched in pain and surprise and tried to bite back at it, but was unable to penetrate its hide, and finally she gaped her jaws and sent a long burst of fire at its neck and shoulder.

Angered, the terra dragon whipped its whole body aside and threw its head over, flinging the little dragoness into a house some distance away.

She crashed partly through one wall back-first and was stopped by something within. She settled on her side into the debris as some of the roof collapsed onto her, and quickly getting her wits about her, she rolled to her feet and from the house and pushed herself up to all fours, and she turned her eyes toward the terra dragon as it lumbered toward her. She tried to back away and give herself some maneuvering room, only to be stopped by a nearby tree. It was only about ten paces away, and now, no matter how fast she went, there was no getting away from it. Still, the young dragoness dug the claws of her feet into the ground and crouched to leap forward, folding her wings tightly to her, and she opened her jaws and blasted it in the face with fire when it was only about ten paces away. When it turned away, she leapt forward with all her strength, tightly folding her wings to her as she found room and retreated.

This time, as it opened its eyes and saw her circling to its left, it opened its jaws and responded with fire of its own!

Boiling flames engulfed much of the dragoness' head and neck and she turned away and screeched as she tried to keep the flames from her eyes and nose, and it would prove to be a horrible mistake.

It charged to her and before she could turn to respond in any way, it crashed into her, knocked her to her side and pinned her there with a clawed forefoot.

Kyshira finally turned her head, her wide eyes fixing on the teeth of the terra dragon as its jaws opened, jaws and teeth that would bring her death. Instinctively, she raised her arm as if to ward off its jaws, and she shrieked as its teeth plunged through skin and deep into the flesh. Movement above and behind the terra dragon drew her attention and she turned her eyes up, seeing a dark red form that was little more than a blur.

Revillee slammed her feet hard onto the top of the terra dragon's head and as she passed, she hit its head hard with the end of her tail. Stroking her wings hard, she turned sharply and gaped her jaws, fire belching forth that hit the top of the terra dragon's head and raked along its back to its tail.

Enraged, the terra dragon abandoned its prospective meal and roared as it turned fully with bared teeth, and it pursued the burgundy dragoness as she turned sharply again and landed.

Her brow low over her eyes, Revillee gaped her jaws and roared a mighty challenge.

This made the terra dragon pause, and with its attention no longer on her, Kyshira rolled to her feet and retreated. She tried to open her wings, but pain ripped through one and it popped loudly, then fell to the ground. She looked to that wing, seeing that it bled from many punctures between the elbow and shoulder. Flying was not going to happen.

Looking past the large terra dragon, Revillee squinted slightly and studied the little blue, how her wing did not hang right, and she seemed to know what had happened. Her eyes found the terra dragon again and she bared her teeth and growled. In her short time as a dragon, she had learned much, especially how to outmaneuver larger predators. She knew her advantages and disadvantages, and one more thing the terra dragon did not know, and she confidently squared off against the much larger predator.

Kyshira backed away, feeling that she had to help somehow, but knowing she could not without getting killed.

Then, her eyes shifted upward as a flash of ocher streaked overhead.

Falloah, much larger than either of the other two dragonesses, did not announce her own approach but instead slammed into the terra dragon's back with all fours, digging claws in and forcing it to the ground. Before leaping off, she bit the terra dragon hard on the back of its neck, driving her teeth in as she opened her wings and leapt off of it. Turning hard, she landed beside the burgundy dragoness and growled something to her, then she stood fully, half opened her wings, and roared a challenge of her own!

Taking to the wing, Revillee flew around the confrontation and landed at the little blue's side, and the two stared back at each other.

Revillee's brow tensed and she admitted, "I was afraid of that smoke wyvern, too."

Her lips tightening and her eyes glossing with tears, Kyshira realized that her friendship with the burgundy dragoness was not over after all.

Raising her head, she informed, "Another is approaching from the shore, one that looks even bigger than this one."

Kyshira clenched her jaw and mumbled, "We can barely handle this one, and there are crocodiles approaching from the south."

Revillee looked that way and growled, then she looked back to her smaller friend, down to her wing, and she shook her head. "Again?"

The little blue growled, and looked back to Falloah and the terra dragon. "Where is Farrigrall?"

"Somewhere with Ralligor," Revillee answered. "I came to..." She looked to the little blue again. "I just wanted to talk. I've missed spending time together." Looking down to Kyshira's wing, she gently took it in her hands and lifted, then abruptly pulled outward and released it with a loud crack.

Kyshira groaned in pain, then she gingerly folded her wing to her and strained to offer, "Thanks."

"How many crocodiles?" Revillee asked as she looked back to the standoff ahead of them.

"Three," the little blue answered. "Farrigrall could easily drive them all away."

"That other terra dragon looked awfully big," Revillee informed. "It might be bigger than him." Her eyes slid to the little blue. "Distract this one here when Falloah needs to rest. I'm going to..." He raised her head and turned abruptly to the struggle before them, and beyond as the second terra dragon scrambled ashore. "Yeah, it's bigger." She grunted. "Wish me luck."

Kyshira watched as the burgundy dragoness swept herself into the sky, then she looked to the standoff before her and heaved a heavy breath. Yelling from the docks drew her attention and she knew the humans were trying to fend off the crocodiles there. Turning back to the duel before her, she raised her head and looked on with widening eyes as the second terra dragon lumbered toward the village center. All that stood between the village and the largest of the terra dragons was Falloah, and she was much smaller and clearly no match for it. Looking back toward the water, she could hear that Farrigrall's humans were losing in their efforts to drive away the crocodiles.

Revillee postured with the smaller terra dragon and circled, and finally the little dragoness felt as if she had some kind of advantage.

Kyshira knew she could not fly, could not even open her wings without dislocating the injured one again, so she stalked closer, crouched and set her feet, digging into the ground beneath her with her claws. The terra dragon may have been nearly twice her size, but it was not paying attention to her, and her eyes narrowed as she rocked back and forth a few times, and finally leapt toward the terra dragon with gaping jaws and her claws ready to dig into its thick hide.

She collided with the terra dragon with all her weight and all the force she could muster, driving her teeth in as hard as she could as she clamped her jaws shut right behind its head. The terra dragon screeched as she plunged her teeth through its thick hide and it stumbled sideways and fell to its side, and Kyshira was thrown over it and to the ground. Quick to roll to her feet, she crouched on all fours and turned to face the terra dragon as it struggled to roll back to its own feet.

Revillee backed away a step, her attention falling on the little blue.

Kyshira looked back at the burgundy dragoness and cried, "The crocodiles! They can't stop them. I'll keep this one occupied!"

With a simple nod, Revillee opened her wings and swept herself into the air, turning hard to the south and flying low over the rooftops.

Her brow lowering over her eyes, Kyshira turned fully on the terra dragon as it got its footing and turned to face her. No more running away. No more surrendering to fear. It was time to fight and show this primitive creature what even a small dragon could do. Her lips slid away from her teeth and a growl escaped her as her brow lowered over her eyes. It was larger and stronger, but she was faster and more nimble, and she intended to make use of this. Unable to use one wing, this fight would have to stay on the ground, but one more disadvantage would not deter the little blue.

A growl rolled from her as it turned fully and widened its stance, its eyes locked on her as if it had found its next meal, and almost defiantly, she gaped her jaws and roared a loud challenge.

Time to fight!

Not waiting for the terra dragon to make its move, Kyshira leapt at him with gaping jaws and belched fire right at its eyes. When it shied away, she slammed her feet hard into its face and kicked off to jump behind it, driving its head to the ground in the process. Not able to use her wings, she twisted in the air and wheeled around to face the terra dragon even before she hit the ground behind it on all fours.

Looking behind her, she could see that Falloah was losing her battle against the larger one. She was trying to keep it distracted, had a wound open and bleeding on her arm near her shoulder. She was backing away from the larger one, and it was advancing.

The larger terra dragon was too far away to use fire, but once again she gaped her jaws and roared, drawing its attention, and this distraction gave the scarlet just enough time to open her wings and sweep herself away, and she gaped and spat fire as she did.

Whipping back as her own opponent turned and charged, the little blue dragoness employed the same tactic, leaping over it, fire to its face, and slamming her feet down hard on its head. This time, she did not spin in the air, rather she landed behind it and looked over her shoulder. It was turning slower, and her eyes narrowed as she turned to meet it. Finally, for perhaps the first time in her life, she was feeling the exhilaration of battle. Sure, it was larger, stronger, but now she knew she could outthink it, and this made her confidence grow.

Perhaps a bit too much.

It charged again, and this time she dodged to the left, and when it corrected and gaped its jaws, she suddenly dug in the claws of her foot and hurled herself the other way with open jaws, flung her head over and slammed her teeth shut around its neck. The momentum of her body carried her to its side, and as it turned to try to get at her, she scrambled backward to stay away from the roaring jaws that snapped at air in a vain attempt to get at her. Kyshira's teeth were sharp, but not well suited for dealing with the scaly armor of the terra dragon. Still, she clung to the mouthful of hide and flesh she had, wrenching her head back and forth to work her teeth in ever deeper. Raising her hand to its back, she dug in her claws as best she could and raked at the thick scales of its side with her foot.

Roaring in anger, the terra dragon turned and turned as it tried to dislodge the stubborn little dragoness, but she held firm and was working her way onto its back even as it spun and wrestled to get at her.

She growled and wrenched her head back and forth again. She pulled upward with the claws she had dug into the hide of its back, and as it turned again with gaping jaws, she lifted a leg and was clinging to its back and side with both hands and both feet, and was refusing to let go even as she found herself quickly tiring.

Bending its body toward her, it continued to bite at her in futility, but it raised its hind foot and began to claw at her, and its claws found her tail and hind leg. Swiping and kicking repeatedly, its claws finally got a good grip between her tail and leg and with one mighty kick, it finally dislodged her.

Her teeth tearing from its thick hide, Kyshira was sent tumbling to the ground and she rolled to a stop on her back. Before she could get her bearings, its heavy, clawed hand slammed down on her chest and crushed her to the ground beneath.

Now was a good time to panic.

Screeching hysterically, she clawed at its arm as she kicked at its side and belly and raked the claws of her feet as hard as she could against its thick hide. She blasted its face with fire and it only shied away for a few seconds before opening its jaws, and her eyes widened further as it lowered its teeth toward her head.

Closing her eyes, she turned her face away and crooned as she awaited the inevitable.

This time it was the terra dragon that screeched as long, spike teeth clamped down on its head with a sickening crunch, teeth that were driven by jaws that were more than powerful enough to plunge those teeth through its thick, scaly hide and crush bone.

With the terra dragon's head clamped in his mighty jaws, Farrigrall stood fully and took a step back as he used all of his weight to fling the smaller predator away from the little blue, and he growled as he watched it hit the ground and roll to a stop about twenty paces away. Looking down to Kyshira, he met her eyes, then he ordered, "Wait here," as he turned back on the stunned terra dragon as it struggled back to its feet.

Looking beyond it, his eyes narrowed as he saw Falloah backing away from the other terra dragon. Glancing up, he opened his jaws and roared a mighty challenge at the larger one, and he turned to stride that way.

The first had regained its wits and gotten to its feet, and as the black dragon strode by, it gaped its jaws and charged when his foe was barely two paces away.

Without even looking that way, Farrigrall slammed his fist down hard on top of the smaller terra dragon's head, knocking it back to the ground.

The larger terra dragon turned to face the new challenger and responded with a roar of its own.

Bleeding from a few scratches and a bite to her arm, Falloah took the opportunity to back away, her eyes on her son as she retreated. This terra dragon was at least as big as the black dragon, likely heavier, and faced off with this new threat with no fear.

Kyshira rolled to her feet and faced the smaller terra dragon as it stood and looked back to the black dragon, then she drew her head back as it turned fully to her. Opening her jaws slightly, she trumpeted a call for help and backed away this time.

The terra dragon charged toward her.

Ralligor's feet slammed onto the ground on both sides of the terra dragon's tail. His hands hit the ground at its shoulders, half a second later and sword size teeth driven by jaws of unimaginable strength plunged through thick, scaly hide, muscle, and bone right behind the terra dragon's head.

The terra dragon shrieked as the Desert Lord stood fully with the much smaller predator clamped in his jaws. He violently shook his head with a deep growl, and after a sickening crunch, his prey went limp. Stepping back with one foot, Ralligor wheeled around and flung the now lifeless terra dragon from him and watched as it rolled to a stop.

As he turned fully and looked to the other battle between his son and the larger terra dragon, Kyshira stood and also looked that way. Farrigrall seemed fearless and roared as he charged this opponent that at least equaled him in size. She feared for him, and at the same time was awed by his apparent fearlessness. Still, she looked up at the Desert Lord and frantically asked, "Aren't you going to help him?"

Ralligor did not even look her way as he casually sat catlike beside her and countered, "He doesn't need me fighting his battles for him."

Farrigrall and the terra dragon collided and pushed against each other with all their strength, kicking up dust and rocks and each growling and roaring as they tried to get in a critical bite. Claws raked at scales and heavy hide. Teeth clacked as they slammed shut against air. The black dragon's tail whipped about, and he finally drew his head back, using his longer neck to his advantage, and sent his gaping jaws down toward the back of the terra dragon's neck.

This wrestling, this test of strength continued for a moment, and it seemed that Farrigrall tired of it and patience abandoned him. Unable to best the terra dragon with strength alone, he sidestepped and used all of his power and weight to twist his body hard and topple his opponent and send it hard to the ground on its side. Without hesitation, he gaped his jaws and slammed his teeth hard around the terra dragon's head and lower jaw with a sickening crunch.

With a loud screech, the terra dragon violently struggled to right itself and free its head of the black dragon's jaws. A hind leg repeatedly kicked and scraped at the dragon's body and finally got enough grip with its claws to push the dragon off balance and send him stumbling away. Long teeth were ripped from the terra dragon's head as its opponent staggered to keep his balance, and it was finally able to roll back to its feet and face the dragon once again.

Farrigrall looked down to his side where three long scrapes went from his belly to his side and nearly to his back, one bleeding slowly. His brow low over his eyes, he growled deeply like distant thunder and turned his full attention back on the terra dragon.

Kyshira watched with her full attention as the young drake launched himself into battle again with his jaws gaping. The terra dragon appeared to be a match for him, but he roared and attacked fearlessly, and she felt her heart thundering hard behind her breast as she watched the raging battle.

Once again, Farrigrall clamped his jaws hard around his opponent's head, and Ralligor just growled and folded his arms, shaking his head in clear disapproval of his son's tactics.

Revillee shrieked and Kyshira raised her head and looked that way with wide eyes. A high-pitched roar from the other dragoness drew a loud gasp from the little blue and she cried, "The crocodiles!"

Ralligor casually looked over his shoulder at her, then his attention strayed to the battle on the south beach. He heaved a heavy breath, looked back to the fight with which his son still struggled, then he looked back to the little blue.

She stared back at him anxiously.

With a thunderous growl, Ralligor shook his head, then he turned and stomped toward the south beach.

Kyshira followed.

They arrived to find three large crocodiles well ashore, several men of the village with gaffs and oars trying to fight off two of them, and the largest squaring off against the burgundy dragoness. This one was much larger than Revillee, much heavier, and was advancing on her with gaping jaws as she held her body low, her own jaws agape, and she was backing away toward one of the unfinished drying huts.

Ralligor growled again and lowered his body almost parallel to the ground, and he charged the largest crocodile with long strides and a nightmarish roar.

The largest of the crocodiles whipped around to face the new threat with its jaws wide, but the black dragon was already upon it and slammed his jaws shut around the crocodile's head and the back of its neck. This crocodile was much larger than the little burgundy dragoness, but was dwarfed by the massive black dragon. There was a loud crunch as teeth plunged through thick hide and bone and Ralligor rose up and backed away a step, hoisting the crocodile from the ground as he crushed it between his jaws with all his might.

The other two crocodiles turned toward the largest as the black dragon whipped his head back and forth hard to work in his sword sized teeth further, and ultimately broke its neck.

Ralligor was not finished. He stepped forward and planted a foot solidly on the middle of the crocodile's tail and wrenched his head the other way, his teeth doing their murderous work as they severed the big crocodile's head with one mighty jerk. Raising his nose, he opened his jaws wide and lunged forward, collecting the crocodile's head further into his mouth. Twice more and he was able to close his jaws and swallow his prize, then, slowly, he turned his full attention down to the other two.

They stared up at him for long seconds and one slowly moved a foot back.

The big dragon's eyes narrowed and he bared his teeth, and when he snorted through his nose, the two crocodiles wheeled around with all the speed they could muster and scrambled back toward the water, splashing in and diving out of sight in seconds.

Raising a brow, Ralligor watched the water calm, then he turned back toward the north, looking over the buildings of the village to find his son still in a pitched battle with the largest of the terra dragons. A growl escaped him and he shook his head again, lowered his body and strode back that way.

Kyshira looked back to the water where the crocodiles had disappeared, then she turned her attention to Revillee, meeting her eyes.

Together, they turned north and followed the big black dragon to the fray that still raged.

Ralligor had arrived back at the field where they had watched the fight with Farrigrall and the terra dragon a few moments earlier, and as the two dragonesses arrived and took his sides, he laid down to his belly and folded his arms before him as he watched the younger black dragon throw himself into his slightly larger opponent yet again.

Locked in a head on wrestling match, each bit at the other, clawed at the other, but neither could find a decisive advantage, nor could either get a good bite in against the armor of the other. Roars were exchanged and the two pushed against each other and circled, but once again neither could overwhelm the other in brute strength alone. It was the terra dragon that found an advantage in footing, sweeping its tail and spinning with all its might, and it was able to throw its opponent off balance and hurl him hard to the ground and toward the audience of dragons and humans who anxiously watched.

Farrigrall rolled to a stop about ten paces from his father and clumsily scrambled to his feet. While he was trying to get his wits back and at his most vulnerable, the terra dragon charged on all fours like some kind of huge and armored monitor lizard, but a look and a warning snort from the bigger black dragon stopped it in its tracks and it raised its bloody head and just stared back from about forty paces away. Clearly, it was not interested in provoking a dragon of that size and power.

With a deep growl, Farrigrall looked to his father, his brow low over his eyes.

Ralligor raised his brow and simply asked, "Learning yet?"

"I trust you have a suggestion?" the young drake demanded.

"Or twenty," Ralligor assured. "We'll start with the basics. First, a terra dragon's skull is much thicker and heavier made than ours or even the crocodiles you are used to fighting. Male terra dragons bite at each other's heads in disputes over territories and mates all the time. You might try using what's inside *your* skull and go with a tactic that hasn't already failed you a dozen times in this fight."

Farrigrall looked back to the terra dragon and snarled, "So what do you suggest?"

The big drake's eyes also slid to the terra dragon. "An experienced dragon would go for the throat or right behind his opponent's head where he can use his teeth to cut through hide and muscle there and crush the bones of its neck." He shrugged. "Works nicely for me, but feel free to fight him any way you feel is best."

The terra dragon backed away and barked a roar.

Turning fully and holding his body low to engage the terra dragon again, Farrigrall said, "Behind the head."

"Behind the head," Ralligor confirmed.

Farrigrall snorted through his nose and slowly lowered his body, his lips sliding away from his teeth as he braced to charge into battle again. With a mighty roar, he hurled himself into the fight head-on with his larger opponent.

And he clearly had taken his father's advice to heart.

Right before they collided, Farrigrall slammed his clawed hand as hard as he could into the side of the terra dragon's head, and as his opponent's head was knocked aside by the brutal impact and it staggered, the young dragon planted a foot and turned as hard as he could. In the same motion he lunged and sent his gaping jaws down hard onto the terra dragon's neck, slamming them shut there as hard as he could and driving the larger predator all the way to the ground. With and angry roar, the terra dragon pushed itself back up, struggling under the weight of the young dragon, and it tried to turn and counter-attack, but its nimble foe remained out of range of those snapping jaws.

Wrenching his head back and forth, Farrigrall drove his teeth all the way through thick hide and dense muscle, and he began to taste blood. His foe struggled harder, his feet scraping against the ground as he groped for traction. Each time it managed to get its footing, the young drake would force it back down, and he slammed a hand hard onto the top of the terra dragon's head, the other on its back, his jaws straining to close fully with his opponent's neck between them.

The terra dragon roared, then screeched as the young black dragon hurled himself backward. Teeth plunged further in and there was a sickening crunch, and the terra dragon's body suddenly became limp.

Farrigrall dropped his vanquished foe and stared down at it for long seconds before turning his attention to his father, his brow low over his eyes as he met those of the Desert Lord.

Ralligor just stared back with no readable expression, and his only reaction was a slight and subtle nod.

The young drake nodded back, and he looked around as the villagers began to emerge from their hiding places, and many began to clap and cheer.

Kyshira's eyes danced about as the villagers approached and cheered and clapped the young black drake, and many walked by her, giving the Desert Lord a wide berth as they did. Looking down at her forearm and the punctures left by the terra dragon's teeth, she could only feel that she had failed these people, these humans who had only just begun to accept her. Her first real test to protect them had ended in dismal failure. With a heavy heart, she pushed herself up and turned, walking away from the budding celebration under the watchful eyes of the black dragon and Revillee.

The two dragons watched the little blue as she strode slowly to the mine, and the young burgundy dragoness looked to the black dragon with her brow tense and she crooned in a low voice.

Ralligor growled and looked back to his son, stood, and strode toward him as the humans fled his path.

The little blue dragoness' heart grew heavier and heavier as she watched the villagers rally around their saviors, the big drakes who had won the day where she had failed. Falloah and Revillee also watched and those villagers seemed to clamor for their attention, and somehow, amid all the cheers, she somehow felt all alone once again. She heaved a heavy breath as she watched the celebration, then she turned around and strode toward the mountain, toward the mine. Stopping just outside, she stared inside, into the torchlight that burned within. Slowly, she lowered herself to the ground and laid to her belly, crossing her arms before her. Her eyes found the wound to her forearm, another reminder of this failure. The blood had not yet coagulated and it still bled slowly, and her wing ached horribly.

Ralligor looked over his shoulder and saw the little blue lying by herself, and his brow tensed. Turning his attention back to his son, he informed, "We need to go. Attend to your humans and I'll look in on you in a day or two. And you should think about staying close by for a few days. If they are going to be drying their fish out in the open then it's sure to draw in more predators."

Farrigrall nodded, staring up at him as he acknowledged, "I'll do that."

Glancing back at the little blue, the Desert Lord added, "And go attend your dragoness." He looked to the scarlet and barked, "Falloah. We are leaving. Revillee, head north and make sure your drake is staying alert."

The burgundy dragoness raised her head and protested, "But I want to stay and... " She fell silent as the black dragon's eyes narrowed, then she growled, lowering her brow as she called, "I'll see you tomorrow, Kyshira."

As she opened her wings and took flight, the two drakes looked to each other again and Ralligor ordered, "Get yourself in order. I'll show you more in the next few days." Humans fled his path as he strode toward the west shore and opened his wings.

Falloah gave her son a long look and a little smile, then she turned and followed the Desert Lord.

He watched them take flight to the cheers of the village, then he turned his full attention to the little blue who lay near the mine, and his brow tensed, his lips tightening as he saw her there.

Kyshira just lay where she was and stared at the ground before her as she pondered what to do next. Ordered by the Landmaster to stay where she was and at Farrigrall's side, she also found this impossible under the circumstances.

Movement to her right drew her attention and her gaze found Josslee just walking up on her with her eyes fixed on the little dragoness' wounded arm.

Folding her arms, Josslee raised her brow as she looked up at the blue dragoness and she spat, "That was really foolish." As the dragoness turned her eyes down, she smiled and added, "And I think that was the bravest thing I ever saw."

Kyshira's eyes snapped back to the girl.

Other people began to approach, and one woman strode to her with clean linens, pushing past Josslee as she laid the cloth over the dragoness' wounded arm and pressed it in place. A man appeared behind her, and he was carrying ropes. As the makeshift bandage was finally settled into place, he looked up to the dragoness and ordered, "Raise your arm up, Lass." When she complied, he wrapped the rope around her arm, running it under and then over the bandage several times to hold it in place.

Still another man, one who she knew as a fisherman who had been helping with the rebuild of the drying hut she had assisted with, strode to her with a rather large carp in his arms, and as he reached her, he ordered, "Open up."

Hesitantly, she lowered her head and opened her jaws, and when she did, he tossed the heavy fish into her mouth. She collected it between her teeth, then raised her head and swallowed the gift whole, and when she looked back down to the man, he was giving her a smile and a nod.

"We'll need to keep your strength up," he informed. "We'll work on that drying hut more tomorrow." He turned and walked away, saying, "Get you some rest, dragoness."

Farrigrall collapsed to his belly right beside her, and when she looked his way, she found him staring down at her with his brow high over his eyes.

She stared back sheepishly as she awaited her inevitable scolding.

"That was amazingly foolish," he informed, and when she lowered her eyes, he added, "And I'm very proud of you."

Her gaze snapped back to him and she raised her head.

"In the future," he continued, "why don't you stick to the smaller ones and let me handle the big ones."

Josslee looked up at him with her brow high over her eyes and she loudly informed, "Maybe if you wouldn't wander away for so long, she wouldn't have to put herself at risk so."

Farrigrall growled and regarded the girl with narrow eyes. "Shouldn't you be off annoying someone else?"

She smiled sweetly back and replied. "No. I've set the whole day aside just to annoy you."

The drake snarled, "That was your invitation to go away, Josslee."

Kyshira's attention was shifting from one to the next as they spoke.

The girl folded her arms and raised her chin, and she defiantly spat back, "What if I don't want to?"

Farrigrall growled again, then he looked behind him and called, "Mama!"

Josslee turned and began to stride away, yelling back, "I'm going! For goodness sake, you are such a big baby!"

"I am not!" the dragon shouted after her. Looking back to the little dragoness, he found her staring up at him with an expression that was somewhere between amused and perplexed. "She's always been a difficult little brat," he explained.

Kyshira nodded in slight motions.

One of the men of the village approached and declared, "Those crocodiles ravaged the fish we were drying. How are we supposed to get through the winter now?"

A mumbling of concern rippled through the people who had gathered to show support for the young dragoness.

Farrigrall's eyes swept the small crowd, then he looked behind him, then back to them. "There's plenty of meat over there that is freshly killed."

Kyshira added before she realized, "Ralligor killed a crocodile down there, too." A cold feeling swept through her as many eyes fell upon her.

Another of the fishermen pointed with his thumb over his shoulder. "Some of the men have already begun butchering it." His attention went to the drake. "We more thought that those you killed were for you and your little wife."

"We've always shared in this village," the dragon reminded. He drew his head back and barked, "Wife?"

In a low voice, Kyshira asked, "What does that mean?"

Also in a low voice, he mumbled, "It's a human word for mate."

An older woman of the village beamed a big smile and declared, "I always knew the day would come when our Farg would find himself a special girl."

Another woman said, "We should plan a binding ceremony!"

A ripple of agreement began among the women in the small crowd.

The older woman took one of Kyshira's fingers and tugged on her, urging, "Come along, dear. Let the men folk figure out the butchering of them crocodiles. We have a ceremony to plan."

As more women gathered toward her, the little dragoness looked up at her drake with her brow high over her eyes.

He heaved a hard breath and mumbled, "You should go with them. They're never going to let it rest."

Urged on by the tugging on her finger, Kyshira stood, her eyes still on her drake as she began to turn, and a little smile curled her mouth, one that widened as he smiled back, ever so slightly, and nodded to her.

Finally, she turned and followed the small group of women, about seven in number, as they led the way toward a part of the village where there were many shops, and an open space near the village hall where they could gather.

And for the first time in her young life, she felt accepted, was not afraid, and for the first time, felt as if she were, somehow, loved.

CHAPTER 18

Nearly a month passed with no further incidents involving large predators, even crocodiles. Most of the village was rebuilt, with the help of a couple of dragons, firewood was brought in by boat to keep homes and shops warm through the long winter, but the fish they lived on had seemingly disappeared, going to the deepest parts of the lake or migrating as far south as they could to find the warmest water. The air was growing colder and in the mornings the people's breath was as smoke as they exhaled. While the first frost was still seemingly weeks away, there was a definite chill in the air, and the people of Peak Lake Village found themselves bundled up against it most days.

The only residents who did not seem to be very uncomfortable were the dragons, and often they spent the afternoons at each other's sides and would lie in the open and bask in the sun for hours, and more often than not, they would doze during this time.

Once a day, Farrigrall would patrol the western border, occasionally meeting his father as he flew toward the north to spend time with him, learn from him, and acquaint himself with his own kind as best he could.

He and the village he protected had settled into a routine, but it was time for his identity as a dragon to be tested once again, and it would happen on what all considered to be the start of just another normal day.

High sun meant that it was time for a nap in the sunlight and Farrigrall and Kyshira lay in their favorite spot on the west side of town, sprawled in the sunshine and facing the village of Shoreline only a third of a league away. With Terrwrathgrawr gone, the people had returned there and trade with Peak Village had resumed with great vigor.

The two dragons watched the bustling activity across the lake with absent interest, those crossing the long bridge, and the fishing boats that now ferried people and supplies from the island to the mainland and back. It seemed that things had finally returned to normal, but for the addition of one more dragon.

In short order, eyes grew heavy and they drifted off to sleep lying side by side.

An unknown time later, some subtle commotion among the villagers alerted the young drake and his eyes slowly opened, and they focused on the little white unicorn who stood a few paces before him.

Shahly stared at him, and long seconds later, she informed, "I have questions."

He blinked as he stared back at her, and finally mumbled, "Questions."

"Questions," she confirmed.

Leedon walked into view and took the unicorn's side, leaning on his walking stick as he smiled and said, "Unicorns are far more inquisitive than most realize."

Kyshira opened her eyes and raised her head, showing a little alarm at a unicorn suddenly standing so close to her.

Shahly glanced at her and greeted, "Hi."

Farrigrall also raised his head, his attention on the wizard as he said, "It's good to see you again."

"Always good to see you," the wizard assured. "Just thought I would pop by and see how you are faring, now that the crisis has passed."

The young drake shrugged. "Falling back into my old routines, I suppose, with a few others added to them."

Leedon's eyes slid to the little dragoness, and he raised his brow. "Changes are often difficult, but as you can see, wonderful things can result." He leaned his head and looked behind the dragons. "Seems to be a bit of commotion over there.

The two dragons looked behind them.

There was, indeed, a commotion behind them, one that was moving away toward the east side of the island. Something of great interest was over there and it seemed that most of the village was in a hurry to go and see.

"The east docks," Farrigrall observed. "No fishing boats went that way this morning." He pushed himself up and turned that way, his full attention on the other side of the island. Leaning his head slightly, he hesitantly began to stride that way, his body low and almost parallel to the ground as he fell in behind the crowds of people who were already on the way.

Stopping behind the many people who were gathered at the east docks, he looked beyond and out into the lake as he saw three large barges approaching. The closest of them was also the largest and was about thirty paces from the end of the pier. It was at least fifty paces in length, over ten paces wide, and was propelled by forty long yellow oars on each side, each of which was pulled by two men. Its wooden hull was thick and rather solid, curled upward in the front where a platform was built, one where half a dozen men stood who watched the big craft approach the modest timber pier. A hut rose from the center of the barge, one what was covered with a canvas roof over the timbers of its construction, and was about ten paces long and four wide with dark yellow canvas walls and flaps for windows. The whole thing was painted a dark green and was trimmed in yellow, as were the smaller two, but the largest was much more elaborately decorated. Yellow tassels hung from the roof of the hut in the center and a banner flew over it, a green field with a yellow bird of prey in the center. It was trimmed in gold ribbon which took easily to the wind.

Many soldiers were on board and formed four rows in straight lines just inside the oarsmen.

Farrigrall watched as the big barge turned its right side to the pier and ropes were thrown to it by the many men who would help to bring it in and tie it off.

Even holding his body low, Farrigrall's head was still over a full man's height above the heads of the men present, and he garnered a few looks from the villagers as he stared at the barge that was tying up to the pier. His eyes narrowing slightly, he asked in a low voice, "What is happening?"

One of the men half turned and looked up at him, answering, "Looks like an emissary from that king on the north end of the lake."

The dragon's brow lowered and he snorted through his nose. "This the same king who claims our village as part of his kingdom but doesn't lift a finger to aid us in our times of need?"

The man looked back to the barge and replied, "The very one."

"What do you figure he wants this time?" The young drake asked.

Another man, still watching the barge, replied, "They haven't come here looking for taxes for quite a number of seasons. Could be they're finally calling on us for that."

With a growl, Farrigrall scoffed, "Always looking to take what they can and never giving anything back."

The first man nodded and agreed, "That is how you define royalty."

Kyshira took the drake's left side and also looked to the barge, but she did not ask questions nor even speak her mind, she just watched.

Leedon and Shahly took his other side, though they could not see what was happening through the crowd, but watched nonetheless.

Before anyone noticed, Leedon looked to the little unicorn and simply said, "Shahly."

She huffed a hard breath and mumbled, "Okay." Folding her essence around herself, she concealed her presence from all but those who already knew she was there.

Josslee pushed her way through the crowd and toward the dragons, and once she reached them, she walked between the two and behind them, and she stopped halfway down Farrigrall's tail. Looking up at it, she reached and leapt upward, getting a good grasp on one of his dorsal scales with both hands. Pulling herself up, she swung her lower body and got a leg up over his tail and was able to climb upon it, and once up there, she stood and made her way up his tail, along his back and neck, and finally reached his head where she straddled his neck and laid over his head between his horns. Resting her elbows on the top of his head, she settled her jaw in her hands and watched the final docking of the barge from one of the best vantage points in the village.

Farrigrall glanced up and asked, "What are they saying down there?"

"Just a lot of guessing," the girl replied. "They are not even flying the King's banner, so I'm guessing he's not even on board."

The dragon growled. "Couldn't be bothered to leave his comfortable castle for a visit."

The first man he had talked to before grumbled, "Typical."

A woman ahead of him kept her attention on the barge, but added, "The nobles no more care about us than they do about animals in the field.

The crowd made a path for the village elders as they approached in a single file line, led by the foreman in the black drape.

There was only a low mumbling of discussion among the crowd that had gathered as the village elders strode to the pier, then spread themselves out in their respective places to await the emissary.

First to walk from the barge to the pier were twelve soldiers or guards, each carrying a long spear that was over a man's height long. They wore the green and yellow tunics of the kingdom, more elaborately embroidered than the other soldiers who waited on the barges. They walked in twos about halfway down the pier before stopping and turning toward each other, leaving just enough room for someone to pass between them.

Two more soldiers stepped onto the pier, these with the same tunics, but with much more gold embroidery. They also wore gold-colored helmets. They did not carry spears, rather they had swords on their sides in elaborate scabbards, and they strode between the rows of soldiers and right to the village elders.

Behind them was a well-dressed, plump man who also wore an elaborately embroidered tunic, a green hat with gold embroidery. His trousers were that dark green with yellow stipes down the sides that were trimmed in gold, and he wore tall black boots halfway up his shins. This was the emissary, and he walked with slow, purposeful steps, and he seemed to be taking his time as he strode between the soldiers and toward the village elders. He was followed by two young women, one of whom carried a short board with parchments fastened to it. They wore gowns in the kingdom's colors and largely kept their eyes down, their heads slightly bowed as they followed about two paces behind the Emissary.

Farrigrall made his way a little closer to hear what was said, turning his head slightly as he did. Dragons are already endowed with excellent hearing, but this could still be a strain from almost forty paces away.

Reaching the elders at last, the emissary smiled and extended his arms, revealing that his sleeves draped almost half an arm's length beneath them. "Good people," he began pleasantly. "I come bearing the good and just will of the realm."

The elders all bowed their heads to the emissary.

The emissary continued, "We have not visited for many seasons, and it has been brought to our attention that this village has not offered its taxes for at least three seasons."

A ripple of nervous murmuring began.

"But," he continued, "his Majesty has graciously extended his forgiveness for this oversight, given that this village may not be of great means. Still, a debt is owed and I am here to offer a solution to resolve this debt."

One of the men in front of Farrigrall mumbled, "A debt for what?"

"Therefore," the emissary went on, "It is decided that, instead of the gold or silver owed by this village, you shall, instead, pay the debt with conscripts of not less than thirty young men of the village who will serve in his Majesty's army for a period of not less than five seasons."

Voices could be heard among the villagers growing louder in protest, and the village elders all turned and gestured for them to be silent.

The Emissary stood still, folding his hands before him as his eyes swept from one end of the gathered villagers to the other and back. His lips were tight with disapproval. When, finally, the crowd was orderly and quiet again, he resumed. "In addition, his Majesty decrees that this village shall offer as conscripts no less than ten girls over the age of ten seasons and no older than twenty to serve the kingdom for a period of not less than five seasons." His eyes became hard as he fixed them on Farrigrall. "He has also decreed that your dragon shall be delivered to the castle the day your conscripts are delivered to us."

The young drake drew his head back.

Josslee shrieked a loud gasp and breathed, "No!"

"Upon delivery of the dragon," the emissary continued, "the taxes of this village shall be forgiven for a period of no more than ten seasons." He glanced at Kyshira. "The small blue one you may keep, but the black one is now the property of the realm." His eyes returned to the elders. "I shall return at high sun tomorrow to collect the debt owed to his Majesty."

The elder in the yellow drape stepped toward him and protested, "You cannot just take our people like this!"

"It is done," the emissary sternly informed. "You may choose the young men and girls by lottery or whatever means you wish, but I *will* return here to collect them tomorrow."

The gnome elder wearing the green drape offered, "What if we can scrape up the gold to pay this tax debt? I think, perhaps—"

"I think," the emissary loudly interrupted, "that if you could have paid your taxes with gold as you should have over the last three seasons then I would not be standing here today." His eyes swept the elders. "You *will* have the conscripts ready when I return tomorrow." Those cruel eyes narrowed as he turned them to the dragon. "Do believe that your village will pay a terrible price if I return here and your debt to the realm is not ready to be satisfied. A terrible price."

Farrigrall swallowed hard as he stared back, knowing that the threat was directed at him.

"High sun tomorrow," the emissary barked loudly before turning on one heel and striding back down the pier.

The crowd did not disburse as the emissary and his entourage boarded the barge and it was pushed away from the pier. All watched as the three crafts slowly made their way toward Shoreline to spread the fair and just news to them, too.

Finally, the elders turned and strode back toward the village.

As they passed near the dragons, Josslee hung over the side of Farrigrall's head, hanging onto one of his horns as she shouted down to them, "What are we going to do?"

The man in the yellow drape was the only one to look up at her, and he replied, "We will convene." He looked to the wizard who watched them and offered, "Leedon, perhaps you will join us."

Farrigrall looked to the wizard, then to the little blue dragoness, and the distress and fear in her eyes broke his heart.

**

Hours later, near nightfall, the two dragons lay side by side in the field near the west shore once again, but this time there was no dozing or napping, nor any conversation. Kyshira lay with her head down and facing the south, away from the dragon on her right, and from time to time a pitiable coo would escape from her. Farrigrall stared at Shoreline, watching as they were also preparing to pay this so-called debt to this king. The more he thought about it, the tighter his chest felt inside, and the angrier he became. Once again, he felt cornered, trapped by circumstances that were well beyond his control. Defiance would mean more death and destruction for the village. Compliance would likely mean much the same. His life had just begun to come together as it should with the respect and acceptance of his own kind and a lovely young dragoness finally at his side. Now, once again, his life was unravelling, and he knew there was nothing he could do about it.

Footsteps drew his attention, but he just stared blankly at Shoreline and did not acknowledge the lone human who strode around the little blue and stopped near his head, and he stared longer as he felt eyes on him.

Josslee stared up at the dragon with strain in her eyes that was well beyond her seasons. Her hands were folded before her and it was clear that she was struggling to hold back the horrible avalanche of emotions within her.

He finally turned his head and looked down to her.

She offered a strained smile and informed, "The council decided on a lottery." She held up an old tile, one that was decades old and painted gold. "Looks like I'm going with you."

He growled and looked back to Shoreline.

Josslee raised her brow. "Well, someone has to go along and keep you out of trouble."

"We likely won't even see each other," he snarled. "Our fates are too much separated. I'll be a weapon to enforce this king's will, and you..." He closed his eyes, bowing his head.

"It can't be that bad," she assured. Folding her arms, she snapped, "And you'd better stop your brooding. Mama and Papa will be here in a moment and they will want to see that you're happy and not upset about this new chapter in your life. You'll be getting us out of ten seasons—"

"Are you happy with this decision?" he barked, looking on her with his brow low over his eyes.

She just stared back, then she bowed her head and looked to the ground, and finally breathed, "No."

Ucira and Eston finally arrived and also walked around the little blue, and Eston paused to pat her head as she crooned yet again.

Farrigrall did not wait for them to speak and instead told them, "Tomorrow I am flying Josslee to Caipiervell. The princess there has promised me already that she would look after her and give her all of the education and training that she desires. At least there I know she will be safe and will not be mistreated."

"The council has decided," Eston reminded. "If Josslee does not go, then another girl will have to be selected. I don't believe that would be fair to another family."

"I can at least look after mine," the dragon informed. "I don't want that king marching his army over the village, this one or any other, but he will *not* have my sister."

Leedon announced as he approached, "The nobility of dragons amazes me in its boundlessness." When all looked to him, he stopped about ten paces to Farrigrall's right and looked up at him, raising his bushy white eyebrows as he commended, "It takes one of great strength to put aside his own desires for the good of his people."

Shahly took the wizard's side and also looked up at the dragon, but a look was all she would give him.

Josslee's full attention fell on the unicorn and her lips tightened, then she fought back more tears and dared to ask in a tiny voice, "May... May I approach you?"

Shahly's looked to the girl, and without a word, paced to her and nuzzled her shoulder and neck, and tears finally streamed from the girl's eyes as she reached up and stroked the unicorn's mane with both hands, and as she cried, she laughed.

Ucira hesitantly approached her daughter from behind and placed a hand on her shoulder as she watched this mystical creature show such affection for her daughter. She tried not to feel envy, but she could not help it, and she drew a loud gasp as the little unicorn took a couple of steps past the girl and nuzzled her, too.

All of this was of very little interest to the dragon and he looked to the wizard, finally asking, "You came up with no solutions to this?"

"I can only advise," the wizard informed. "Your council made the decision as best they could under the circumstances."

Farrigrall looked out over the lake again, his brow low over his eyes as he grumbled, "Their decision stinks of rotting fish. Everything about this does."

Leedon nodded, and he would only say, "Agreed."

The young drake glanced at his human sister and he ordered, "We'll leave at first light tomorrow."

Josslee turned her eyes down and clenched her jaw, and long seconds later she said, "No."

Farrigrall turned his full attention to her and he growled, "You're going to Caipiervell in the morning, now quit arguing."

She looked up at him and shouted, "I will not be the cause of another family having to go through this because you want me to hide at Caipiervell! I am going to just run away tomorrow and that is final!" She threw the tile she still held at his head and wheeled around, storming back toward their house, and ten steps later, she broke into a run, and it was clear that she was crying.

With a growl, the dragon grumbled, "She has to go to Caipiervell."

Leedon informed, "And yet, her sense of duty to her village will not be swayed by you or any other." He walked toward the dragon's human parents and patted the unicorn as he strode by. "Come along, Shahly. Ucira has promised us a wonderful meal this evening."

Farrigrall watched as the wizard strode on, as his parents gave him one last, pitiable look before they turned to follow.

The unicorn turned to follow the humans, then she stopped and looked back at the dragon, then turned fully to him, informing, "When I need to find answers that nobody seems to have, there is always one that I can turn to who can help me find them."

The dragon stared back at her for long seconds, and finally he asked, "And who is that?"

Shahly just stared back, then she raised her head and replied, "Your father."

He watched as she turned and followed the humans back toward the south shore and when she disappeared into the trees and structures on the way, he looked back over the water as darkness began to descend, and he heaved a heavy breath.

CHAPTER 19

Even this late in the season, with winter perhaps only weeks away, the sun warmed the desert quickly and already radiated off of the tan and orange stone of the mountains there and shined brightly all the way to the end of a box canyon that ended in a large cave, illuminating into the cave about forty or fifty paces.

Farrigrall sat catlike about eighty paces from this cave, facing his parents who lay on their bellies just outside of it. Falloah the Scarlet had her head lying on the ground and her eyes closed as she seemed to doze in the morning sunshine. Beside her, the huge Desert Lord was propped up on his elbows with his forearms crossed before him and his neck almost vertical as he stared at the younger drake with an expression that was somewhere between annoyance and disbelief.

Ralligor drew then vented a deep breath through his nose, then said as calmly as he could, "Let me see if I understand you correctly. Some human king of a small kingdom at the north end of your lake has decided to take conscripts from your village, the human girl you call your sister is one, you are one, and now you come to me looking for advice."

The young drake glanced aside and confirmed, "You seem to understand the situation and I'm hoping you find it as terribly unfair as I do."

"In ways you cannot imagine," the Desert Lord agreed. He looked down to Falloah, then back to his son. "And, you are afraid of the consequences that will befall your village should you refuse all of this nonsense."

Farrigrall nodded. "He promised terrible consequences. I can only image he would bring his army down and take what they want by force."

Ralligor nodded in slight motions, then he looked back down to the scarlet and asked, "Are you understanding the situation here?"

She stirred slightly and replied, "Yes."

Turning his attention back to the young drake, Ralligor just stared at him for long seconds, then he slowly shook his head.

Farrigrall felt himself becoming more anxious and a little angry, and he demanded, "So what am I supposed to do? If I comply to save the village then other predators could move in and attack like they did before. If I don't..." He looked away and growled. "There seems to be no way to win!"

Ralligor just stared at the young drake, then he finally blinked a few times and mumbled, "Unbelievable."

His brow tense and now low over his eyes, Farrigrall glared back at his father and grumbled, "Well, what would *you* do?"

With a deep growl, the Desert Lord laid his head down and closed his eyes, replying, "I would not be in such a predicament to begin with."

A growl rolled from the young drake and he looked down to the scarlet. "Is he always this difficult?"

Falloah did not open her eyes as she replied, "Always."

Farrigrall snorted through his nose and looked back to his father. "Well, I'm in this situation and I came here thinking you might just have some advice for me!"

Slowly, Ralligor opened his eyes, and he heaved a heavy breath that blew sand and dust away from his nose. After a few long seconds, he raised his head and looked back at the young drake, and he asked, "Farrigrall, were you granted part of my range as your own by the Landmaster?"

Drawing his head back, the young drake answered, "Yes, you know I was. What does that have to do with this situation?"

Ralligor looked down to Falloah and informed, "I swear, I was never this much an imbecile at that age!"

"If you say so," she answered back.

Farrigrall snorted through his nose again and demanded, "What is it I am missing?"

Ralligor's brow was tense and low over his eyes as he regarded the young drake as patiently as he could, and he heaved another breath that growled out of him.

Still lying still with her eyes closed, Falloah ordered, "Be kind."

The Desert Lord simply glanced at her, then his full attention returned to his son and gave him a hard, unblinking stare. Finally, he drew a deep, calming breath and asked, "That range is yours, is it not?"

Raising his nose slightly, Farrigrall confirmed, "It is."

"That means you are the most powerful creature in that range, does it not?"

The young drake blinked and agreed, "I suppose so."

"You suppose so," Ralligor snarled. His expression hardened and he raised a scaly eyebrow. "If that's the case, why do you think you should you answer to some human king?"

Farrigrall looked down and pondered, and pondered. Slowly shaking his head, he stammered, "Because... He's a king. Like the village answers to the Council of Elders. Without some kind of law, there would be chaos." He raised his eyes as the big dragon pushed himself up and stood.

A growl rumbled from deep in the Desert Lord's chest and throat as he loomed over his son, and with bared teeth, he roared, "Are you human or are you dragon?"

Wide eyed, Farrigrall also stood, looking up at his father with his jaws agape, and finally he replied, "I am dragon."

Ralligor growled again, louder, and he opened his wings and yelled as loudly as he could, "Declare it with the conviction of your kind!"

Farrigrall also opened his wings, bared his teeth, and he roared, "I am dragon!"

Folding his wings to him, the Desert Lord closed the distance between him and the younger drake with two steps and grasped his shoulder hard. "Then it is time that you quit allowing lesser creatures to hold dominion over you. The range granted you is yours to defend, and if the humans who reside within that range look to you for protection, then so be it." His brow lowered over his eyes. "You are the law there, Farrigrall of the Lake, not some human king, not your village elders. You are. If this king would act in defiance of your law, then he has no place in your range. I have many human kingdoms in my range and all of them know not to cross me, and they know the consequences of doing so. I razed several to the ground that did, and others learned from that and kept their heads down." He raised his head and growled. "Humans and other lesser creatures must answer to you, not you to them. If this human king demands a pet of a dragon, then it's time you deliver a message, a message that *you*, not him, not his minions, rule over that range, the lake, the mountains, the fields, and all inside your borders. He will not have a pet; he will *be* a pet!" Ralligor held his fist before him and added, "Or he will be crushed." He leaned his head. "Do you understand?"

Farrigrall looked down and allowed his father's words to penetrate his mind. When he looked up again, there was a confidence in his eyes that he had only felt when defeating crocodiles, and the few dragons he had defeated. "Still, the village may not like this."

"How is that your problem?" Ralligor growled. "If they will have your protection, then they will accept your law." His eyes narrowed. "As will this human king." He motioned behind the young drake with his head. "Go on. Claim that range and all in it for you and... and... the blue one."

"Kyshira," the young drake reminded.

"That one," the Desert Lord confirmed. "Let them know that Farrigrall of the Lake has arrived."

Farrigrall nodded, then he turned and walked away, toward the mouth of the canyon, only to stop and half turn, looking behind him to his parents. "Thank you, Father."

Ralligor nodded to him, then watched as the young drake strode toward the wider part of the canyon, opened his wings, and took to the wind.

Falloah finally raised her head and looked up at the Desert Lord, a little smile on her mouth as she observed, "I think that is the proudest I have ever seen you."

Glancing back at her, Ralligor nodded and looked back to his departing son, and he admitted, "He makes it easy."

CHAPTER 20

The barges were approaching as before and were only a hundred or so paces out. As before, the largest was heading for the pier, but this time there were three smaller ones, not two, and there were about thirty soldiers on each, waiting to disembark and take possession of what this king had demanded.

The thirty young men were dressed as usual and lined up near the shore where the smaller barges would land to take them aboard. The then girls and young woman were made to dress in white gowns with long skirts that were too narrow to allow them to run or even walk with long strides. These gowns fit them very tightly around their waists, were low cut at their chests and had long and large belled sleeves. The conscripts' families stood behind them. Many wept. All but one of the girls wept.

The tallest of the girls, Josslee stood on one end, and was really more annoyed and angrier than anyone else present. She looked up and scanned the sky, clenching her jaw as she grumbled, "Where is he? He's going to get us all into trouble again." She turned around and broke from the line, striding as best she could to her parents, and she demanded, "Where did he go?"

"He did not say," her father informed. "He would only say that he had something to do and he would be back by high sun."

Josslee raised her brow and set her hands on her hips. "Well, it's high sun and he's nowhere to be found."

"He'll be here," Eston assured. He reached to the girl, pulled her in close and hugged her as tightly as he could.

Hesitantly, she slid her arms around him to hug him back, and now the reality of what was happening began to drive home. She felt tears coming and buried her face in his shoulder as she did not want anyone to see her cry, but her body quaked as the issue forced itself.

Seeing this, Ucira stepped toward them and wrapped her arms around them both as she also began to weep.

One of the village policemen approached and took Eston's shoulder, reluctantly informing, "The barges are about to land. She will need to take her place in the line."

Eston nodded and pulled away from his daughter, and he offered her a smile as he said, "I hope you will find all of the grand adventures you can out there. Maybe you'll return home a princess, eh?"

Josslee rubbed tears from her cheeks and forced a smile back as she assured, "I'll do my best, Papa."

He nodded, and watched as the policeman escorted her back to her place in the line.

Moments passed and the emissary's barge was pulled up to the pier and was tied off, and as this was happening, the three smaller barges beached on the white and gray sand of the eastern shore. When they were solidly on the sand, ladders were lowered down and about ten soldiers climbed from each of them and began to walk toward the young men who awaited them.

As before, the emissary's soldiers disembarked first, but this time they went all the way to the shore and formed up there. His two escorts followed, and then the emissary himself. All were dressed as they had been and the village elders stood where they had before to greet him.

He strode right up to them and looked around, his brow high over his eyes as he demanded, "Where is the dragon? I don't see the dragon."

The foreman assured, "He should be along any moment now. He said he had a matter to attend and would return by high sun."

The emissary looked up and turned his palms upward. "It's high sun, and I don't see him." He turned a hard look on the foreman. "If he does not return, it will not go well for your village."

Clearly feeling anxious, the foreman raised his hands between him and the emissary and assured, "He will be here. I would stake my life on it. He would never betray us."

The emissary looked around him again and said, "Then it's a wager." He turned to one of his personal escorts and ordered, "Go and have the girls taken aboard my barge. I'll inspect them once we leave." As the guard went to task, he looked back to the foreman and raised his brow again, folding his arms before him. "I was quite clear about this matter. Thirty young men, ten girls, and one dragon. I don't even see the little blue one anywhere."

"She's atop the mountain," the foreman informed. "She goes there when she is upset."

"Not my issue," the emissary scoffed. "If the black one does not appear before I leave, we will take her, and you can explain to his Majesty..." He turned his eyes up and they widened as he took a step back.

Farrigrall slammed onto the ground very hard and dropped to all fours, and he bared his teeth and roared a nightmarish roar as he stroked his wings forward to kick up a hurricane of dust and sand.

Many in the gathered crowd screamed or yelled, and most retreated from his path, scattering in all directions. Even activities on the beach stopped as the young drake made his sudden appearance.

Farrigrall stood fully, towering over all around as he scanned the scene before him, and his eyes narrowed as they fixed on the emissary. A growl rolled from him as he began to slowly stride forward with heavy steps, his brow low over his eyes and his lips slid half away from his long teeth.

The Village Council backed away and fled from his path as the dragon approached with thumping steps.

The dragon stopped only twenty paces away and slowly folded his wings to him as he loomed over the elders, the emissary, and his escorts. The soldiers held their spears ready, but many had backed away when the dragon had approached.

Snorting through his nose, Farrigrall glared down at the emissary, and he snarled, "Well? Here I am." His eyes narrowed. "I see this king could not be bothered to come and face me himself." He growled again. "Oh, and *I* have decreed that it is time for you to leave my village." His eyes slid to the soldiers who had been trying to get the boys on the barges, and those who were escorting the girls to the pier. "And you'll be taking none of my people with you. Back away from them."

Kyshira glided down from the mountain top and circled to land behind her drake.

The emissary swallowed hard as he backed away a step, and he was less than confident as he reminded, "I am here to collect the conscripts for his Majesty."

Seeing that the soldiers were not quite following his commands, Farrigrall turned slightly and stomped toward them, and he roared, "I told you to back away!"

The soldiers on the beach complied, many raising their hands before them as they did.

Another deep growl rolled from the young drake as he turned his attention back to the emissary.

The emissary swallowed hard and retreated a couple more steps, and he repeated, "I... I am here to collect his Majesty's conscripts. He will be expecting everything he commanded from this village when I return to the castle. He will be expecting you as well."

Farrigrall leaned his head. "Will he? Well, I certainly would not want to disappoint *his Majesty* now, would I?" His eyes narrowed and he bared his teeth again. "You'll be leaving now." He glanced at the barges. "Abandon that barge on the end and leave it here. Consider it a tribute for me allowing you to leave with your lives." He looked to the north, his brow lowering over his eyes. "As for his Majesty..." Turning, he looked to the little blue and ordered, "Make sure they are gone within the hour and they leave that barge like I told them to. If they do not obey me, then fire the barges and all of the invaders they brought with them." He lowered his head and gently rubbed the side of her snout with his. "I'll be back shortly, dragoness."

A little wide-eyed, she drew her head away and smiled up at him, and she complied, "I will do as you command, my drake."

He winked at her, then turned back to the emissary and raised a brow. "Your time is running out. Get aboard your barges and go. Move against this village while I am gone and you and your entire kingdom will burn."

That was his last command, his last warning. He opened his wings and swept himself into the air, stroking his wings hard as he climbed higher and turned toward the north.

**

It was simply called Northshore Castle and was the only inhabited kingdom left in this part of the country. A modest castle of four levels, it had five tall towers topped with conical copper roofs that had long since turned green with the weather. Its wall was only about four heights high with one way inside that was closed by two heavy timber gates. The stone was all whitewashed and the castle itself stood out against the dark stone of the mountain behind it. About half a league to the north, a waterfall seemed to sprout right out of the middle of the dark limestone mountain and cascaded into a wide, circular pool below that in turn flowed toward the castle and into the lake. The castle itself was only about three hundred paces from the shore of the lake, and a sprawling village was all around it. Five piers jetted from the shore and out into the lake, and a couple of sizable ships were tied to the ends of the piers, their masts bare of canvas as it was furled and tied to the crossmembers. They appeared to have been recently constructed, recently painted, and it seemed that this king had gone to great expense to expand his influence to other areas. Four more barges were also tied up to the piers, along with other, smaller fishing boats.

For a visiting human or gnome or elf, this would be an impressive sight, a newly established kingdom that had built up quickly and was still gathering its strength. But to an approaching dragon, this was merely a representation of the attempted oppression of the village he called home, and with narrow eyes, he pulled his wings back and descended quickly and slammed his feet onto the ground only about fifty paces from the castle's perimeter wall. This put him near the middle of the village.

Humans fled in all directions, many screaming, and he ignored them all as he turned his full attention to the castle.

As he strode toward the castle with heavy steps, the humans within frantically tried to close the gates, and he almost laughed as he shook his head. His chest and throat swelled as he drew his head back, then he lunged with gaping jaws as he sent a deadly blast of fire at the gates that exploded as it hit them. One gate was blasted from its hinges and the other was forced back open, knocking many men to the ground as it did.

Farrigrall turned his eyes up, then he opened his wings and swept them hard as he leapt up and in seconds was perched atop the perimeter wall.

Several arrows and crossbow bolts hit him from the right and a growl rumbled from him as he slowly looked that way.

The attending soldiers and guards slowly backed away, and when the dragon's jaws swung open and he roared, they turned and fled.

Farrigrall looked to his left, and his eyes narrowed, and those soldiers fled as well.

"Loose!" someone from the courtyard below shouted.

The young dragon looked that way and saw five catapults evenly distributed close to the palace, and one had just hurled a large stone at him. The aim was not even almost accurate and he watched the stone pass by just outside of arm's reach, then he looked back down to the catapult and growled again as the men there worked quicky and frantically to get it pulled back and reloaded. The other four were also being loaded and prepared to shoot, and teams of men were trying to get them turned and aimed at the dragon.

Shaking his head, Farrigrall leapt from the wall and opened his wings, gliding down to the catapult that had shot at him, and as he slammed onto the ground twenty paces away, the soldiers manning it fled. Once again, his chest and throat swelled, and he gaped his jaws and blasted the weapon with hellish fire, blowing it apart and setting its pieces aflame.

As the catapult settled to the ground and burned and more soldiers fled, the dragon backed away a couple of steps, then he looked to the main doors going into the palace, then up to the defensive positions two stories above it, just below his eye level.

"Here's what is going to happen," he announced. "I am going to count to twenty. If his *Majesty* has not come to greet me by the time I get to twenty, I will destroy something else. Like this." He turned to the left and fired the next catapult, blowing it into flaming pieces. He growled as he looked back to the windows of the castle again. "You do not want to keep me waiting!"

He would not have to wait long for action.

A middle-aged man in black trousers, a white shirt and a green cloak and long black hair ran out of the main palace door on knee high, polished black boots, and once outside, he waved his arms and bade, "Wait!"

Farrigrall regarded him with cruel eyes as he observed, "You don't look like this king, and I'm nearing twenty."

"Please!" the man begged. "His Majesty is on the way, but he was holding an audience at the other end of the palace and assures you he is coming as fast as he can. Please!"

The dragon looked away and cocked an eyebrow up. "I do wonder if Peak Lake Village would have been granted such quarter. Hmm." He reached up and stroked his chin, then he looked back down to the man and concluded, "I don't think they would be. In fact, your emissary arrived with a small invasion force and, on your king's orders, was there to kidnap forty people, friends and family of mine. That irritates me." He looked to his right and saw the last intact catapult, opened his jaws, and destroyed it as he had the other two.

The messenger fell to his knees and covered his head. When the blast of fire ended, he slowly lowered his arms and looked up to see the dragon staring down at him again.

Farrigrall smiled. "And, we start counting again. Why don't you count this time? Count aloud to twenty, and if I don't see your king—"

"I am here," a plump man informed as he emerged onto a second story balcony with three archers.

Farrigrall looked to see the king standing in the center of the large circular balcony that was build onto the castle's second level, and just under eye level for the young dragon. It was about three paces across and just over a pace deep from the stone baluster to where one would enter the palace itself, and made of stone and heavy timbers. There were several of these at this level of the palace and the next, and the rest were manned by archers and soldiers. The king clearly had not missed any meals and wore oversized clothes and robes that were trimmed in gold and red. His loosely fitting trousers were a dark red and were also trimmed in gold. Above his brow was a golden crown that was adorned with many jewels. On his fingers were many gold rings. This was a man who loved to show off his wealth, and as other archers and spearmen emerged onto balconies, windows, and from the palace itself, he made it clear that he loved to show off his power.

The dragon was not impressed. He glanced about at the soldiers and archers who assumed defensive positions around their king, and he shook his head. "Is this supposed to be a demonstration of power or are you offering them up as sacrifices?" He leaned his shoulder on the palace wall next to the balcony and folded his arms as he looked down at the king. "Do you know who I am?" When the king did not answer right away, he said, "I am Farrigrall of the Lake. This is part of my range, where your little kingdom sits, so we are going to have a conversation, and by that, I mean I am going give you my law and you are going to listen and accept it." His brow lowered. "Understand?"

The king swallowed hard and raised his chin.

Farrigrall looked down to his claws, raising his brow as he continued, "You may be the king here, but understand that I am in control of everything in this range, which is vast. The lake is mine, the mountains, the fields, the villages... " His eyes slid to the king. "And you."

His eyes widening, the king took a step back and clenched his hands into tight fists.

The dragon looked back to his claws. "Kyshira and I will lair on Peak Island in the center of the village. I am not to see your soldiers within twenty leagues of there, or Shoreline. In fact, you may consider all of the villages along the lake to be out of your realm. They belong to me now."

"Outrageous!" the king shouted. "Those villages have been duly and legally annexed by the Kingdom of Northshore and I'll not simply—" A shrieking gasp sucked into his mouth as the dragon turned fully, and in seconds he was staring at his nostrils from half a pace away.

Farrigrall snorted through his nose and bared his teeth, then he reached to the balcony, grabbed onto the stone wall that surrounded it, and he pulled a section away and allowed it to fall to the ground far below. His eyes were wide, his brow low over them, and he growled, "Are you going to be a problem for me? That will not go well for you. You may be a king here, but I am king everywhere! You raise my ire even once and I will show you in the very worst of ways why your kind fears mine."

Swallowing hard, the king nodded in quick motions.

With another growl, the dragon stepped away from the wall balcony and turned toward the perimeter wall, only to stop and turn back to the king. "Oh, one other thing. I will expect tributes from your kingdom every full moon." He leaned his head. "Consider those tributes... taxes, for me allowing you to remain here." He raised a brow, then he turned away again, opened his wings, and took to the wind.

**

Farrigrall found himself anxious to get back home, just in case that emissary decided to do something treacherous in his absence. But, to his delight, he looked down at the lake and saw the three barges paddling north and already over two leagues from Peak Island, and he smiled a wicked little smile. Angling downward, he spiraled toward them, and when he was less than ten men's heights from the water, he turned again and passed right over them—and roared a mighty and echoing roar as he did so. Turning back south, he passed close again, and this time he belched fire right over them, inciting panic among those aboard. As he stroked his wings for more height, he laughed a little laugh, feeling terribly amused at his prank.

He arrived home to the cheers of the villagers, and the loud, high pitched trumpet of a certain little blue dragoness. There was a smile on his mouth as he landed near the middle of the village where it was clear enough for him to do so, and as he folded his wings, people ran to him from every direction, and even some gnomes charged from the mine to greet him.

Farrigrall sat catlike among them, his eyes darting from one to the next as they crowded around him, cheering him as their hero as they had done before. This time seemed different. He no longer felt so much as one of them, more a leader, a guardian. His father had been right. He had no reason to answer to any of the humans, and yet this put a nervous crawl into his belly. Now was the time to tell them, and he knew it would be difficult.

The council foreman stepped forward through the crowd, smiling, and yet there was an anxiousness in his eyes as he stopped three paces away and bade, "Farrigrall!" When the dragon looked to him, he raised his chin and asked, "Word from the King?"

One of Farrigrall's eyebrows cocked up slightly. "He is no longer king here. He will not be back to take our people, impose his laws or collect taxes. All the villages of the lake are free of him."

The crowd broke out into cheers.

"No more king!" someone shouted.

The woman on the council waited for the cheers to die down, and she raised her hand and announced, "We should elect our own king, then!"

Farrigrall turned his attention to her and informed, "There is a king." His eyes narrowed. "Me."

A fearful hush fell over the crowd.

His eyes swept them. "The Landmaster has granted me range here and dominion over all in it. It is the dragon way, and it is the way things shall be from now on."

The council foreman glanced about, then he turned fearful eyes back up to the dragon. "You... You are declaring us your subjects?"

"It is declared," Farrigrall snarled. "I am the law here, now. As the most powerful creature in this territory, all shall answer to me." His eyes swept the crowd, and a smile slowly, forcibly curled the edges of his mouth. In a moment, his jaws gaped and he began to laugh hysterically.

The people of Peak Lake Village exchanged confused looks.

Farrigrall recovered his composure just enough to manage, "Oh, that was hilarious. You should have seen the looks on your faces!" He broke into laughter again, and many of the village began to laugh along with him. He recovered his composure again and said, "Oh, that was amazing. But, in sooth, I really am king here now." With that, he stood fully and strode toward the mine in the center of the island through the parting crowd of people who were once again silent.

All watched as the dragon stopped at the opening to the mine, turned, and laid to his belly, settling his head to the ground and close his eyes. More fearful, looks were exchanged, and concern was rippled in low voices, and an older man grumbled, "I told you all this would happen in time."

One girl in the crowd did not feel the same as the rest, rather she folded her arms as if she was annoyed. Josslee stormed through the people who and right up to the dragon, right up to his nose, and she loudly cleared her throat.

Farrigrall slowly opened his eyes.

People approached apprehensively, led by those in the council.

Josslee just stood there, her arms folded her eyes narrow, and she spat, "King? You think you are a king now?"

A growl rumbled from him. "I've had a long day, Josslee. What do you want?"

"King?" she barked.

He raised his head slightly and snarled back, "Yes, king. It's the best translation for what I am into human tongue."

One of Josslee's eyebrows cocked up. "What you are is still a big lizard that eats crocodiles, you've just had someone tell you that you are somehow in charge of everything now."

"I'm in charge of everything in my range," he spat back. "You're just too feeble minded to understand that."

She rolled her eyes and snarled, "Whatever, Farg."

He mocked back in a nasally voice, "Whatever, Farg."

She turned and walked away from him, ordering, "Stop imitating me. I don't sound like that."

In the same nasally voice, he repeated, "Stop imitating me. I don't sound like that."

She looked over her shoulder and shouted, "You aren't king!"

"I am too!" he roared back.

"Are not!"

He raised his head fully and yelled, "Mama! Josslee's being difficult again!"

The councilman in the blue drape dared to approach the dragon and loudly cleared his throat to draw his attention. "Um, Farrigrall, there are questions about your new station that must be answered."

The young drake drew his head back slightly. "What questions?"

Leedon appeared with his usual friendly smile and the unicorn still following him and he posed, "There are many questions bounding about that your people will need answers to, my boy. For starters, what does this title mean to them? How can your subjects expect to be treated by their new king?" He stopped before the dragon, about seven paces away, and leaned heavily on his walking stick as he stared up at the young drake before him. "Most of all, what will be your role as king? What kind of king will we find in Farrigrall of the Lake?"

Farrigrall stared back at him for long seconds, then his eyes shifted to the unicorn, who also looked on inquisitively. He looked over his shoulder, to the young dragoness who sat catlike beside him, then his eyes swept the people of the village who looked on anxiously. "I suppose I hadn't thought about it," he admitted.

"No better time than now," the wizard informed.

The full council gathered to the dragon's left and he looked to them, then back to the wizard. "To be honest, aside from what I've heard in stories, I suppose I don't know what a king is supposed to do."

"Well, then," the wizard began. "Perhaps it is time for the King, Farrigrall, to decide what his roll will be. How shall your subjects see you?"

He looked away and growled. "These people are not my subjects. They are..." He looked to the crowd again. "They are my family. Peak Lake and Shoreline and everyone else I grew up among," His eyes found Josslee, who stood among the other villagers, "all family."

The girl smiled at him.

Shahly had taken the wizard's side and offered the dragon a little smile. "It looks like you will be a king who is a protector, like the elders of my herd." Her ears drooped slightly. "I still have questions."

"Mama probably has the answers you want," the dragon informed.

With a little shrug, the unicorn turned and strode toward the villagers. "Okay, I'll go find her."

The council foreman stepped toward the dragon and informed, "Farrigrall, your council will always be here to advise you."

Farrigrall nodded to him, then he looked over his shoulder to Kyshira again and raised his brow.

She leaned her head and just stared back.

He heaved a heavy breath, then he looked back to the wizard and said, "I don't want things to change here at Peak Lake Village. If I am truly to be king, then my role will be to protect my people."

With that, the crowd exploded into cheers once again.

CHAPTER 21

The air had gotten cold very quickly as the boat travelled north on the lake toward its destination. There was not yet ice, but the air signaled that it would bring ice very soon, likely after dark. Onboard were crates of cargo, large bags of burlap that contained more, and about twenty passengers. The dingy white sails were full of the wind as the craft, about twenty paces long and a third that wide, cut across the lake with purpose, leaving a white wake behind it. The journey had been less than half a day, leaving its port on the south side of the lake and travelling north toward the opposite shore. Ahead was its destination.

And sanctuary.

The girl looked to be in her twenties and was covered with a gray hooded cloak that was a little too thin for the cold air that blew by. The baggy sleeves rippled in the wind as she clutched the bundle that was shrouded in a faded, dark green cloth and wrapped as a baby would be. The hood covered her entire head and one could barely see her eyes from beneath it, and there was strain on her face, her tense mouth as she watched from the bow of the small ship as the distant pier drew closer. Her boots, covered by the cloak she wore, were tattered and worn from many leagues of travel with her heavy burden, and one nearly had a hole worn in the sole. She was of average size for a woman with a slight build, but seemed to carry her heavy burden almost easily.

The cloak was damp and she was very cold, shivering at times, but she could not risk interactions with others, could not risk the possibilities of spies finding her, could not risk comfort and warmth.

Her big, yellow eyes looked to the right where she saw a mountain peak that seemed to sprout from the depths of the lake itself, and the seed of a new but risky plan had been planted.

At long last the small ship slowed and came along the long pier that led about fifty paces across the wooden planks to the village that lay ashore, and one of the first to disembark was the woman in gray, and she walked with rapid steps as she clutched the bundle to her.

Something within the green cloth squirmed and a little coo escaped it.

"Shh," she soothed as best she could as she hurried toward the village.

Once ashore, she paused to look around her. There were many people coming and going, many heading down the pier to assist with the unloading of the boat while others appeared to be attending to their own business. This would be an easy crowd in which to get lost.

First things first. With very little money left, only a few copper and silver coins, she would have to find shelter and warmth for them both, and food.

She walked at a more casual pace in an effort to fit in better, to not be noticed, but still she glanced about frequently, and stared down at the gravel path she walked when she was not glancing about.

The walk seemed like a long one, and when she encountered someone on the trail, she would step off of the trail and turn toward the lake as if admiring it until they passed.

Between the villages was a long, timber bridge, one that was thankfully not in great use this day. She found herself walking it alone for the most part, and only encountered a few people as she made her way toward the island, and she hid her eyes even from them.

Finally on the island, she found a grassy field where much of the grass, now mostly tan and brown from the coming of winter, to be laid flat while small sprigs and blades struggled stubbornly through the longer stalks that were laid to the ground. Here she stopped and dared to look around her. In the village ahead among all of the buildings, some of which looked new or freshly repaired, there was about the same number of people as she had encountered before but now in a smaller space.

First order of business was to find something to eat.

Once again, the bundle she held stirred and a faint cry came out this time, something not quite human, and she looked down and soothed, "Shh." Pulling the cloth in closer, she whispered, "I will find us something to eat, but you must be quiet."

She found a main road through the center of the village that went by a large structure, some kind of village meeting hall, and she turned away from it, toward the water on the south side, and she moved with quick steps. When her bundle stirred again, she held it tighter and looked down to soothe her little ward, and did not notice the small group of women who had stepped out into the road before her, and she walked right into the robust woman in the middle of the small group. With a loud gasp, she looked to the women with wide eyes and found herself frozen where she stood, realizing these were eyes she should keep hidden.

The bundle she held squirmed and she barely held onto it, and as the three women stared back, the green cloth fell away before she could act to keep it covered. A dark blue reptilian tail fell out of the bottom of the cloth. A short, scaly snout pushed out of the top of the cloth, light blue at the sides with darker blue over the top where its short dorsal scales were laid flat against its head and down its neck. Silver scales separated light and dark blue. Yellow eyes blinked open and the tiny dragon turned its full attention to the three surprised women who stared back.

Now her secrets were fully revealed and the young woman could only stare back as her mind scrambled for some kind way to respond, some way to get away.

Panic would set in any second, bursting from the three middle aged women who were seeing the little dragon and the yellow eyed woman who held him, a panic that would spread like wildfire through the entire village, and she would have to flee quickly once again.

Much to her surprise, the three women all smiled and a collective, "Aw!" sounded from them, and all of them stepped toward the woman and her ward. She shrank away as the woman on the left actually reached to the dragon but found herself astonished as the woman simply pulled more of the green cloth from him.

The woman in the center drawled, "How adorable!"

A rough looking man with a full beard also approached, drawn by the commotion, and he, too, looked to the little dragon and simply raised his brow before he just walked on.

The woman on the right stroked the little dragon's head and the dragon responded with a coo and closed eyes as he raised his nose for more such cuddles. This woman took the girl's hand, then finally looked to her fully and announced, "Dear! Your hands are like ice! Come inside where it is warm."

The woman in the center of the group asked, "What is your name, dear?"

Turning her eyes down, the girl managed, "I am Elleesh."

The woman on the left bade, "And the little baby?"

Her gaze fell on the baby dragon and she heard herself answer, "He is called Gallador."

"You should come inside," the woman in the center insisted. "By the by, my name is Ucira, and these are my friends Tarami and Rorta." She held her arms out and clutched at the young dragon, eventually taking him from the arms of his protector. "Oh, he's heavy! Come along, dear. You two look famished, and I know young dragons can get fussy if they do not eat regularly."

As she was led to one of the houses near the south shore with the other two women taking her sides. She felt nervous about the young dragon in someone else's arms, but was also glad to be free of the burden of carrying him. She also found herself more and more curious about why these women had no fear of him, or her.

Rorta, on the young woman's left, leaned toward her as they walked, and she informed, "Ucira is no stranger to caring for a baby dragon."

They arrived in short order and Elleesh entered right behind Ucira, and she glanced around at the spacious house she had entered. There was a fireplace on the right with two wicker chairs facing it and a table between them, a wooden table in the center of the room, and at the left end what appeared to be a kitchen with an iron stove right in the center of the wall, a large barrel with a wooden cover, and a flat, stone counter that sat atop wooden shelves to the right of the stove. Above the stove was a black metal box with a hinged door that seemed to be built into the stone chimney at the back of the stove. Wonderful smells filled the house, including the smell of some kind of bread! Something was also sizzling in one of the pans, and a teenage girl who wore a long, dirty apron over her blue and white dress toiled away there.

As the door was closed, Ucira called, "Josslee."

The girl looked over her shoulder and announced, "The bread is ready and just came out and I've... " Her eyes found Elleesh, and she turned fully and greeted, "Hello."

Elleesh only bowed her head to the girl.

Seeing the little dragon that Ucira held, the girl smiled broadly and squealed as she darted toward the woman, and much to Elleesh's surprise, she took the little dragon as she would any human baby and held him to her, hugging the little reptile as tightly as she could as she barked in a very high voice, "He is so cute! I want to hug him forever!"

Even more surprising to Elleesh was how the dragon wrapped his arms and legs around the girl and cooed as he nuzzled into her shoulder and neck.

Josslee giggled as she swung back and forth, the little dragon's tail swinging the opposite direction with each movement.

Elleesh looked on with confusion in her eyes. Not in the half a season she had been fleeing with this little dragon had they been greeted so, and never had the little dragon taken so easily to anyone but her. He seemed to know something about them, and this put her at ease about them.

Tarami, standing behind Elleesh, pulled on the wet cloak and said, "Let's get that wet cloak from you and get you warmed up."

Elleesh realized it was not tied at the front and anxiously protested, "No, wait!" as it was pulled from her—and the hood fell from her head.

The four other women in the house saw her and froze.

Elleesh was a lovely young woman. Her hair was yellow and much of it was worn in a long braid nearly to her lower back. Long locks swirled to each side of it and shorter locks hung from her temples. She was not modestly dressed, only wearing a white shirt that dropped to her thighs almost halfway to her knees and was belted at her waist with a thick, black belt that held three pouches on each side, a drinking cup on the left and a hand length dagger to the right. Most notable about her, other than her big, bright yellow eyes, where long, pointed ears that swept back from beneath her hair, ears that were covered at the tops with shorter yellow hair, very thin hair that made her ears look almost fuzzy.

As silence gripped the room, Elleesh stared at the floor and did not seem to know what to do.

Slowly, Josslee approached, still hugging the little dragon to her as she asked in a whisp of a voice, "Are you an elf?"

Elleesh was long seconds in answering, but finally shook her head and confessed, "No, not as such." She wrung her hands together, and finally said, "I should go."

Ucira took her hands and pulled her a step closer, insisting, "No, you need to warm up and eat something."

"People are looking for us," Elleesh informed in a low voice.

Rorta took her shoulder and insisted, "No one will find you here. You should rest and get something to eat."

Gallador grew restless and squirmed, and Josslee finally barked, "Fine!" as if she knew what the little dragon wanted. She set him down on the table and strode to the stone counter beside the stove, and the little dragon stood right at the edge of the table, opened his wings and flapped them hard a few times as he watched the girl with anxious eyes.

Josslee turned with a large slab of meat in each hand, and as she walked back to the women, she threw one at the dragon and did not even watch as he caught it mid air in his mouth and voraciously gobbled it down as he pivoted to keep facing the girl.

Rorta asked, "Who is chasing you?"

Josslee tossed the other piece of meat at the dragon, then she wiped her hands on the apron and folded her arms.

Heaving a heavy breath, Elleesh just stared at the floor and finally shook her head again. "He is a barbarian king, a leader of many tribes and many different beings, not just human or elf or orc, but a number of others. He is a ruthless, evil man and he decreed that he shall have the little dragon. I think he means to eat him or some other heinous such act." She raised her eyes to the young dragon, who still stared at Josslee. "He had him in a cage. I don't know from where he captured him, but..." She looked down again. "One night, about six months ago, I took him and fled. I could not bear what would happen to him. I've seen the fates of other prisoners, even children." Slowly, she shook her head yet again. "I could not bear the thought."

Ucira took her shoulder and assured, "You and he are safe here. I promise."

The door burst open and all turned to see a rather large, bearded man in dirty black trousers, a gray shirt and a black leather jerkin, enter a few steps.

The man scanned the women and did not seem to notice the little dragon or the non-human woman who stood among the others, and he said in a gruff voice, "Boats. Many soldiers among them including some rather giant and hulking gray skinned barbarian creatures."

"Oh, no," Elleesh breathed, her eyes wide.

The man continued, "Their leader has demanded that the entire village gather at the western shore." His eyes finally found Elleesh, and he calmly turned and was oddly at ease as he left the house, leaning heavily on a cane, and left the door open.

Josslee took the apron from her and reached to the right of the door, took a forest green cloak from a wooden peg and replaced it with the apron. She threw the cloak around Elleesh's shoulders, then turned toward the stove and walked that way.

Gallador watched the girl as she took the pan from the stove top and laid it on the stone counter, then he stroked his wings again before folding them to him, and he reached to the girl with both arms and jumped into her, and she pulled him to her and held him as if she were holding a young child.

Ucira looked to the girl and raised her brow. "You know what to do, child."

Josslee smiled and confirmed, "I most certainly do." She led the way out the door and bade, "Come on, ladies."

Elleesh glanced about and nervously asked, "What are you doing?"

Tarami answered, "We are going to the west shore."

Finding herself near panic as the other four women simply walked out of the house, Elleesh insisted, "He cannot find us here!" She followed and took Ucira's shoulder. "Please! Give him back to me and we will flee, and he will spare your village!"

Ucira looked to her—and actually smiled.

Josslee was hurrying into the village, and she looked over her shoulder. "Do you trust us?"

Shaking her head again, Elleesh found herself unable to answer, but finally managed, "You don't know the evil this man is. He will kill everyone here!"

Josslee smiled. "No, he is about to have the worst day of his life."

They got to the middle of the village and Josslee continued north. Elleesh tried to follow, but Rorta took her hand and shook her head as she pulled her toward the west, and all she would say was, "Trust us."

They arrived at the western shore to find four large barges had landed along the shoreline and a big three masted ship had tied up to the pier. A couple of hundred soldiers in leather and metal plate armor, mostly leather helmets and brandishing all manner of weapons were already ashore and taking up positions, assembling in formations to attack. Already at the end of the pier, this king, who wore gold colored plate armor, a gold helmet and a large axe at his side, scanned the assembling people with cruel yellow eyes. He also had long, pointed ears that were covered with black hair at the tops. He was tall, very thick in the arms, legs and body, and his thumbs were hooked into his heavy leather belt. His stance demonstrated to all that he now considered himself in command.

At his flanks were two hulking, gray skinned warriors who wore only leather trousers, shoulder and arm armor, and each held a long spear with an iron warhead. They were a height and a half tall. One had long black hair hanging like moss from his head. The other had no hair. Both had small, cruel eyes that also scanned the people who had gathered.

The village council, standing in their places before this gold clad, barbarian king, proudly wore their drapes and seemed oddly at ease as they stared at the considerable force before them.

The barbarian king's eyes swept the villagers once more, and he announced in a very loud, very deep voice, "Is everyone here?" He looked about again. "I do not like to be kept waiting!"

The council foreman assured, "Enough are here." He folded his arms. "What is it you want here?"

The barbarian king did not even look his way, he just scanned the crowd again and bellowed, "A girl came here, a stranger to your people, likely trying to conceal herself. She has something of mine. You will deliver them both to me and you will do it now."

Even as Elleesh cringed and pulled the cloak closer to her, the hood closer to her head, Ucira took her under her arm and pulled her possessively close, as if clutching a child to her.

Raising his brow, the barbarian king prodded, "Well? No one here has seen a stranger about? Perhaps she just disappeared into the mist." His eyes swept the crowd again. "Nobody." Suddenly, he shouted, "Someone here is lying!" He drew his long sword. "I do not care for those who lie to me." Looking down to the blade as he laid it across his other palm, he pursed his lips and nodded, then he raised his eyes to the council. "Who leads here? You? No king to rule you?"

The foreman folded his arms and assured, "We have a king, and he is not so fond of invaders."

"Where is he?" the barbarian asked in a calm tone.

Folding his arms, the foreman replied, "He will be here in his own time, and you will want to be long gone when he arrives."

With a wicked smile, the barbarian king nodded in slight motions and acknowledged, "I see. I do not see an army, either." He huffed a hard breath, then he raised his chin and announced for all to hear, "Well, since your king could not be bothered to come and greet me, then someone will have to die in his place. I will kill everyone in this village, one by one, until someone remembers seeing this girl who has my property." His eyes found the foreman again. "You will choose who I kill first."

"I will do no such thing," the foreman insisted.

The barbarian king smiled. "Then I will choose."

Josslee pushed her way between the foreman and the next elder, and she stopped right in front of the barbarian and folded her arms. Raising her brow, she smiled and loudly asked, "Who are you going to kill?"

His eyes slid to her and he raised his chin slightly. "I will kill your entire village, little girl."

The eyes of the invaders were filled with the ominous black and red form that emerged from the mine in the mountain that stood in the center of the village, and they all backed away a few steps.

Farrigrall stomped toward the barbarian king with heavy, ground shaking steps, and the villagers cleared his path. In a moment he was looming over the invading king, his head four men's heights above the ground, and a thunderous growl rolled from him as he bared his teeth.

Even the barbarian king's huge bodyguards backed away as the king himself looked up to the king of this island with wide eyes.

Josslee motioned behind her with her head and informed, "Our king has arrived."

With his brow low over his eyes, Farrigrall growled, "Going to kill everyone in my village, are you?" He slammed his fist into his palm. "Then I suppose you should just start with me."

The reign of Farrigrall of the Lake had begun in spectacular form.